Breaking News

Books by Fern Michaels:

Betrayal
Southern Comfort
To Taste the Wine
Sins of the Flesh
Sins of Omission
Return to Sender
Mr. and Miss
    Anonymous
Up Close and
    Personal
Fool Me Once
Picture Perfect
About Face
The Future Scrolls
Kentucky Sunrise
Kentucky Heat
Kentucky Rich
Plain Jane
Charming Lily
What You Wish For
The Guest List
Listen to Your Heart
Celebration
Yesterday
Finders Keepers
Annie's Rainbow
Sara's Song
Vegas Sunrise
Vegas Heat

Vegas Rich
Whitefire
Wish List
Dear Emily
Christmas at
    Timberwoods

The Godmothers
    Series:

Breaking News
Deadline
Late Edition
Exclusive
The Scoop

The Sisterhood Novels:

Home Free
Déjà Vu
Cross Roads
Game Over
Deadly Deals
Vanishing Act
Razor Sharp
Under the Radar
Final Justice
Collateral Damage
Fast Track
Hokus Pokus

Hide and Seek
Free Fall
Lethal Justice
Sweet Revenge
The Jury
Vendetta
Payback
Weekend Warriors

Comfort and Joy
Sugar and Spice
Let it Snow
A Gift of Joy
Five Golden Rings
Deck the Halls
Jingle All the Way

Anthologies:

Making Spirits Bright
Holiday Magic
Snow Angels
Silver Bells

FERN MICHAELS

Breaking News

**Doubleday Large Print
Home Library Edition**

KENSINGTON PUBLISHING CORP.
http://www.kensingtonbooks.com

Kensington and the K logo Reg. U.S. Pat. & TM Off.

ISBN 978-1-62090-432-9

Printed in the United States of America

**This Large Print Book carries the
Seal of Approval of N.A.V.H.**

Breaking News

Prologue

Teresa Amelia Loudenberry, aka Toots to those who knew and loved her, smoothed a wrinkle from the cream-colored duvet at the foot of her bed. Restless after spending the night tossing and turning, she'd been up for over an hour. Toots glanced at the clock on her night table. Five fifteen, and she was already showered and dressed. Most likely Bernice would be up and about, even though technically she was no longer Toots's housekeeper and was *not* to do anything without assistance. After Bernice suffered a massive heart attack and underwent coronary bypass surgery,

Toots had put her foot down to her dear friend of almost twenty-five years. It was time to call it quits, but like Toots, Bernice wasn't one simply to stop working just because she'd had—Bernice's exact words—"a little setback." The "little setback," unfortunately, just happened to be five clogged arteries, which required open-heart surgery, extensive physical therapy, and major changes to her diet and lifestyle. Toots had categorically refused to allow Bernice to do anything strenuous since being released from the hospital. Toots had hired a temporary service to do the heavy cleaning in her Charleston home.

Bernice might moan and groan until the cows came home. Toots was absolutely not going to let her wash windows and mop floors. Bernice's days as a housekeeper ended the day Jamie, Toots's partner at Charleston's finest bakery, The Sweetest Things, found her curled in a heap on the kitchen floor. Had Jamie not paid a visit that morning, poor Bernice would most likely be six feet under.

Toots did not want to say good-bye to Bernice, certainly not yet. She'd already buried eight husbands in her lifetime. Doing the same for one of her dearest friends was nowhere to be found on her agenda. Not now. Not tomorrow. Not next week, next month, or next year. They still had too much life to live, they meaning Sophie, Mavis, and Ida, Abby's three godmothers, Toots, and Bernice.

Bernice had acted strangely since coming home from the hospital, but Toots put it down to her age and the fact that she'd almost kicked the bucket. Bernice swore she had died and gone to heaven but had to return to help Sophie investigate the odd events that were going to take place at the house of Mrs. Patterson, Toots's recently deceased next-door neighbor in Charleston. Mrs. Patterson's house was empty, up for sale. She'd passed away while they'd been in California, at the beach house.

Toots feared that Bernice might be skirting the edges of dementia, but refused to discuss the possibility with anyone. Not even Sophie. But for now, Bernice was alive—above the grass, not below—and that was really all that counted.

And, of course, there was Ida, who'd lived in New York City, where she'd spent almost all of her adult life. She'd married three or four times—Toots lost count after the second time. Ida's last husband, Thomas, had died of E. coli, or so everyone had thought. Following Thomas's death, however, Ida had morphed into a different person. Since she'd believed Thomas had died from eating a piece of tainted meat, Ida developed OCD, obsessive-compulsive disorder. With the help of Toots, Sophie, and Mavis, plus the unsavory Patel Yadav, who'd been impersonating the famed Dr. Benjamin Sameer, a very successful doctor in Los Angeles who specialized in treating obsessive-compulsive disorder. The fake Dr. Sameer had tried to bilk Ida out of the three million dollars she had inherited from her deceased husband.

Nonetheless, Ida had overcome her bout with germs very quickly with the aid of the unscrupulous Patel, who was also her lover at the time. It was after Ida's almost miraculous recovery that Sophie made contact through the spirit world and learned that, unknown to Thomas or Ida, he had an illegitimate daughter. His death was investigated, and it was determined that he had been the victim of a homicide. His daughter had poisoned him in hopes of gaining access to his fortune. *After* she got rid of Ida. The daughter was successfully prosecuted, sentenced to life without the possibility of parole, so she would not have another day of freedom in this lifetime.

Ida, a former photographer, now had a successful line of cosmetics for the deceased, Drop-Dead Gorgeous. She was quite content with her new business venture and life, one lacking any morbid fear of germs.

Mavis, another of the childhood quartet of friends, had barely been surviving on the pension she received as an English teacher when Toots had e-mailed, inviting her to Charleston. Living on the coast of Maine, with nothing for company except her little Chihuahua, Coco, and daytime television, Mavis had ballooned until she was more than one hundred pounds overweight. When Toots had first seen her that day as she struggled to walk through the airport, she'd had her doubts about Mavis ever having had any quality of life. Right there, on the spot, in the airport, before

Mavis barely had a chance to say hello, Toots knew she would do whatever it took to help her friend lose all that weight.

Toots immediately called Dr. Joe Pauley, her longtime friend and physician. Dr. Pauley announced that Mavis was physically sound in all the areas that mattered. Toots took this as a sign. After a visit to Catherine's, a clothing store for plus-size women, which outfitted Mavis in gorgeous clothing, boosting poor Mavis's self-esteem tenfold, all Toots had to do was sit back and watch as the pounds practically dripped off Mavis. Now a hundred pounds lighter, and a successful businesswoman as well, not only was Mavis new and improved, but she was hip, sexy, and proud of it. Coco still tried to rule the roost, but Toots figured that was okay as long as Mavis didn't fall back into her trap of eating and feeding the little dog more than they needed. Mavis had truly worked her ass off.

Over months, unbeknownst to Toots, Sophie, and Ida, Mavis had created a secret Internet business. During her period of massive weight loss, Mavis had insisted on remaking the clothes Toots had purchased for her when she was so heavy.

As she was doing so, she discovered that she truly loved making her old clothes into new ones, and it was in this way that she started her own line of clothing for those in mourning, aptly naming it Good Mourning.

The line became so successful that Mavis went one step further by designing clothing for the dearly departed themselves. This, too, was another moneymaking venture. Between Mavis's clothing and Ida's makeup, both women were sought after by morticians and funeral directors across the country. Once the two began to work together, they attended special classes in San Francisco that enabled them to "lay out" the deceased. They were more popular than ever in the world of those who dealt with the dearly departed.

And then, of course, there was Sophie. Toots was closest to Sophie. Why? Maybe they were more alike in some ways. She didn't know why, but Sophie had always held a special place in her heart, just a wee bit more than Ida and Mavis. Sophie had always been the toughest of the bunch. Strong and street-smart in ways that Toots, Ida, and Mavis would never be. Sophie had met and married only one man in her life—Walter Manchester, an alcoholic banker who'd kicked the bucket just about a year ago. He'd died of cirrhosis of the liver. Big surprise there. He'd spent most of their marriage slugging Sophie around as though she were his own personal punching bag.

Sophie was a great believer in her marriage vows. She would not divorce him, because, as bad as her situation was, divorce was contrary to her Catholic upbringing. Toots had always known that something was not kosher in her friend's marriage. Once, when Toots had made an unannounced visit to New York City, she'd found Sophie with her arm in a cast. She didn't have to ask her friend what had happened. She just knew. Toots had tried to convince Sophie to leave Walter, told her she deserved better, but Sophie had been adamant in her decision not to divorce him. "Till death do us part," she'd said, all those years ago.

And so she survived. And she'd been smart. Working as a pediatric nurse her entire life had taught her a couple of things. One: people don't live forever; and two: she was going to outlive Walter so she could collect the five-million-dollar insurance policy she'd worked her tail off to pay for. After Walter's death, Toots took control of the "event" so that Sophie could mourn for a few minutes, about all the mourning she had in her. Walter was laid to rest efficiently and quickly. Toots even honored the old sot by singing a very off-key version of "Ave Maria" before they sent him to the fires of hell via one of New York's finest crematoriums. They'd done what was required and not a single thing more.

It wasn't too long after Walter's death that Sophie's psychic abilities blossomed even more than they already had. And now she was sought after like those Hollywood starlets whose lives and loves Abby reported on at *The Informer.*

Though Bernice wasn't an official godmother in the true sense of the word, she'd helped raise Abby when the three of them had moved to South Carolina a little less than twenty-five years ago. Not one to wallow in self-pity or overanalyze a situation, Toots put all negative thoughts aside. They would only depress her, and her life was anything but depressing. She had more reason than ever to greet each new day with an abundance of enthusiasm and a positive attitude.

First and foremost, Toots no longer had to hide behind the screen of LAT Enterprise as the owner of the tabloid paper *The Informer*. She'd purchased the paper a little less than two years ago, when she had learned that the former owner and editor in chief had gotten himself into such a humongous financial disaster that Abby and the team of reporters employed by *The Informer* feared losing their jobs. Toots, being Abby's multimillionaire mother and also being addicted to reading the tabloids, saw this not only as a possible business venture, but also as an opportunity to make sure Abby kept the job she loved so much. Knowing how independent her daughter was, Toots, along with Sophie, Mavis, and Ida, agreed to keep the new owner's identity a secret until the right moment came along to tell Abby. That moment happened shortly after Bernice was stricken with her heart attack.

Toots was very sure that Abby would disown her and the three godmothers when she learned that the four of them had been lying, if only by omission, since *The In-former* had been sold to LAT Enterprise. However, when an unexpected situation presented itself, Toots had known it was time to reveal that she was the secret owner of *The Informer.*

Abby's reaction hadn't been what she'd anticipated. It brought tears to her eyes just thinking about it. Though that had been quite the emotional time for all of them, the fact was that Abby listened to the explana-tion of why Toots had felt compelled to purchase *The Informer* and had felt the need to keep her identity a secret. Her daughter's reaction had practically blown her away.

Abby had phoned Toots to tell her about how the noted physician from Cedars-Sinai Hospital in Los Angeles, Dr. Bruce Lowery, whom Toots had engaged to per-form open-heart surgery on Bernice in Charleston before discovering in a séance that he had been involved in a homicide, had been arrested for murder in an en-tirely different case. Toots recalled asking for details, the who, what, when, where, and why. Abby laughed, telling her she'd never make it as a news reporter, tabloid or otherwise. At that exact moment, Toots knew it was time to reveal her secret.

Toots remembered holding her breath, waiting for Abby to reject her, to tell her she was the worst mother alive, tell her she would never speak to her again, but what she heard was anything but a rejection. Prepared for anger, Toots would never forget her daughter's words.

"Mom, come on! I'm not three years old! I can't believe you'd go to such lengths. Oh, what am I saying? Of course you would go to whatever length necessary to see that I was happy. Oh, Mom, I'm not angry at all. I'm honored that you would do something so phenomenally, fabulously, off the wall just to make me happy. There isn't another mother in the world who would do something so gigantically crazy. Why should I be angry? I'm humbled and bowled over, but angry? No way."

Toots smiled at the memory. Abby was "good people," even if she was her daughter. Toots had been around the block more than once in the marriage department. Abby had never acted bratty, hateful, or spoiled with any of her stepfathers. In fact,

Abby had loved all her stepfathers, except the last one, Leland, whom she'd met only once before attending his funeral, or rather, his *event,* as Toots had taken to calling them. A snicker escaped her lips as she had a quick thought: Abby hadn't missed a thing. Leland had been cheap and petty. Why she'd married him, she hadn't a clue, but at this stage in life, it didn't seem to hold much significance. *It is what it is,* she thought as she switched off the lamp.

Heading downstairs, with the tantalizing scent of coffee teasing her olfactory senses, Toots was more than a little surprised to find Jamie bustling about in the kitchen. "I thought you'd be at the bakery this morning. What gives?" Toots asked as she poured herself a cup of coffee, gazing at her much-loved kitchen. The old pine floors glistened like shiny gold. The custom-made red cabinets still made her smile. Leland had hated them, thought they were tawdry and cheap. And the fireplace was unique, one of a kind. She'd gathered the large stones herself in a mountain stream in North Carolina. Toots's South Carolina home was truly the home of her dreams.

Jamie bustled about the kitchen, her

pretty face flushed. Her once-shoulder-length warm brown hair now reached the middle of her back. She held it back in a low ponytail with a pale yellow ribbon. When Toots had first met the young woman, she'd had short, spiky blond hair. Jamie liked to be different, she'd once explained, when she'd dyed a chunk of her hair green. Toots felt sure that Jamie was past that stage now. Not only was she an excellent baker, but she'd turned out to be one heck of a businesswoman as well. The bakery was making a hefty profit. So much so that Jamie had dropped a few hints about opening up another bakery in Summerville, a small town close to Charleston.

Jamie was clad in her usual jeans and T-shirt. One could never miss the custom-made aprons with THE SWEETEST THINGS emblazoned in bright pink letters against the red material. Toots liked the colors red and pink. She thought the two of them went well together, especially in a bakery. The color pink brought forth images of fluffy frostings, and red brought up all kinds of sweet goodies. There were red velvet cakes, cupcakes, candies, and sprinkles in every color of the rainbow, and some Toots never even knew existed. The bakery's specialty was its pralines. When Toots had first tried one of Jamie's pralines, she knew she'd never tasted anything so sweet and sinful. And Toots was a die-hard sugar addict, something she didn't bother to hide. Jamie's sugar-sweet concoction had put them on the praline map. People pre-ordered and often waited in long lines to purchase the sweet, sugary delight.

So far, Toots had been nothing more than the bakery's financier. However, now that she planned to stay in Charleston for a while to oversee Bernice's rehabilitation, she thought that she might decide to take more of an active role.

If Jamie would allow her, she would learn to bake. One didn't have to know how to *cook* in order to bake, did one? If so, Toots was in a heap of trouble. She was not known for her culinary skills. Indeed, her cooking was an absolute disaster.

"What are you doing up so early? I thought you'd sleep in for a change. I wanted to have breakfast ready for you girls before I left. Lucy came in early this morning. She's really becoming a great assistant. We're lucky to have her."

Jamie had hired Lucy a few months ago to assist her at the bakery. She'd turned out to be an excellent baker and, from what Toots understood, a great friend to Jamie. They were close in age and Lucy had no family to speak of. Their closeness pleased Toots immensely as Jamie had no family, either, since her grandmother had passed away a few years ago. They'd all taken Jamie under their wings, especially Bernice, and now Jamie was becoming a part of their little family. Toots didn't believe it took shared bloodlines to form a family. Sophie, Mavis, Ida and, of course, Bernice were the only family, besides Abby and Chris, she had left. Adding Jamie, and now Lucy, was even better. The more the merrier.

"Oh, you know me. I'm up with the chickens. Sleep is simply a waste of time as far as I'm concerned," Toots said as she scooped liberal amounts of sugar into her cup. She removed the half-and-half from the refrigerator and filled her coffee cup. Sophie always teased her, asking if she wanted a little coffee with her cream and sugar.

Jamie laughed. "I agree, though there

are times when I relish the thought of staying in bed all day."

Toots grinned. "Well, I suppose it would depend on who is lying next to you."

Both women laughed heartily.

"Only you, Toots. But you do have a point. I just don't have time for a boyfriend at this point in my life. Maybe later," Jamie added before taking two red and white checkered oven mitts from the countertop and slipping them on her hands. She opened the oven door, filling the kitchen with the savory scent of cinnamon.

Toots eyed the baking sheet as Jamie removed it from the oven. "Smells yummy. What is it?"

"Cinnamon rolls," Jamie said. "Better than those at the mall. Guaranteed."

"I'm sure," Toots acknowledged.

"Give me a minute, and I'll ice one for you," Jamie said over her shoulder. She removed a bright yellow bowl from the refrigerator. With a large spoon, she dropped sizable globs of thick cream-colored icing on top of the rolls, their warmth causing the icing to spill over the sides and in between the flaky layers of golden crust.

Toots removed a stack of small dessert plates from the cupboard and forks from the drawer. She held her plate out to Jamie, who forked a cinnamon roll onto it. Not bothering with the fork, Toots didn't waste any time delving into the sugary sweet roll. She closed her eyes, a slight smile lifting the edge of her mouth. When she'd consumed every last bite, she held her plate out for another. "As usual, you were right. This sure as hell beats those sticky-ass buns in the mall. I think we should add this to the menu at the bakery."

Jamie placed another roll on Toots's plate. "Good. I was hoping you would say that. Since we've expanded into coffees, too, customers have been asking for a sweet roll. I know we have all kinds of baked goods, but a cinnamon roll and a hot cup of coffee would appeal to the vast majority, don't you think?"

Jamie removed the rest of the rolls from the baking sheet, placing them on a gleaming red platter. Toots was about to take a third when Jamie stopped her. "Let the others try one. I only made a dozen."

Toots laughed. "I'm a pig when it comes

to sweets, but okay. I doubt Mavis or Ida will want an entire roll, so maybe I can share what they don't eat."

Both women giggled.

"You're lucky all that sugar hasn't trans-planted itself to your hips and thighs," Jamie teased.

"Trust me, it has. I just hide it well," Toots said, then gave Jamie a wicked little grin.

"Who's hiding what?" Sophie said, en-tering the kitchen.

Now seated at the table with a second cup of coffee, Toots motioned to the plat-ter of rolls. "I was explaining to Jamie how I have to hide my fat thighs. All those sweets."

Sophie removed a mug from the cup-board, filling it with coffee. She reached in-side her robe pocket and pulled out a pack of cigarettes. "Yes, you're a real fat ass, Toots."

Toots rolled her eyes. "I didn't say that. I said I hide it well. What do you think that young gal in Atlanta invented Spanx for? My God, it's better than a panty girdle. Re-member those? I can't believe we actually wore the silly things, though they did keep

my nylons from falling to my ankles. I suppose there is a blessing to be found in just
about anything."

"A girdle?" Sophie quizzed. "I think that
damn Spanx has squished something
loose in your brain is what I think." Sophie
sat across from Toots.

The three women laughed.

Ida chose that moment to make her
grand appearance. "What's so funny at this
godforsaken hour?" Ida asked. As usual,
there wasn't a hair out of place. Her blond
chin-length pageboy was styled to perfection. Her makeup, too. Though she was
known as a makeup expert for the dearly
departed, she used her skills on the living
quite well.

"Toots thinks she's a fat ass," Sophie
said.

Ida smirked, raking her gaze over Toots's
frame. "Well, if she is, then she must hide
it very well."

"I didn't say I was a fat ass," Toots stated
firmly. "I said I was thankful for my Spanx."

She'd poured herself a cup of coffee, no
sugar, no cream. "What are Spanx?" Ida
asked as she made her way over to the
table.

Jamie, Toots, and Sophie stared at Ida as though she were one slice short of a loaf.

Sophie laughed. "I can't believe you, of all women, queen of appearances, don't know what Spanx is."

Ida rolled her eyes, normally something Sophie would do. Ida was picking up her bad habits. "Well, I don't, so there!" Ida shot back. "What's the hoopla, anyway?"

"You ever watch that show *What Not to Wear* on cable TV? You've never heard of NVP?" Toots questioned Ida.

Showing her impatience with the conversation, Ida took a deep breath. "I might've seen it a time or two, but what in the world is NVP?"

"No visible panty lines," Toots, Sophie, and Jamie chorused.

"That sounds rather tacky if you ask me," Ida replied dryly, sitting down. "However, since we are on the subject of looks, I might as well tell you"—Ida took a deep breath—"I've been invited to—"

"Wait!" Mavis practically raced down the stairs to the kitchen. "Don't say anything yet." Somewhat winded in spite of her excellent physical condition, Mavis poured herself a cup of black coffee before coming to the table.

"Now you can tell us," Mavis said with a grin.

Chapter 1

"Should we wake Bernice?" Ida asked. "I'm only going to tell this story once."

"Leave her alone. She doesn't give a rat's ass what you do," Sophie said. "Hurry it up, Ida. I'm dying to go smoke."

Toots nodded. Though she and Sophie had managed to cut down on their habit, big-time, they both still required a puff or two in the morning. Pretty soon they'd be down to only a single cigarette a day. When that day finally arrived, they had both vowed to toss their cigarettes away for good.

Ida looked down her slim, patrician nose. "All right, I suppose you all have a right to know." She gazed at the three other women seated around the table. "I've just learned that I'm going to have an opportunity to audition my new line of cosmetics for The Home Shopping Club." There, now it was out.

Toots looked at Ida as though she had a horn growing out of her head. Sophie curled her lip in disgust. Even Mavis looked shocked. Jamie, ever the diplomat, busied herself washing the baking sheet.

Toots finally took control. "Ida, darling, I realize how successful you've become, and I completely respect and admire you for all you've achieved." She paused, thinking of what to say next. "But this . . . There are limits to one's entrepreneurship! Don't you think this is taking your cosmetics just a bit too far?" For a brief second, Toots had to wonder if Ida had totally lost her marbles.

Ida rolled her eyes. "I am not referring to Drop-Dead Gorgeous. Good grief. Did you actually thing I would . . . Oh, never mind. Of course you would think that."

Sophie pulled her chair away from the table and got up. "I'm going outside. Now. Something tells me that whatever is about to come out of her mouth is about as important as this hot smoke I'm about to suck into my lungs."

"Sophie, you're being rude," Mavis said. "Now, sit back down and let us hear what Ida has to say. She would do it for you, wouldn't you, Ida?" Mavis sent an overly sweet smile winging across the table.

Ida raised her perfectly arched eyebrows. "Truthfully? Probably not, so go ahead and blacken your lungs. I want another cup of coffee, anyway." Ida got up and brought the pot of coffee over to the table. Meanwhile, Sophie scurried out the door, where she lit a cigarette and took several quick puffs before stepping back inside.

"Quick, grab a camera," Sophie said as she made her way over to the table. "This must be special, because I don't think I have ever seen Ida carry a coffeepot. Period."

They all laughed. Even Ida smirked as she took her seat again.

"Shut up, Soph. Let's hear what Ida has to say," Toots declared, becoming impatient with the silly bantering.

"Okay, but don't expect a drumroll from

me," Sophie said as she plopped back down on her chair.

More rolling of eyes around the table. Jamie, who still had not said a word, continued to scrub the baking sheet until it gleamed.

Ida straightened in her chair and adjusted her shoulders before responding. "You all act like a bunch of teenagers. I swear, it's hard to believe you're as old as you are."

"And you're just as old, so go on. Spit it out. I have things I have to do today," Sophie said, her voice full of annoyance.

"Sophie's right. We all have a busy day ahead. I have to take Bernice to rehab today. Spill it, Ida, so we can all go on with our day."

"The Home Shopping Club is interested in my *new line* of cosmetics, and before you say another word, they're for the living. The long-lived, actually. I'm going to call the new line Seasons."

For a few seconds, the kitchen was totally silent. Then they all started talking at once.

"When did this happen?"

"How did you manage to do this without our knowing?"

"It's the best news I've heard all day," Mavis finished.

"It's early, Mavis," Sophie added. "Just wait. Maybe they'll find a cure for cancer this afternoon."

Toots actually clapped her hands. "Girls, be quiet! Ida, that's fantastic news. Of course you'll share the details," Toots said, more a question than a statement.

"I've been trying to tell you for the past ten minutes. If someone"—Ida looked across the table at Sophie—"can keep her thoughts to herself for a moment, I will be able to tell you exactly what I know."

The three women and Jamie waited for Ida to continue.

"I've been working with a group of top-notch chemists. We've come up with a line of creams and cosmetics that promises to improve wrinkles."

"Oh, for crying out loud, Ida, there are a gazillion products on the market that make such stupid promises. What makes you think that your cosmetics are any better? You need scientific proof before you can legally make such claims. Doesn't the FDA have some kind of say in these kinds of products? These are for the living, right?" Toots said, all traces of her earlier humor gone. The last thing any of them needed was legal issues.

Sitting on the edges of their seats, Mavis and Sophie waited with bated breath for Ida to explain her new venture to Toots.

"Toots, do I look like an idiot?" Ida asked.

"Oh, is that ever a loaded question," Sophie teased. "And yes, there was a time when you did look like an idiot. Am I the only one who remembers the hot pink hair?"

"Please, don't remind me," Toots said, grinning broadly. Goebel Blevins, a former New York City detective turned private eye, had assisted them in locating Chris Clay, Toots's stepson, when he disappeared after preventing the now-infamous B-grade actress Laura Leighton from setting fire to World Con Studios. The two-bit actress had learned that she would not be reprising the role of Ella Larsen in *Bloody Hollow Two,* the successor to a teen horror flick that, through a fluke of luck and crazed teenagers, had become one of the hottest movies over the summer. Luckily for Ms. Leighton, her disappearance and the news that she was not to play Ella Larsen again led to her teenage fans picketing the studio, which promptly changed its mind and gave her the part.

Toots had suspected that Ida was planning to seduce Goebel, who'd already laid claim to Sophie. Since his feelings for Sophie were reciprocated, Toots decided that she had to do something. So, she'd called Ida's new hairstylist and asked her to give Ida Hollywood's most popular hairstyle. When Ida returned from the salon a few hours later, she sported spiked hot pink hair.

Ida glared at Sophie. "I knew *you* would never forget this."

"Stop, girls! Ida has reached another pinnacle on the ladder of success. The least we can do is hear her out," Mavis insisted.

"Mavis is right. Let's listen to what Ida's been up to. I, for one, am curious where she found the time to work on another project," Toots replied.

Jamie chose that moment to place the platter of warm cinnamon rolls on the table, along with plates and forks. "I can leave if you girls need some privacy."

"No, you're family now. Whatever Ida has to say is for your ears, too. Right, Ida?" Toots asked.

Ida looked at Jamie and gave her a genuine smile that reached her eyes. "Of course you can stay. This might be something you'll want to take note of now, while you're still young enough."

Jamie nodded and took a seat beside Toots.

Sophie spoke up. "We're all ears."

Ida cleared her throat and viewed the women as though she were about to address the nation. "Cosmetic companies are not, in point of fact, required to register their cosmetics establishments with the FDA. Even companies that produce cosmetics for the living." Ida stared fiercely at Sophie, as if trying to make sure she was listening to every single word she said.

"Companies are mandated to register their establishments. Once they do that, they then file what's called a Cosmetic Product Ingredient Statement with the FDA's Voluntary Cosmetic Registration

Program, commonly referred to as VCRP. From there, the FDA often inspects these facilities in order to ensure that the cosmetics are safe and to determine that the cosmetics are not adulterated—"

"What the hell did you just say? Please tell me I heard you wrong? I know you just said something about adultery," Sophie interjected before allowing Ida a chance to finish explaining the ins and outs of her new venture.

Toots burst out laughing. "Sophie! She isn't talking about adultery. It's *adulterated*, meaning debased by the use of foreign or inferior materials. Right, Ida?"

"Yes, Toots. Sophia Manchester, I know you must be the only woman alive who manages to insinuate something sexual into every conversation you have." Ida's eyes twinkled.

"Oh, shoot, I know. I'm just yanking her chain, okay?" Sophie explained. "I can't help it if she sets herself up for stuff like this."

Toots rolled her eyes. "Go on, Ida. Please finish explaining what this entails." Toots turned to Sophie. "And please, let her speak without interrupting."

"Yes, your frigging highness," Sophie shot back.

Toots flipped Sophie the bird, their usual silent method of communication. Sophie followed suit, using both hands. Jamie laughed out loud. Mavis giggled, and Ida simply pursed her lips.

"If you're going to make fun of me, I'm not going to tell you anything." Ida directed her fiery gaze at Sophie, then Toots.

With mock seriousness, her tone that of a drill sergeant, Toots ordered, "Yes, everyone, let's all be quiet and give Ida the floor."

Immediately, Sophie saluted Toots, letting her know she "got" her. Toots gave a shake that only Sophie could see, then mouthed, "Not now."

When Ida saw she finally had her friends' undivided attention, she resumed her explanation. "I've had a panel of testers trying the products, and they all agree, they're top of the line when it comes to smoothing out wrinkles and fine lines. We've added the secret ingredient to the makeup as well, so the consumer will really be getting much more than just a facial cream. All the lipsticks, eye shadows, blush, and foundations will have it, too. Plus, I've added an SPF factor of fifty. The Home Shopping Club doesn't accept just any company. Their criteria are quite rigorous. Of course, they're aware of the chemists I worked with, so they know that the quality of my cosmetics and creams is outstanding."

"And we would expect nothing less from the queen of beauty," Sophie added. "Dead or alive. So what is *your* secret ingredient?"

Ida smiled. "Pumpkin."

"OMG, I can just see it all now, women out there during the holidays, trying to watch their weight and resorting to licking the makeup off their faces. Pumpkin pie, yum."

"Sophie! You should be proud of Ida's accomplishments!" Mavis exclaimed in her usual perky voice.

Sophie refilled her mug. "And who says I'm not?"

Mavis appeared crestfallen. "You were . . . a bit harsh, that's all. And I've heard pumpkin has wonderful purifying qualities."

"She's a smart-ass to everyone. You

should know that by now, Mavis," Toots reminded her friend. "Sophie wouldn't be Sophie if she were nice like the rest of us."

Sophie took a loud slurp of coffee before answering. "Well, you can just kiss my wrinkled old ass! I am, too, nice. Just ask Goebel," Sophie informed them. "He likes me just fine."

"Hey, stop that right this minute! That's my line, and you can't have it," Bernice said as she entered the kitchen.

"Well, I'll be a monkey's uncle," Toots said, a grin the size of the moon on her face. Then, just as quickly as it appeared, a frown took its place. "You are *not* supposed to come downstairs without assistance. Next thing, you'll have a broken hip. And then we'll be changing your diapers."

Since Bernice's bypass surgery, Toots and the godmothers had been super careful, making sure that Bernice wanted for nothing and did only what the doctor allowed. Walking up and down the staircase was not on the list. A stair lift was going to be a must.

"I wanted a cup of coffee. If I waited on your lazy butts to bring it to me, I'd be as good as dead."

"She's feeling better," Toots said dryly. "And it isn't even dawn." Toots glanced over her shoulder, just to make sure. "Yet. You're supposed to rest today, or did you forget that, too? We have an entire afternoon of rehab ahead of us. You need to be well rested, Miss Smarty Mouth."

"Just think of all the stress and strain you're putting on your wrinkled ass. Maybe with all this rehab, you'll firm it up a bit," Sophie tossed in.

Everyone laughed, including Ida.

"See what I mean? She *always* has to speak of a . . . a body part! You really need to get a life, Sophia," Ida said in her know-it-all voice. "You need something other than ghosts and goblins to occupy your time. Isn't anyone interested in what else I have to say?"

"Nope, not me." Sophie turned to Bernice, who'd seated herself next to Mavis. Jamie poured Bernice's coffee and plated a cinnamon roll for her.

"Did I hurt your feelings, Bernice? Tell the truth." Sophie asked, her voice laced with concern.

"Oh, for crying out loud, you didn't hurt my feelings at all. What hurts my feelings are those dirty plates next to the sink. If someone doesn't hurry up and put them in the dishwasher, I'll have no other choice but to do it myself."

Toots, Sophie, Mavis, and Jamie practically leapt across the kitchen, where they each took turns putting a dirty dish in the dishwasher.

"Thank you. All of you. Well, not *all* of you," Bernice said, directing her gaze at Ida, who remained at the head of the table, sipping her coffee.

Again, the group of women giggled like a bunch of schoolgirls.

Ida had the grace to appear chagrined. "Just so you know, I did bring the pot of coffee to the table."

Another chorus of laughter.

As was the norm, Toots took control of the conversation. "And it's appreciated, really. Now, I, for one, want to hear more about The Home Shopping Club deal. Who knows what it could lead to? Maybe you'll become famous touting your old-age cosmetics."

"At least they're not for dead people. That's a real bonus," Bernice stated. "How you can put makeup on a dead person is beyond my comprehension." She shook her head and pushed the cinnamon roll aside. "Jamie, you know I can't eat this." Bernice moved her plate across the table, in front of Toots.

Jamie's face reddened. "Oh, Bernie," she said, using her pet name for the older woman, "I wasn't thinking. I'm sorry. I'll make something for you later. A heart-healthy dessert. And I promise not to tempt you again."

Bernice waved her hand in the air. "Forget about it, kid. It's up to me to resist temptation. But for the record, let me know when you're baking. I'll sit on the porch and keep an eye on Mrs. Patterson's place. Something is about to take place over there, and it's not gonna be pretty."

"You've been saying that since you came home from the hospital. What exactly do you mean?" Sophie asked for the millionth time.

Bernice hadn't been herself since the surgery, and they were terribly concerned about her.

Bernice rolled her eyes. "I'm not psychic. That's your gig, Sophia. I've told you all a dozen times. Something big is going on over there. For the hundredth time, I died on that damn operating table, and I don't care what that doctor says. I died and was told to return so that I could keep an eye on that place." Lest anyone doubt which place she meant, Bernice tilted her head toward the large property next door.

"You should let Sophie read the tarot for you. She's good, knows her stuff. If anything is about to take place, she'll know. Right, Soph?" Toots asked.

The old woman shook her head so hard that wisps of gray hair came loose from her tightly wound bun. "No! You know I don't believe in all that mumbo jumbo. I know what I was told to do, and it didn't involve a bunch of crazy old ladies with a deck of cards and a glass."

Mavis giggled.

Ida raised her chin a notch higher.

Toots and Sophie grinned, and Jamie, as usual, didn't utter a word.

Chapter 2

"Crazy old ladies?" Sophie chirped. "I'm ashamed of you, Bernice. I saved Ida from being killed by that fake doctor, talked to Marilyn Monroe's ghost, solved the JFK assassination, well, sort of, and found that silly starlet who caused Chris all that trouble. You think I can't help you with a little . . . *premonition?* Give me a break!" Sophie reached for the coffeepot in the middle of the table and refilled her mug. "In short, I got it going on."

"Who said anything about a premonition, or whatever the heck you want to call it? I've been telling all of you for weeks now that something is going to happen at that place next door. I don't care if you believe me or not. I died on that operating table. I distinctly remember hovering above my body, wondering what the hell was going on. That good-looking doctor, you know, the one Toots has the hots for, had his hands on my heart, and the next thing I knew I was observing my own surgery. From there, well . . . you all should know the story by now since I've told you girls a thousand times exactly what I experienced. But you still won't believe me. What is wrong with you people? And to think, you call yourselves *psychics*."

"That's Sophie's department," Toots corrected. "What I don't understand is why you won't let her read for you."

"I do," Sophie interjected. "She's afraid of the unknown."

Bernice had been home from the hospital for several weeks when Toots began to suspect that something was up with her. They were closer than sisters, and Toots had tried on several occasions to speak to her, to find out what was bothering her. She knew from her many conversations with Joe Pauley, her good friend and physician, and Dr. Phil Becker, Bernice's cardiologist, that it wasn't uncommon for people who came out of surgery to claim they'd had a near-death experience. Both he and Joe assured Toots that Bernice had not *died* during her surgery. Of course, Bernice disagreed.

"I am not afraid of the unknown. I *know* something evil, bad, whatever you want to call it, is going to happen at Mrs. Patterson's old place. When I was hovering between life and death, I knew it wasn't my time when that beautiful bright being, and no, before you ask again, I don't know what *it* was, but it was the brightest, most phenomenal experience I've ever had. I've told this story a dozen times. When I was pulled back into my body, the message I received was clear. *It's not your time. Go back. Watch the empty house next door.* And I don't give a flying hoot what you say. A tarot reading, a séance, whatever it is you all do, isn't going to change things, isn't going to prevent it, whatever *it* is, from happening. I'll know when *it* happens. That's all I can tell you," Bernice said adamantly, then tipped her coffee mug back and drained the last of her cold coffee.

Toots decided then and there they'd all be better off if they just went along with Bernice and her tale of a near-death experience. Knowing the three g's as well as she did, she knew that they would pick up on her cue. "I believe you, Bernice. So much so that I think it's time we started observing Mrs. Patterson's house. We can all take turns, each take a shift. Sophie, do you still have all your cameras and psychic mumbo-jumbo stuff?"

"Now, wait just a minute," Bernice contested. "I don't want you to start playing ghost hunters. This is my problem, and I'll . . . deal with it. Right, Jamie?"

Flustered at being brought into the middle of a discussion she didn't want to take sides in, Jamie raised her shoulders, as if to indicate no opinion either way. "This is your story, Bernie. You have to do what you feel is best."

"I don't believe a stakeout is in order. I am supposed to watch the place, not move in," Bernice articulated. "Now, can we discuss something else?"

Toots, always the leader of the group, spoke up first. "We're not talking about a stakeout, just one of us paying extra close attention to Mrs. Patterson's place. Since it's empty and has that huge FOR SALE sign in the front yard, I'm thinking there could be vandals. If we're watching the place, and something happens, we'll just report it to the police. I really don't believe something evil is going to go down. What about you, Soph? Is your gut telling you anything?" They all knew that Sophie's gut instinct was almost always spot-on.

Sophie, her brown hair trailing down her back, shook her head vigorously. Then she took a deep breath and closed her eyes. For a few minutes, the kitchen/dining area was completely silent. Suddenly, Sophie's large whiskey-colored eyes opened wide. "Oh my—"

"What? Do you *see* something?" Toots asked.

"No, I just have to pee really bad. I'll be right back." Sophie practically flew out of her chair and up the stairs, leaving the other women clueless.

Bernice broke the ensuing silence. "Why, I swear, if I were in better shape, I'd run after that old girl just so I could smack her in that smart mouth of hers."

Seconds later, Sophie ran downstairs

with an armload of books. "Damn, this getting old sucks. I thought I was going to pee all over myself. Now"—she plopped the stack of books on the table—"I've had these for a while. I just haven't gotten around to reading them yet. So, Bernice, you believe you've had an NDE, correct?"

Mavis's face reddened. "Oh, please tell me what you just said. Isn't that . . . well, you know, that pump thing that George needed?"

They all broke out in hysterical laughter. Mavis had met a gentleman while they were in Malibu. He owned a string of dry cleaners across the country. He and Mavis were just getting ready to take their relationship to another level when he mentioned he would need to use a VCD, a vacuum constriction device, if they were to become intimate. Mavis had been mortified, and she'd broken it off with George, sparing herself his inability to rise to the occasion, so to speak. They'd all had quite a few laughs over that incident.

"You're talking about that VCD, right? No, this is something entirely different. Not a sex aid, Mavis," Sophie explained, a mile-wide grin spread across her face.

"None of you will listen to me, and yet as soon as . . . Miss Cleo appears with her magic books, you . . . you"—Ida sniffed— "give *her* your undivided attention. I was going to ask all of you to act as my models on The Home Shopping Club. Now I think I'll consult a modeling agency and give other senior citizens the opportunity of a lifetime."

All the chatter stopped instantly. Toots, Sophie, and Mavis focused their gaze on Ida. Bernice rolled her eyes, and Jamie could not help smiling.

"Okay, you have our undivided attention," Toots said.

Content now that she had their complete attention again, Ida blotted her obviously fake tears with a napkin, then spoke as though she'd never been interrupted. "As I said, The Home Shopping Club wants to help launch my line of new cosmetics. In order to demonstrate, I will need real women to show how well my product works. Of course, you all *are* my best friends and were the first women I thought of when I was approached by their CEO."

Ida paused, waiting to see what, if any, effect her words had on her longtime friends. Seeing that she still had their un-divided attention, she continued, "For the next four weeks, once a week, I get to highlight my products live on national tele-vision. I'm so sure of this that I've guaran-teed the executives their sales will reach record highs."

"Don't you think that's a bit much? Every beauty product on the market makes simi-lar claims," Toots said, an edge coming into her voice.

"Not at all. I believe I have a big advan-tage, something that will put Seasons right up there with Estée Lauder, Lancôme, and many of the other high-end cosmetic com-panies. As I was saying, I'll be using live models. Each week, we will show their progress live on television, nothing like those still shots from infomercials that have been airbrushed. This is going to be the real thing, no gimmicks, not one stroke of an airbrush. So"—Ida grasped her palms in front of her, then rubbed them together—"are you girls in or not?"

Toots weighed her words before she spoke. They'd been involved in so many projects the past few years. Wasn't it time for them to settle down a bit? Enjoy their golden years? Stop running all over the country in search of excitement?

Hell no!

"I'm in. Just tell me what I have to do," Toots all but yelled.

"OMG! I knew you'd agree to this. You vain old woman," Sophie announced. "I guess if Toots is willing to show the world how ugly she is without her makeup, then I can, too. I'm in, Ida, but just so you know, I do not under any circumstances want to be referred to as 'seasoned,' 'ripened,' 'aged to perfection.' We'll have none of that crap."

In her sweetest voice, Ida cooed, "Why, I would never refer to you as anything but . . . beautiful. Though the line is called Seasons, we can let the consumers assume whatever they want. When ladies of our . . . *experience* see how well my products work, women both young and old will line up just to get a sample of my cosmetics. So, Mavis, are you game? You're almost as expert as I am with a makeup brush. Do you want to model, too?"

Mavis smiled. "What about our other work? Are you saying you don't want to continue with Drop-Dead Gorgeous? I have no intention of putting a halt to Good Mourning. I've become a very rich woman and have all those workers making garments. I just couldn't put them out of a job, especially in this terrible economy."

"I'm not giving up anything, Mavis. You should know me better by now," Ida said. "I love what I do. As a matter of fact"—Ida raked her gaze over each one of them—"the more I do, the better I feel about myself. I'm happier now than I've ever been in my entire life. So, there. Now, Mavis, are you in or out?"

Mavis took a deep breath and reached for Coco, who'd slipped into the kitchen without making a sound. She scooped the little pooch onto her lap. "If Toots and Sophie are in, then count me in, too. We don't need to sleep that much. I only need three or four hours as it is."

Ida turned to Bernice and Jamie. "Bernice, would you like to join us? We have room for another pretty face."

Bernice's eyes doubled in size. "I can't believe what I just heard. Toots, did I hear what I think I heard?"

"You did," Toots said.

"So I'm to assume that you think I'm . . .

pretty, Ida? And that I need to work? And that people would want to turn their television sets on and look at my wrinkled ass?" Bernice started to laugh, then Toots. Jamie giggled, followed by Mavis. Sophie laughed so hard, she snorted and choked.

And Ida wore the biggest shit-eating grin ever.

Chapter 3

"It's a lovely thought, but I don't have time. Remember, I was allowed to live in order to keep an eye on Mrs. Patterson's place. I don't think I'll have time to do anything else. Between that and physical therapy, I'm just too danged busy," Bernice said.

Ida smiled. "I understand. But if you change your mind, you know where to find me."

"So now that we're all official models, aren't we supposed to start jet-setting around the world, changing our clothes every three hours, eating celery sticks, and having affairs with married men? Isn't that what models do when they're not *modeling*?" Sophie teased.

Basking in the attention, Ida replied, "I wouldn't know. Of course, I would expect that you ladies would always be on your best behavior while representing Seasons. None of that flipping Toots the middle finger, Sophie. That isn't the image I want to create."

"Yep. I got it, Ida. I promise not to pick my teeth in public, and I'll be sure never to say 'Shit,' even when I have a mouthful," Sophie retorted.

"Good grief, that's trashy even coming from you, Sophia," Toots admonished. "I know you're just trying to yank Ida's chain, but the visual is disgusting."

"On that note, I'd better go. Lucy will wonder what happened to me if I'm not there soon," Jamie announced. "I'll make the cinnamon rolls tomorrow and take note of the customers' reactions."

"Perfect. Do tell as soon as you can. I'm anxious to see if the rest of Charleston's sweet tooth is as bad as mine," Toots said. She realized she hadn't mentioned anything about her going to work at the bakery. *Later,* she thought. When this modeling stint was over. Lucy's position was safe for now, not that it was ever in jeopardy. Froot Loops and coffee were Toots's only claim to culinary fame.

On her way out, Jamie stopped at the screen door. "I'll call or stop over and let you know." Without another word, she left the others to continue their discussion.

Cutting straight to the chase, Sophie asked, "So when does this *modeling* job begin?"

"Right now," Ida said succinctly. "The sooner the better. I want all of you to start using the products immediately."

"I think she meant to ask, when will we make our television debut?" Toots corrected.

"Yep, that's exactly what I meant. When do I need to make sure my legs are shaved and my upper lip is waxed?" Sophie asked.

Mavis chuckled. "Oh dear, Sophia, we are going to have so much fun. I can see it now. And who knows? Maybe one of us will meet the man of our dreams." She sighed, a wistful look on her thin face. Coco chose that very moment to lick her chin, and Mavis embraced the little pooch tighter.

Sophie rolled her eyes, grabbed her

pack of cigarettes, and headed for the screen door. Before going outside to smoke, she responded to Mavis's musing. "I doubt that. Men in the modeling business are gay. Most of them. And I, for one, am *not* looking for a man. You either, right, Toots?"

Toots jerked to attention. She followed her friend to the small stoop without muttering a word. And once they were outside, she took the offered smoke Sophie held out for her. Placing it between her lips, she inhaled when the flame from Sophie's lighter touched the tip of her cigarette. Then she took another deep puff.

"God, I don't know if I can give these disgusting things up completely. There's nothing like a good hit of nicotine after a meal. Maybe I'll just smoke after I eat. I won't tell Abby, either. She hates that we smoke. You know that, right?" Toots inhaled again. "And to answer your question, no. I am not 'looking for a man.'"

Sophie nodded, her cigarette dangling from the corner of her mouth. "Of course you're not, and I know Abby hates these cigarettes. She isn't bashful about telling me. I plan to quit. Just not today."

They both laughed.

"Well, I plan to quit, too. I'm just not sure when. I know they're nasty, and the smell is absolutely, positively atrocious. It was hip to smoke when we were young, remember?"

"A lot of things were hip back when we were young, Toots. Some good, some not so good. The not so good, for me, was Walter, that lazy, wife-beating lush. You know, I actually thought I would miss him when he kicked the bucket. But the truth is, I've hardly given him a thought since his timely demise. I can't even imagine my life with him in it now."

"Do that eight times. Trust me, you won't forget, though I must admit, since Leland's death, I haven't thought too much about him, either. I have to think very hard just to recall what the cheap buzzard looked like," Toots observed, an evil grin spreading across her face.

"Well, I, for one, will never forget what Walter looked like. I've had enough visions to remind me. His is the one face I wish I could forget." Sophie took a deep drag from her smoke. "But I am not going to dwell on the past. Our future just keeps getting better and better. Who would've thought we'd be so happy in our old age?"

"Good grief! What the hell has gotten into you this morning? Where is Goebel? I think you need to get laid," Toots said, then crushed out her cigarette in the coffee can they kept on the side of the steps.

"Ida is right, you know?" Sophie said as she stood up.

Toots stretched her neck, then arms. "Ida's right about a lot of things. I'm just not going to be the one to mention it to her. God, she's already so full of herself. But what are you referring to?"

"About the sex stuff," Sophie explained. "It does seem to pop up a lot in our conversations. I mean, I thought once you reached a certain age . . . well, I just thought, you know, I thought . . ."

Toots held her palm out in front of her. "I don't want to know what you thought, but I can imagine it's along the same lines that all women our age have."

"And that would be?"

Toots returned the coffee can to its former place. "That sex isn't important at our age."

Sophie blushed. "It's not. Really."

Toots opened the screen door, cast a glance over her shoulder at Sophie, and replied, "Yes, it is. *Really*. Now, if you know what's good for you, you'll do whatever needs to be done to get Goebel beneath the sheets."

Toots headed inside, not giving Sophie a chance to come up with a snarly response.

"Who's to say that I haven't already?" Sophie asked in a loud voice the second they entered the kitchen.

Toots stopped dead in her tracks. "I know you. You would have told me."

"Told what?" Ida asked as she watched the pair.

"None of your damn business, that's what."

"Sophie Manchester, you don't need to be so hateful! It will make you . . . ugly, and you won't be able to model for Ida. Tell her you're sorry before I sic Coco on you," Mavis threatened. Two years ago, she would never have spoken up. Losing a hundred-plus pounds did a great deal to improve her self-esteem.

"I don't have anything to be sorry for!"

Sophie tossed back. "Do I?" She glanced at Toots.

"The list is long, but it's not for me to say."

Sophie did what she knew best. She flipped up her middle finger, directing it high in the air for all to see. Toots immediately followed suit.

Exasperated, Ida said, "That's exactly what I'm talking about. I'm afraid one of you will do this on live television." And she pointed to Sophie.

Sophie directed her single-digit salute directly at Ida. Whereupon Ida rolled her eyes and turned so that her back was to Sophie.

Dropping her arm to her side, Sophie asked, "Do you really believe I would do this on live television?"

Toots, Ida, and Mavis all spoke at once.

"You're damn right I do!"

"Of course!"

"That's my Sophie."

"Well, I wouldn't. I do have some class," Sophie offered, her way of promising Ida she'd behave.

"It's very difficult for me to believe that," Ida said, a smile lighting up her face. "As long as you keep that finger where it belongs, and your potty mouth to yourself, you'll be a wonderful model. You have excellent bone structure."

"Miracles never cease! The beauty queen has complimented Bernice, and now she's telling me I've got good bones. What's come over you, Ida? Are you screwing around with some man we don't know about? You're never this nice unless you're getting laid," Sophie stated, her voice laced with suspicion. She gave Ida the evil eye. "Are you seeing someone on the sly and not telling us?"

Haughty as ever, Ida planted both hands on her hips. "If I were, you would be the last person I would tell. What I do in my private life is not your"—she glanced at Mavis, Toots, and Bernice, seated at the kitchen table—"or anyone else's business."

Sophie gave her the finger.

"See? This is exactly what I'm talking about! You have absolutely no control over that middle finger of yours! I can just see it all now. Sophie in the makeup chair, a call comes in from a prospective customer, and she flashes that finger at the camera."

The outrageous image caused all of them to laugh.

Always having the last word, Sophie answered, "Okay, okay, I promise not to flip the bird and cuss when we're on television. Anything more than that, you'll just have to take your chances."

Chapter 4

"And you'd better not smoke," Ida added. "I'm quite sure they don't allow smoking in the studio, either."

"For crying out loud, Ida, if you're ashamed of what I *might* do, then why in the hell did you ask me in the first place? I can take it or leave it," Sophie cracked. "You'd think we were going to the White House or something."

Toots decided then and there it was time to put an end to all their bickering. "I think you two have said enough. I'm tired of listening to your arguing. Sophie, you will not under any circumstances cuss or

smoke or flip the bird while we're on television. Ida, you can stop treating Sophie
like she's an . . . *igmotard.* Okay?"

"What the heck is an *igmotard*?" Sophie
asked.

"I'll tell you later. It isn't very politically
correct."

"Since when did that ever stop either of
you?" Ida questioned. "You're both known
for saying what's on your mind."

"Okay, if you must know, it's a combina-
tion of *ignorant, moron,* and *retard.* Are
you happy now?"

"That's really bad, Toots, coming from
you. Even I haven't heard that one," Sophie chastised. "If I had, I don't think I'd
use it. Too tacky, and cruel besides."

"Let's forget I said it, then, okay? It's not
a nice word, any of it. And for the record, I
heard it in a teen horror movie. One that
Laura Leighton starred in."

"Figures," Sophie said. "She's the worst
actress in Hollywood. I can't believe they're
making another part of those stupid vam-
pire flicks. Abby told me that she refused
to cover anything even remotely connected
to her or her movies. I think it has something to do with Chris."

"When did she tell you that?" Toots asked. Her daughter called her at least three times a week since they'd returned to Charleston. She'd never mentioned this to her, but Toots figured that just because she was her mother didn't mean she told her *everything.* It was only fair that she saved a few tidbits for her three god-mothers.

"Last time I spoke with her. She didn't say anything specific about Chris, but I could tell from the tone of her voice. She is so massively in love with him, I would bet you my last dollar that something major is about to happen between the two of them."

"Oh, that would be lovely. Just think of the beautiful children they'll have," Mavis gushed. "I can't wait to be a grand-godmother."

"Is there such a thing?" Ida asked.

"It doesn't matter. We'll make it 'such a thing,'" Toots said. "Is this a gut feeling you're having or just godmother intuition?"

"Both," Sophie said succinctly.

Toots had high hopes that the two of them would acknowledge their feelings for one another. It had been quite obvious for the past two years. When they were in the same room together, the air around them was electric. You could practically feel the sensuous magnetism that passed between them. They'd had several dates, but Abby kept the details to herself. Chris wasn't so reluctant. He'd hinted for the past several months that Abby meant much more to him than she knew. When authorities had cast him as a person of interest in Laura Leighton's disappearance, Abby had been an emotional wreck, though she didn't come right out and say so. Toots knew. When Chris and Laura were located in the Sierra Nevada mountain range during a blizzard, holed up on Mammoth Mountain, in a cabin owned by Joshua Kline, a friend of Chris's, the relief on her daughter's face when she learned Chris was safe, and that he was *not* romantically involved with the B-grade actress, was obvious.

"Let's keep this to ourselves for now. I wouldn't want to spoil any good news they might share with us. When the time is right, it will happen. Until then, I'm content to let Abby run the paper while Chris looks out for her. Now"—Toots stood up—"Bernice, you and I have a date with your physical therapist. I'm going to run upstairs and change first. I'll just be a few minutes."

"My appointment is at noon, Toots. I really don't want to arrive earlier than I have to. It's not fun at all," Bernice stated dryly.

"She wants to get to the hospital early so she can catch a glimpse of Dr. Pecker. . . . I mean *Dr. Becker.* Am I right, Tootsie?" Sophie teased.

Toots couldn't help but laugh. "How many times do I have to tell you to stop calling him that? And for the record, Bernice's therapist called yesterday and said her day was open, and I could bring her in at any time I wanted. So there. Does that answer your question?"

Sophie stood up and stretched, a sneaky grin on her face. "Sure. Bernice, whatever you do, keep her away from this good-looking doctor. She swore there would never be a husband number nine. If she continues to hang around that hospital, Dr. Becker and his pecker are in deep doo-doo."

"Sophia Manchester, I ought to kick your skinny tail! I am not interested in Dr. Becker or any part of him . . . *that way.* He's simply a new friend, and he just so happens to be Bernice's cardiologist."

"Who just so happens to have a pecker. I see how your face lights up when his name is mentioned. I've also observed the two of you together. He's got the hots for you, too. Big-time, Tootsie," Sophie added.

"Sophie has men and sex on the brain," Ida interjected. "She needs to take her relationship with Goebel to the next level. It's been long enough."

"Why, you old rip! Just because you bop every man you meet on the first date does not mean I'm going to follow in your trampish footsteps. You have no clue what goes on between me and Goebel. Like you said, my personal affairs are not your concern."

Mavis had remained silent for too long. She clapped her hands together in order to get their attention. "Ladies, please! We have wasted the entire morning on idle chitchat. Do I need to remind you that we are not in seventh grade anymore?" Coco growled in agreement with her mistress.

"Our bones, to my utmost regret, are quite aware of our age. At least mine are," Toots replied as she headed toward the staircase. "Bernice, unless you want to ride a Lark to the hospital, I suggest you get your wrinkled butt in gear."

"What the hell is a Lark?" Bernice asked of no one in particular.

Showing her amusement, Sophie replied, "The last I heard, it was a damned songbird. Toots, are you expecting poor old Bernice here to ride a frigging bird to the hospital?" Sophie could barely contain her laughter.

Toots paused on the staircase and turned around to face Sophie. "Remind me why we're friends again. Please."

"Because you love my sense of humor and my great beauty?"

Toots rolled her eyes, her lips upturned in a grin. "How could I forget? And for the record, the Lark that I am referring to is a motorized chair."

"Hey, I resent that! I am not *that* old, Miss Smart Mouth," Bernice said. "I've seen those commercials. No way will you ever catch me buzzing around doing laundry in a wheelchair with an engine."

"I was teasing, Bernice. You should know me better than that. By the time you're finished with your physical therapy, you'll be able to run a marathon."

"I guess I should thank you for the vote of confidence, but I am not exactly planning to run any marathons. I just want to be healthy enough to observe Mrs. Patterson's place, and if I'm needed over there"—she directed her gaze to the property next door—"then I want to be able to do what it is I was sent back to do in the first place."

Toots gave a slight nod. "Whatever your motivation is, Bernice, I suggest you find it soon, or as I explained before, you will be arriving at the hospital by another means. Bird, bus, taxi, or me. The choice is all yours."

Continuing in the vein of the morning's giddiness, Bernice threw both her hands high in the air, then slowly positioned her fingers until both middle fingers, gnarled with arthritis, stood out from the others and prominently displayed a double single-digit salute.

Chapter 5

"I think you have too much perfume on. It's making my eyes water," Bernice said. "I don't know why you bother getting all gussied up just to watch me sweat bullets."

Toots steered the Range Rover into the handicapped parking space. Bernice insisted on using the permit she'd been issued even though there was no way in hell Toots would allow her to drive herself to the hospital. But if it made her happy, then Toots was all for it.

"I like watching you sweat. It makes me smile."

"Bull. You like watching my doctor examine me."

"Oh, stop it! I don't know what's come over you and Sophie, but you'd better keep it to yourselves. If you so much as hint to Dr. Becker about such . . . nonsense, then you *will* be riding a bird to the hospital. Or a taxi."

Toots shut off the engine. Pulling her sun visor down, she peered in the small vanity mirror. She smacked her lips together and fluffed her hair before closing the mirror.

"I guess you like what you see. I wonder if Dr. Becker will?" Bernice asked as she retrieved her handbag from the floor.

"I don't know and don't care. Come on, let's get this over with. I have much more exciting things to do than hang around a hospital."

Bernice clambered to get out of the Range Rover. But before she had a chance to close the passenger door, Toots was at her side. "Be careful. I don't want the therapist to think you're not well taken care of." Without being too pushy, Toots led Bernice through the hospital doors and then inside the elevator and up to the third floor, where the physical therapy center was located.

The center was divided up into sections according to the patients' different levels of ability, beyond the required initial phase tackled while still in the hospital. Bernice had completed that phase with flying colors. After three days, she'd walked up and down the halls like a prostitute searching for her next john. Toots smiled when she recalled Sophie telling this to Bernice. She had recuperated faster than expected of a woman her age and had been sent home, promising to change her lifestyle. Bernice had followed the doctor's orders to the letter, and then some.

Now she was nearing the end of phase three. When it was successfully completed, she would be allowed to continue her therapy at home, as long as she continued to go to doctor appointments and all of her blood work remained normal. And so far, good old Bernice had passed this third phase with flying colors, too. Toots intended to keep her friend around for a while and did whatever she could to assist Bernice in her quest for good health.

Though she would not smoke around Bernice, she knew she had to seriously give up the habit. Yes, she'd cut way down, but cutting down and quitting were two different things.

When they reached what Toots called "perspiration paradise," a room filled with all kinds of exercise equipment, and the smells to go along with it, Bernice shooed her away. "Go have coffee, or have a piece of cake in the cafeteria. I'm going to be here for a while, and I don't need you to babysit."

They went through this same routine three times a week. Toots rolled her eyes, took Bernice's handbag for safekeeping, then headed for the bank of elevators. "Just so you know, I don't eat the dried-up cake they serve in the cafeteria. I plan to have a bowl of Froot Loops." Toots was noted for her sweet tooth. For a period of time, she'd actually called herself a vegan; but when she had to resort to using soy milk, she'd given up her attempt at a vegan lifestyle. It was either whole milk or nothing at all for her.

"Yeah, you just watch what happens if

you keep eating that junk and smoking those nasty cigarettes. You're going to be right here alongside me, only I'll be the one running after that sexy, hot doctor," Bernice said to Toots right before the elevator doors opened.

"Did I hear someone say 'sexy, hot doctor'?" Dr. Phil Becker asked as he entered the physical therapy room.

"You did, but you just missed her." Bernice nodded toward the elevator. "She's going to the cafeteria. And then I'm sure she'll run outside to huff a smoke or two."

At sixty-eight, Dr. Phil Becker could've passed himself off as ten years younger if he were of a mind to do so. More than six feet tall, with the lean build of a runner, a thick mop of curly brown hair, and eyes so blue that one noticed them from a distance, he was far from the public's image of a cardiologist. Some might mistake him for a college professor. That day, he wore a pale blue polo shirt, khaki slacks, and Sperry deck shoes. To distinguish himself, he wore the obligatory white jacket with DR. PHILLIP J. BECKER, M.D. F.A.C.C., embroidered in thick black letters above the upper left pocket.

Dr. Becker glanced at the closing elevator doors. "I'll catch her later. Now, my friend, let's see how you're progressing."

A pretty blond physical therapist made a few notes on Bernice's chart before handing it over to the doctor. He scanned the information and signed his name at the bottom of the chart before giving it back to the physical therapist.

"Looks like you've more than surpassed the normal expectations. This is good. Now, I know the answer to this, but I have to ask, anyway. Are you prepared to continue to follow a strict diet and exercise regimen when I formally release you?"

Walking on the treadmill, Bernice nodded. "You ask this every week, and my answer is still the same. Yes. I want to live a while longer, so I will follow the rules. Now, can you leave me alone for a while? I want to listen to my music." Toots had given Bernice an iPod. She had learned to download music and books and brought this with her for her required sixty minutes on the treadmill.

Dr. Becker laughed. "Yes, all right. But remember, you still have two more sessions here at the hospital before I can allow you to start working out on your own."

Bernice took a deep breath and nodded. She had her earbuds in place and clicked the START button. She waved the doctor away and began her stint on the treadmill.

Seeing that he wasn't needed to assist or advise, Dr. Becker raced to the elevator, where he pressed C for cafeteria. He was going to find Ms. Loudenberry before she made an excuse to leave. He'd tried to corner her on several occasions, and each time she'd raced off to some urgent errand. *Not today, she won't.*

As soon as the elevator doors swished open, he raced down the short hall to the cafeteria. Midmorning, and it was already packed with medical staff, a few ambulatory patients, and several visitors. The hum of voices and the clatter of dishes, along with the smell of baking bread and burnt coffee, greeted him as he stood on the threshold, searching for her. He spied her sitting alone at a table against the back wall, farthest from the exit. *Perfect,* he thought as he made his way across the cafeteria. It wouldn't be so easy for her to avoid him this time. He would follow her if he had to. That sounded scary even to him. He laughed to himself. A stalker he was not.

He strode over to her table. He saw three opened mini-boxes of Froot Loops scattered on her tray, plus two empty cartons of whole milk. "You keep eating that junk, you're gonna wind up on my table sooner than you think."

Toots was too surprised to do more than nod, and she needed a few seconds to compose herself. Swallowing the last bite of her Froot Loops, she wiped her mouth with the small square of rough paper disguised as a napkin. "Dr. Becker, I presume." She wasn't going to say more, nor was she going to stand up and invite him to join her.

"Ms. Loudenberry," he said. Then, without waiting for an invitation, he sat down in the chair across from her.

Toots suddenly remembered why she was at the hospital. "Is Bernice all right?"

"She's better than all right. I just left her. She really doesn't need to come back for therapy. She's progressed enough to move on to the next phase."

Toots's heart lurched, then slowed to a steady beat. *Figures Bernice would recover quickly.* Not that she didn't want her to, it was just that she thought she might have a chance to . . . *Never mind. It is what it is.* She cleared her throat. "Well, that's the best news I've heard all day." And it was. Really.

His full lips twisted into a cynical smile. "Then why, I cannot help but wonder, do you not look very happy?"

No way was she going to allow him to get under her skin. "And what is that supposed to mean? You don't know me. I don't see how you can make such a statement. It isn't like we're . . . friends or anything. You haven't even . . ."

He reached across the small table and took her hand in his. "I haven't even what? Had the opportunity to ask you out? Hold your exquisite hand in mine?" His gaze went to their clasped hands. Toots yanked her hand away.

His smile turned into a chuckle. "I see. You want to play hard to get. Okay. I'm game. It's not like I'm going anywhere. Nope, just staying right here in Charleston. I don't have a home in Los Angeles, or anywhere else, for that matter. So you see, I have all the time in the world."

Toots's eyebrows rose in amazement at his gutsiness. In spite of herself, she smiled. She liked this man. He had . . . chutzpah. She was thinking of something else when she had the sudden thought that she really didn't know if he had . . . *those,* what she thought of instead of nerve. Just the thought forced her to laugh out loud.

"You think this is funny? I've been trying to corner you for weeks, and now that I have, you're laughing at me?"

Totally unaware of the captivating picture she made when she smiled, Toots waited, sure the good doctor was about to say something she wanted to hear. She raised her brow, inquiringly. "No, I'm not laughing at you." He was going to work for this, she thought as she waited for him to spit out whatever it was he had to say. She liked playing hard to get. Was actually surprised at how much she'd missed the chase, playing the game of cat and mouse.

The noise in the background stilled to a low drone. Toots felt the blood gush to her head, and her ears felt like they had when, as a child, she'd held a seashell next to her ear. She was sixty-six years old. This was *not* supposed to happen at her age. Nope. Not at all. She'd been there, done that. Eight times. Seven times too many. No way. It was not going to happen again. She was finally in complete control of her life. The last thing she wanted was a man to complicate things. Her life was nearly perfect—she could come and go as she pleased, answering to no one but herself. She was not going to be like Ida. Just comparing herself to her man-hungry friend had the power to frighten her.

"Then you must be afraid of me," Dr. Becker said.

Toots shook her head. "No, not at all."

"Your red face says otherwise."

Good grief! She was actually blushing. Trying to think of a quick comeback, she said, "I have . . . rosacea."

Phil Becker laughed so loud that several patrons in the cafeteria turned to stare at him. Toots felt her face . . . her *rosacea* . . . turn crimson. Damn him for making her feel like she was a . . . a kid! She was anything but, and was just getting ready to tell Becker a thing or two when a young woman in her early thirties approached their table. She wore green scrubs and a light blue cover over her head. Her shoes also sported the protective covers.

"I'm sorry to interrupt, but Dr. Miller has a patient in ER he wants you to examine. He said you'd be here."

Toots wondered why he hadn't been paged over the intercom system, beeped on his pager, or called on the cell phone she knew he kept strapped to his hip.

"Of course. Tell him I'm on my way."

The young woman nodded before racing out of the cafeteria.

"Ms. Loudenberry, you have been saved by the bell once again, but before I let you off the hook, just so you know, I know what rosacea is, and trust me, you do not have rosacea. What you do have, I think we doctors refer to as blushing." He stood up, grabbed her tray, and motioned for her to stand as well. "I would really like to discuss something very important with you. Since I'm needed in the ER, would it be too much to ask you to walk with me?"

Shit! He was not going to leave her alone, and frankly, Toots admired a man with persistence. Given her rosacea lie, the least she could do was listen to what he had to say.

"I'll walk with you," she replied, following him to the area where garbage and trays were disposed of. "Of course, if this is an emergency, please don't wait for me."

He raked the cereal and milk boxes into the garbage, then stacked the tray on top of the others. "No, I knew Miller was going to ask me to have a look at his patient. They've been there for a while. It's not a real emergency."

Out in the hall, Toots walked beside him but was careful not to get too close. She didn't want to give him any ideas.

"A person is in the emergency room, waiting for you, and you say it's not an emergency?" The disbelief in her voice was obvious, but she didn't care.

"I know what you're thinking. I really can't divulge patient information, but let's just say this 'emergency' is here at least three times a week. I believe this emergency was diagnosed with panic attacks. It seems a cardiologist is needed in order to reassure the patient that he or she is not having a heart attack. Now, forget I told you that, okay?"

They were in front of the bank of elevators. Toots knew that the emergency room
was farther down the hall and around several corners ahead, but he'd stopped here,
and she wasn't going to ask any questions.

"Forget what?" she asked with a smile.

"I like smart women. Did I ever tell you
that?" he asked as they proceeded around
a corner.

Smiling inwardly, Toots thought about
how she really liked this guy. *Really.* And
that was not a good thing. No way could
she even think about going down *that* path
again. Eight times, and she'd worn it out.
Nope, she did not see Dr. Becker in her
future. She slowed her pace at the next
turn. "Look, I really should go. Bernice is
probably finishing up and wondering what
happened to me. I have her handbag."
She touched the strap to the large white
purse hanging from her shoulder.

He glanced at his wristwatch. "No, she
has at least another hour. According to
what her physical therapist wrote in her
chart, Bernice is going to learn the fine art
of weight lifting today. It's all part of the
usual process."

Toots didn't know what to say, so she said nothing. Dr. Becker picked up his pace, and she decided to follow him. They turned two more corners and walked down another long hall. Neither spoke, but Toots knew they were close to the emergency room. She heard a blue page code over the main speaker, and before she had a chance to comment, Dr. Phil Becker was gone.

Not wanting to stand out, but curious, Toots slowly made her way down the remaining connecting hallways that led to the emergency room. Rushed footsteps, beeping sounds from the many lifesaving machines, and firm commands greeted her as she rounded the corner. From a distance, she spied a curtained-off area, where she viewed several sets of protective-covered feet as they raced around the small space. Sure this was the room in which the code blue patient was being treated, Toots gave a quick prayer that whoever it was, Dr. Becker could save their life. Knowing what bad shape Bernice was in when they'd admitted her, she had high hopes that the patient would survive with the help of the good doctor. Understanding that it was useless to remain lurking in the hallway of the emergency room, Toots decided she'd best return to the third floor. She could watch television while Bernice did her weight lifting.

The second she decided to leave, she heard her name. "Teresa, wait!"

Only those who didn't know her called her by her given name. She smiled. It sounded much better than Ms. Loudenberry.

She stopped but didn't turn around. Toots felt a hand touch her shoulder, giving her a warm, tingling sensation. She wanted to push his arm away but knew that if she did, either he would think her incredibly rude or—and this was what she feared most—he would think his touch had an effect on her. Slowly, she turned around, making sure her features were completely normal. Hopefully, she wouldn't blush again.

"Sorry to take off like that, but I hear a code blue, and, well, you know what that means?" he asked, a grin on his handsome face.

She could've played dumb and said no, but after burying eight husbands, she would look totally stupid if she did. "I take it the emergency is under control?"

"There wasn't an emergency. That patient I told you about? Seems that he or she initiated the code blue when messing with the instruments above the bed. I calmed the patient down, and now that patient is ready to be released." He raked a hand through his thick curls. "At least until next week. He took her hand in his and followed the same route as before. "Now, I have to say this before I'm interrupted again. For weeks, I've been dying . . . No, forget I said that. I've wanted to invite you to dinner. Either you're off and running, or I am. So, now that that's out of the way, will you have dinner with me? Tonight?"

Toots felt her heart rate increase, and for a moment she feared she might wind up next to the patient he'd just left. With her hand in his, she called up every power in her not to tremble, not to blush like a teenager. She took a deep, cleansing breath.

Why not? It wasn't as if he was going to ask her to marry him. She could have dinner with a man without it leading to marriage or anything more. She was not like

Ida, who hopped into the sack on the first date and wanted a lifetime commitment. *No,* she thought, *I just marry them as soon as they ask. Then I bury them. Marry and bury. Could I be a jinx to men?*

"Dinner would be nice," she answered. Had she just doomed Dr. Becker to becoming number nine? *Unlucky* number nine. No! She was just suspicious of everything these days. She'd have Sophie read for her; maybe she'd reassure her that she wasn't bad luck when it came to men.

Dr. Becker squeezed her hand. "Where would you like to go?"

She thought for a moment, then recalled a new restaurant that had recently opened three doors down from The Sweetest Things. She couldn't recall its name but gave Dr. Becker, *Phil,* the location.

"Okay. I'd like to pick you up and drive you there." He let go of her hand then. "I'm an old-fashioned kinda guy."

Of course he is, she thought. She liked a man with old-fashioned manners. As independent as she was, it was still nice to know there were a few men left who still followed society's unwritten rules. Sophie would croak if he knew her thoughts.

The idea of an evening alone with the good doctor sent her spirits soaring. "That would be wonderful, but I want you to stop calling me *Ms. Loudenberry.* My friends call me Toots." There was a trace of laughter in her voice.

He threw back his head and chuckled. "I love it! Toots, huh? How'd you end up with that?"

Coming from anyone else, Toots would've been insulted, but seeing the merriment on Dr. Becker's, *Phil's,* face, she was anything but. "Toots. My father started calling me Toots when I was an infant. Said Teresa was a mouthful for such a small girl." Wistful, Toots smiled at the memory. "I was very young when my father died. He was a great man." Not wanting to get too personal, she blinked several times in order to keep her happy tears at bay.

"It suits you much more than Teresa."

They continued down the hall, stopping when they reached the bank of elevators. The doors opened, and they stepped inside. Confined in the elevator for the short ride to the third floor, they both remained silent. The air was electric, so much so that Toots had a brief flash of what it might be like to crawl beneath the sheets with the handsome doctor. Luckily, before she had time to pursue that thought further, the doors swished open.

By then, she knew she was in deep brown stuff.

The buzz of activity on the third floor brought her back to the present. She clung to Bernice's purse strap like to a lifeline. Was she biting off more than she could chew? What would Abby think if she knew her mother was in the throes of having a major case of the hots for Phil Becker? Toots answered her own question: Abby would be thrilled.

"I hope I'm the reason for that gorgeous smile lighting up your face."

If he only knew. "Oh . . . well, I'm just happy Bernice is finished with her therapy. She's convinced that something terrible is going to happen in the empty house next door. Despite all the evidence to the contrary, she believes that some sort of celestial being said she had to remain on earth to watch that house. Now she can devote all of her time to her 'project,' as she calls it." Toots made air quotes with her index fingers.

"She's got a couple more rounds of therapy before I release her. Just make sure she doesn't overdo things. She's come a long way. We wouldn't want her to have a setback."

Toots stopped in the middle of the hallway. "Could you tell that to her? If I say a word about her doing too much, she tells me to kiss her wrinkled old . . ." She paused. Did she really want Dr. Becker, *Phil,* to see this side of her? Yes, she did. *What you see is what you get.* Nothing phony about her. "Ass."

He laughed, drawing the attention of two nurses walking past. They both smiled at Toots. Was Phil a ladies' man?

"I'll make sure to tell her to take it easy. I wouldn't want to . . . Well, let's just say I wouldn't want to be subjected to kissing anything that's not visible."

The visual made Toots giggle. "I understand. I haven't had to view her . . . derriere, and with luck, I'll never have to. Bernice is a good soul, though. She's like a sister to me. I couldn't imagine life without her.

She's been with me for almost twenty-five years. If not for Bernice, I don't know where I'd be now." What she wanted to tell Phil was that Bernice had been with her through eight husbands, but she figured since she had yet to go out with him on their first date, it probably wasn't a good idea to bring that up. Maybe later, if and when she got to know him better, but for now, she'd keep her past to herself.

He chuckled, then looked at his watch. "How does seven o'clock sound to you?"

"Perfect, Dr. Becker. Just perfect."

Chapter 6

Since learning that her mother was the face behind LAT Enterprise, Abby Simpson had doled out assignments as she saw fit. In doing so, *The Informer*'s sales had quadrupled, and they were now running neck and neck with the *National Enquirer.* They'd surpassed the *Globe* months ago. And Abby couldn't be happier. Though she missed her mother and her three godmothers being in Malibu, Abby knew it was best that they stayed in Charleston in order to monitor Bernice's condition after her bypass surgery. Bernice was like a favorite aunt to her. She'd moved with her mother, her father, and Abby from New Jersey when Abby was only five. She couldn't imagine life without Bernice any more than she could imagine life without her mother and her three godmothers, or the three g's, as she affectionately referred to them.

Tonight she'd been invited to attend the premiere of what Hollywood insiders were calling the movie of the year, a shoo-in for an Oscar and a Golden Globe Award. Sandra Bullock had the starring female lead, with George Clooney as the leading man, in *As Time Goes By,* a love story that took place during the Holocaust.

Abby had splurged on an exquisite Carolina Herrera gown, a two-tone satin gown in Paris Poppy red with a one-shoulder neckline and a mermaid pleated back. She'd had to have a few alterations done, given her petite size. Abby would wear the diamond earrings given to her by her mother for her sixteenth birthday, would carry a small matching clutch, and would wear heels, but that was it. Nothing too flashy for her. She didn't want to be accused of trying to upstage the stars, but she didn't want to show up in some off-the-rack garb from last season, either. She thought that she'd reached a happy medium with her choice.

The icing on the cake—Chris was going to attend the event with her. Wanting to stay out of the limelight as much as possible since his much-publicized nightmare with Laura Leighton, he'd dropped most of his clients, telling Abby he was easing out of entertainment law. Said it was time for a second career. Abby had asked him what he had in mind, but he had yet to reveal any plans to her.

"Woof! Woof!" Chester, her six-year-old German shepherd, barked, letting her know he wanted her attention.

"Yes, I know. You want to go outside." Abby dutifully opened the French doors that led to her fenced-in backyard, where Chester would watch the squirrels and occasionally give chase, though he never tried very hard to catch them. She'd adopted him from a shelter as a Christmas gift to herself. He'd been her constant companion ever since. When she was working as a reporter at *The Informer,* she would take him to work with her, and when she was on what she thought of as a Hollywood stakeout, she always brought him along for protection. He'd become a permanent fixture at the paper, and she hoped to keep him around as long as humanly possible. He was her very best friend.

Leaving him outside to do his thing, Abby glanced at the clock. It was getting late. She needed to start getting ready for tonight's event. Her dress hung in a plastic bag in the closet; her shoes were still in the box. Unlike most of tonight's attendees, she'd opted to do her own hair and makeup. Besides, she wasn't one for all the glitz and glamour. Abby liked to observe and report, nothing more. But she had to admit that she was excited about tonight's premiere. Not because of the movie's star-studded cast. No, she was excited because it was really the first time she would be attending such an event with Chris as her date.

Since his nightmare experience with Laura Leighton, Chris had treated her like an entirely different person. Especially since they'd admitted their love for one another. She recalled quite clearly the night they admitted this to each other.

Abby had written about Chris and Laura being stranded in a blizzard, though she omitted the part about Laura Leighton wanting to blow up World Con Studios. They'd shared a phone call; then, out of the blue, he'd called her back. She recalled the conversation quite clearly.

She answered on the first ring. "What?"

"Did I ever tell you your telephone etiquette sucks?"

"What?" Abby said again.

"You need to learn how to answer the phone properly."

"You called me just to tell me that? Chris Clay, have you been nipping at the bottle?"

He cracked up laughing. "Nipping, Abby? What's that? A new Hollywood term for drunks?"

She couldn't help but laugh. "No, Chris, it's not. Now tell me, why are you calling me at this ungodly hour? I have to be at work in a few hours. Unlike some people I know."

"Didn't you just call me half an hour ago? What's changed, Abby? The dog's not keeping you warm enough?"

"Chris, the next time I see you, I swear I'm going to smack you right up-

side the head. What in the hell has gotten into you?"

"You, Abby. You've gotten into me.
And that's why I called. I couldn't wait
another minute to tell you that I love
you."

Abby remembered that it took her a few
minutes to get her bearings. She wasn't
sure she'd heard him correctly.

"Did you hear what I just said, Abby?"
Silence.

"Abby?"

"I heard you, Chris. I heard you."
Abby was breathless.

"And? Aren't you going to tell me
what a jerk I am? Call me a few choice
names? Smack me right upside the
head?"

She was stunned, surprised, and
over the moon. Totally over the moon.
The three words she'd been waiting to
hear from him for longer than she cared
to admit. She was over the moon. Big-
time. Very, very big-time.

"No, Chris, I don't want to do any of
those things to you. What I want is for
you to get your butt in that boring Toyota Camry you drive and come out here

so I can tell you I love you back to your face."

"I'm on my way, sweet girl. I'm on my way."

They'd been practically inseparable ever since, though they'd yet to take their relationship to an intimate level.

Soon, Abby thought. *Soon.*

We've definitely waited long enough.

Chapter 7

Chris Clay wiped an imaginary speck of dust from the lapel of his newly purchased Calvin Klein tuxedo. He was attending a movie premiere with Abby, and he wanted to look his very best. Though he'd been to many such events in the past, he'd never attended them with a woman with whom he was madly in love.

He grinned just thinking of Abby. She was a pint-size ball of fire, with blond curls and eyes as blue as the sky. He'd been attracted to her for a long, long time. Though their parents had married one another, Chris had never seen much of Abby during the years of their parents' marriage, as he'd been away at college. Then his father passed away, and he thought his contact with Abby and Toots might end, but it didn't. Toots remained his mother in every sense of the word. He'd been in high school when they married, and he adored Toots. She was the only mother figure he'd ever had. Later, when Abby moved to Los Angeles, where Chris was practicing law, he'd promised Toots he'd keep an eye out for her. He had in his own way. Chris didn't want her to think he was stalking her, or that he was an overly possessive step-brother, so he'd stayed behind the scenes as much as possible, allowing Abby to live her life. Occasionally, they'd meet for lunch or just bump into one another, but they'd never really hung out on a regular basis.

Nonetheless, she'd somehow managed to get under his skin, and no matter how much he tried, he simply could not stop thinking of her. He'd kept his feelings to himself. But two years ago, they'd had a date of sorts. He'd taken her to Pink's, a little joint in Los Angeles noted for its hot dogs. They'd sat in the car, chatted, and eaten their hot dogs. Then he'd kissed her fingers. One at a time. With each kiss, his whole being filled with wanting. And it hadn't stopped since.

Trapped on a mountain during a blizzard with that featherbrained Laura Leighton had made him realize just how short life really was and that it could be taken away at a moment's notice. He vowed then that he would tell Abby his feelings. If she rebuffed him, then so be it.

Luckily for him, she'd felt the same way. Ever since, they'd taken things slow and easy. Tonight he planned to change that when he proposed. He had purchased a diamond ring and had it safely tucked inside the pocket of his tuxedo. For that matter, he planned to change a lot of things in his life. He could only hope that Abby would agree to the changes.

With one last look in the mirror, he ran a comb through his hair, knowing it wouldn't stay in place no matter what he did. Then he shut the light out, grabbed the keys to his Toyota Camry, and headed for Brentwood. Since selling his condo, he'd relocated to an apartment just minutes from

Abby's. He liked being close to her, liked that he could be at her house in ten minutes, and that was in heavy traffic.

Five minutes later, he pulled into Abby's drive. Her bright yellow MINI Cooper was parked in its usual place. Abby had spent hours weeding, watering, and planting, and now her front lawn rivaled any in Beverly Hills. In the back, the courtyard had been overrun with elderberry vines, honeysuckle, and morning glory. Abby had artfully trimmed the vines, making her back lawn a place to kick back and relax. If it were up to him, he'd rather toss a couple of steaks on the grill and enjoy the sweet scents and the view. Not that night, though. It was an important night for Abby, as she, or rather *The Informer,* had been invited to attend the movie premiere. In the world of tabloid journalism, it was big news.

A loud bark jolted him out of his reverie. He hopped out of his car and walked behind the house to the fenced-in yard, where Chester was racing around. Chris unlocked the door to the gate, as Chester stood on the other side, waiting to greet him like an old friend. He stooped down to pet the big

German shepherd and received a big, slob-
bery doggy kiss.

"Hey, not tonight, old guy. I've got a hot
date with the best-looking woman in LA. I
don't think she'd like it much if I smelled
like a dog." Chris rubbed the shepherd between his ears. "No offense, buddy."

He left the backyard and went around
to the front, where he knocked on the door.
He could've tapped on the French doors,
and Abby would've let him in, but tonight
was formal, special. He wanted the evening to be perfect, because if he was lucky
enough, both his and Abby's lives were
about to change.

She opened the door, and what he saw
literally took his breath away.

"Don't you look like the sexiest man
alive," Abby said as Chris stepped inside
the entryway. "You could give any one of
those movie stars a run for their money."

Chris grinned but said nothing. He
stared at Abby as though he were seeing
her for the very first time. "And I could say
the same about you. If I didn't know better,
I would mistake you for one of those starlets that you write about."

Abby stopped and turned to face him. She placed a hand on each shoulder, then leaned into him, her lips mere inches from his. In her most sensual voice, she said, "If you ever say that to me again, I will smack you squarely in that delicious mouth of yours."

Chris placed his arms loosely around her waist, then whispered in her ear, "Promise?"

"I'm not making any kind of promise," Abby said, her blue eyes dancing playfully. She stepped out of his embrace. "Though I must admit, you clean up very nicely."

"Only because I wouldn't want to publicly humiliate you," Chris joked.

Abby really took a good look at Chris. "There isn't a chance of that, and you know it very well. I think the tux suits you, kind of James Bondish. I like the all-black look." She scanned the length of him, then smiled.

"I take it I pass your inspection?"

"With flying colors," Abby added, then did a quick swirl. "And?"

Chris laughed. It wasn't like Abby to seek a compliment, but he liked that she did, and from him especially. "That dress looks as though it were made for you. The color brings out your cheekbones."

"You sound like Joan Rivers on the red carpet," Abby said, trying unsuccessfully to suppress a girlish giggle.

"Whatever I sound like, I hope to hell I don't look like her. All that stretched skin. Reminds me of a Halloween mask gone bad."

"Oh now, that's mean, Chris. Even from you. If we're lucky, she'll stop us tonight. She's known for picking on the unexpected guests. *The Informer* isn't at the top of the guest list, I can tell you that much."

"I won't argue with that." Chris glanced at his watch. "Are you all set? Anything special we need to do for Chester? He's in the backyard, admiring the squirrels."

"My new neighbors are going to check on him tonight. Since I had that new doggy door installed, he can pretty much come and go when he wants."

"You didn't tell me you had new neighbors," Chris stated.

"You didn't ask," she replied. "And before you do, they're a retired couple. They bought that ranch two houses down. Their granddaughter urged them to move here.

They said she's going to be a big star someday, and they wanted to do whatever they could to support her," Abby explained.

"Well, good luck. Only her and a zillion others," Chris commented. "But if Chester likes them, then I'll take that as a sign."

"He does, and thanks. I thought the same thing," Abby agreed. "You know, we're both starting to think and act like Sophie."

Chris cackled. "Please don't put me in that category! I love the old gal, but she could use a bit of sprucing up in the mouth department. At sixty-five or sixty-six, she's still attractive, I'll give her that, but she needs to tone down the cussing. Takes away from her good looks."

Abby looked at him as though he had two heads. "You're . . . *shitting* me, right?" She couldn't help herself.

He shook his head, his eyes as bright as fire. He put both hands out in front of him, as though he were reluctantly surrendering. "No, I am not *shitting* you, Abby Simpson. Now"—he glanced at his watch for the second time—"if we don't get out of here soon, we'll miss the walk down the red carpet. And I, for one, do not want to miss an opportunity to be interviewed by Ms. Rivers."

Abby laughed. "Let me get my purse."

Unbeknownst to Abby, Chris had arranged for a limousine service to take them to the movie premiere. He wanted this entire night to be magical, like something out of a fairy tale, an experience Abby would remember for the rest of her life. A story she would tell their children and grandchildren. He smiled at the thought. Life was good, and if he was right about Abby and her feelings for him, it was about to get a whole lot better.

Abby emerged from the bedroom with a tiny matching purse. He couldn't imagine what it could hold.

"It's for my cell and lipstick, okay?" Abby informed him. "I know what you're thinking."

"More and more like Sophie."

She rolled her eyes. "I cuss, but I am not psychic. Now, let's get out of here. I had the MINI detailed just for tonight. No dog hairs on this dress." Abby grabbed her keys from the hook on the wall by the front door. Chris reached up and took them from her.

"Just what in the heck do you think you're doing? Don't you dare go and get all macho—me man, you woman—on me. I can drive just fine, thank you very much."

"Abby." His lips found hers. He explored their soft, velvety fullness, the taste that he'd learned to love.

Gently, Abby pushed him away from her, a smile igniting the fire he saw in her eyes.

"That's . . . nice, but—" She stopped. She wasn't *required* to attend this premiere.

"But what?" he asked.

"We don't have to go, really. We can stay here and . . ." Abby wanted to say "have wild sex all night" but didn't.

Chris wrapped his arms around her, and she placed her head of thick blond curls on his chest. "I know what you're thinking, and there is nothing I would like more, but we can't. Our wheels just arrived."

Abby pulled out of his embrace and peered out the front window. "A limo? This is why you took my keys from me?"

"Yep," he said.

She opened the clasp on her clutch purse and dropped the keys inside.

"Then what are we waiting for?"

Chapter 8

"How do I look?" Toots asked Sophie.

"Like a cheap old woman trying to look twenty years younger," Sophie stated in a steely tone.

Toots whirled around, saw the teasing look on Sophie's face, then fell on the bed next to her. "You are such a witch."

Toots had spent the last hour in her bedroom, trying on clothes. She wanted to look extra special for her date that night but didn't want it to appear as though she was trying too hard.

"I know. Ida reminds me every chance she gets," Sophie said. With several pillows propped behind her, Sophie reclined on Toots's bed in a pose that Queen Elizabeth I might have taken. "She's pissed. You know that, right?"

Toots got up and tossed the cream-colored skirt she'd removed on the bed to join the rest of the clothes she'd already discarded. "Look, Ida is always pissed at someone. It's just her way. She's really excited about her new cosmetics, and frankly, so am I. I just used the face cream when I got out of the shower. It really softened my skin."

"Yes, she instructed me on how and when to use it, too. Mavis likes it. I do, too, but I'm not sure I want to tell her that. Today is day one. Who knows? We could look like old, dried-up prunes tomorrow. That would be just like Ida to do something like that. Make us believe she's discovered the fountain of youth, when, in reality, she's condemning us to something that could cause disfigurement or skin cancer."

"Sophie, your vivid imagination continues to amaze me. Do you really believe Ida would do such a thing?"

"No, of course not, but do not ever tell her I said so."

In the walk-in closet, Toots pulled hanger after hanger from the rod, then piled them on the bed, next to the other pile. "If I told Ida everything you said, she would have murdered you a long time ago. Or at least maimed you in some way. Facial disfigurement?"

Sophie laughed. "You think it's funny, but I don't. I've tried for years to make Ida like me, and she doesn't. Who knows? She might try to—"

"Shut up! Your psychic abilities have warped your mind. Ida is totally harmless. She's simply a self-centered, self-righteous, stuck-up bitch. She knows this full well. I swear, I think she takes pride in it, too. But a killer? No, she wouldn't have the guts." Toots took a black skirt with a sheer black blouse from the hanger. "What about this?" She slipped into the skirt and held the blouse in front of her for Sophie's inspection.

"Older slut. You don't wear see-through clothes when you've been a member of AARP for more than fifteen years."

Toots rolled her eyes. "I wouldn't wear this blouse without a camisole under it. I am not trying to seduce the doctor. I just want to have a nice dinner with him. And I want to look . . . nice. Is there anything wrong with that?"

"Nope, there isn't. But I know you. You've been around the block at least eight times. That I know of. You always start out wanting to look your best. Actually"—Sophie jumped off the bed as though there were springs attached to her feet—"if you were to play down your natural beauty, it might improve your chances. Maybe you've tried too hard in the past, and that's why all your husbands kicked the bucket too soon."

Toots looked in the mirror and saw Sophie behind her. She grinned. "Is that what you think?"

Sophie came to stand beside her. They viewed the sheer blouse and black skirt together. "It was just a passing thought," Sophie stated. "Before you ask, no, it was not a gut-instinct thought." Sophie's gut instinct was always right on the money.

"That's good to hear. At least we can agree that Dr. Becker isn't doomed to die after one measly dinner."

"I didn't say that," Sophie said firmly. "Don't put words in my mouth."

"Trust me, I don't have to. You have plenty spewing out on your own. Now, seriously, which one of these outfits should I wear? Pretend you're going out with Goebel. Which would you choose?"

"I'd probably just go naked. Save a lot of time and trouble."

Toots tossed the blouse on the bed with the rest of the clothes. "You are no help at all. I'm going to ask Mavis. She has much more of a sense of style than you do. I don't know why I invited you into my room in the first place."

"Because you love me? You couldn't live without me?" Sophie suggested, an evil grin pasted on her face.

Toots couldn't keep herself from laughing in spite of Sophie's lack of help. "That's a given, and you should know that by now."

"I do, but I just like yanking your chain. And if it were me, I'd wear the cream skirt and the black blouse. Wear those cream and black heels."

Toots grabbed the cream skirt and black blouse. "Find those shoes, will you?"

Sophie entered the closet and came out with a sleek pair of black heels with a narrow cream-colored stripe along the side of the shoe. "Remember these? You bought them right after Mavis started sewing clothes for dead people."

Toots eyed the shoes. "Hmm, I don't recall buying them, but they're sort of nice. Let me try this ensemble on, see what it looks like." She took the black skirt off, dropping it on the floor, then slid into the cream skirt, grabbed a black camisole out of her chest of drawers, pulled the see-through blouse on, then slid her feet into the shoes. She looked in the mirror, then at Sophie. Part of her wanted to scream, and another part of her wanted to cackle with laughter.

She chose to cackle. "Why, you mean old woman. If I wore this, Dr. Becker would think I was a damned penguin!"

Sophie plopped back on the bed, laughing so hard that tears ran down her face. "And you fell for it!"

Toots removed one of her heels and tossed it in Sophie's direction. It hit the wall, knocking down the one and only wedding picture featuring her and Leland. When she saw what she'd hit, she looked at Sophie, then back at the blank space on the wall, and started to laugh so hard, she fell onto the bed, giggling like a kid. Blotting her eyes with the cuff on the sheer black blouse, she hiccuped, then spoke. Her words were barely audible. "I think that must be a sign!" She continued to laugh, and Sophie joined in, cackling so loud, it was a wonder the others didn't come in to see what was going on.

Again, they were no longer two senior citizens in the twilight of their lives, but two young girls giggling as they talked about Toots's dreamy date with a real doctor, no less.

Chapter 9

Bernice didn't dare tell Toots or any of the other ladies what she had planned. No doubt they would thwart her plans, and she wasn't going to allow that to happen. She'd been given a second chance at life, and she wasn't about to do anything that would jeopardize it. No way. No red meat, nothing sweet, and she'd ride that stupid exercise bike and walk on the treadmill until the cows came home if that was what it took. Not many people her age got a second chance at life. The first half of her life had been decent, except for her son leaving for parts unknown. Sharing Abby with Toots and those other three old women had made for a good life.

When the others had all gone upstairs to check out Toots's attire for her big night out with Dr. Becker, and knowing they wouldn't expect her to climb the stairs, Bernice made her escape.

Careful of all the plant growth and shrubbery that separated Toots's house from old Mrs. Patterson's, Bernice wished she had thought to bring a flashlight. Some spy she was turning out to be. Dusk in Charleston was late, however, and for that she was grateful. Still, she wished she had remembered to bring along a flashlight, or, at the very least, one of those nasty cigarette lighters that were always being tossed on the kitchen table. Then she could have made a torch out of the dried limbs she was constantly stepping on, no matter how hard she tried to avoid them. She saw people do it on television all the time. With her luck, however, she'd catch herself on fire, along with the entire estate. No, her eyes and ears still worked pretty darn good for a woman her age. She'd just watch and wait. Something was bound to happen.

Carefully, she inched her way through

the thick shrubs. Dried sticks cracked beneath her feet, the sound amplified in the early evening air. Most people were having dinner then or watching the evening news. She wouldn't be missed for at least another half hour, when Dr. Becker was expected to arrive.

The Patterson home was on the South Carolina Historical Society's list of homes.

It had been neglected since Mrs. Patterson's death. There were all sorts of wild green vines trailing up the side of the house that faced the back of the guesthouse where Jamie lived. Bernice noticed that seaweed-colored moss fanned the glass windowpanes, preventing anyone from seeing inside or outside.

Bernice pushed one last thorny bush aside, then stepped fully onto the side lawn, where she encountered knee-high grass much in need of a big drink of water. Adirondack chairs, faded from too much time in the sun, were turned over on their sides and backs. Out of the corner of her eye, Bernice saw something move. Her heart drummed in her chest, and for the briefest moment, she was frightened.

"Ah, crap, I'm a wuss," she said out loud,

hoping to calm her fears. She wasn't afraid of whatever was hiding under the chairs. No, she'd felt her heart race, and that had scared her more than anything. Remembering when she'd last felt such a flutter in her chest reminded her that she was in decent shape, at least heart-wise. Her fear, reasonable though it might be, was nonetheless unfounded. Her mission clearly at the forefront by then, she pushed all negative thoughts aside.

As she walked across the neglected yard, she spied movement under the wooden chairs for the second time. Before she walked any farther, she searched for a weapon. To her left, she spotted a large limb lying on the ground. Must have been from that storm last month, she thought as she reached down to pick it up.

"Perfect," she said out loud. "If there's a snake, or a . . . *goblin,* I'm gonna have the first swing." Maybe Sophia and all her psychic mumbo jumbo were having more of an effect on her than she realized. No, she refused to go there. She was here because she'd died on that operating table. She was on a mission, had been sent back to earth to watch this old place, and that was precisely what she was doing. Though, come to think of it, wasn't this mission along the same lines as Sophie's séances and her ability to reach out to the netherworld and beyond? Maybe she'd been a bit too hasty in judging Sophia. Could it be there was something to that mumbo jumbo, after all?

Distracted by her musings and knowing she had to hurry before Dr. Becker arrived to pick up Toots for their evening out, Bernice carefully inched her way over to the Adirondack chairs, her large stick held out in front of her just in case something jumped out at her.

Eyes darting in every direction, searching for the movement that had caught her eye minutes ago, Bernice jumped back a few paces when she heard a low growl, the sound coming from beneath the overturned chairs. Unsure what she might find, she walked closer to the chairs, then lowered herself into a kneeling position. Listening intently, she peered down, hoping to see what she'd heard before *it,* whatever *it* was, saw her first. Another low growl. It wasn't a snake, she thought, because she'd never heard a snake *growl.* She strained to hear one more time. She didn't want to mistake a growl for a hiss.

Nothing.

Overcome with an attack of bravery, Bernice used her stick to push one of the large wooden chairs over on its side. What she saw just about did her in.

Frankie, Mrs. Patterson's seven-year-old dachshund, lay cowering in the overgrown weeds. Bernice reached down to pick him up. When she did so, he growled again. "Frankie, it's me. I won't hurt you, little guy. I thought someone took you away."

Tears welled up in Bernice's eyes. She was a sucker for animals, though she didn't tell this to just anybody. Very carefully, she held her hand in front of Frankie's long reddish brown muzzle so he could identify her scent. As soon as he did this, he peered up at her with his big brown eyes, and Bernice swore he cried when a pitiful wail came from him. "Well, let old Bernice here see what's the matter." She plopped down on her knees, which wasn't an easy feat. Then, being careful, because she didn't know where the little dachsie was injured, she gently picked him up. Frankie yelped, and Bernice set him back down. The little dog tried to stand, and as soon as he did, she saw that his hind legs refused to cooperate.

"Poor little man. You just wait right here. I'm going to get someone to help me get you out of here."

The little reddish brown dachshund that Mrs. Patterson had adored, along with her cats, sat down in the tall grass as though he understood exactly what she had said.

"I'll be right back," she added, before heading back to the shrubbery she'd just pushed her way through. In less than three minutes she was on the back steps leading to the kitchen.

She opened the door and shouted, "Toots! Help. It's an emergency. Come quick!"

Chapter 10

Toots and Phil were saying their final good-byes to Sophie, Ida, and Mavis when they heard Bernice hollering from the kitchen.

"Oh my God, she's having another heart attack! Phil, follow me!" Toots said, her words leaving no room for questions. He trailed behind her, stopping only when they reached the back door.

Apparently, Bernice was *not* having a heart attack.

Miffed that her evening with Dr. Becker was starting off on such a sour note, Toots wasn't nice when she spoke. "Bernice, what are you doing? You're supposed to be in your room, resting. You look like you've just had a roll in the hay."

"Your friends' dirty minds have rubbed off on you. And no, I have not had a roll in the hay. I was . . ." She wasn't about to tell Toots she was spying over at the Patterson place. "Sitting on the stoop and heard this growling sound. I followed it to the Patterson house. Remember her little dachshund, Frankie? It looks like he's been left alone, and he's hurt. We need to get him some help. Now!" Bernice turned around and headed back the way she came. Toots and Dr. Becker followed her.

When they saw the little dog cowering from pain or fear, most likely both, Dr. Becker immediately ran his hands along Frankie's spine. "He's got a spinal injury. Let's get him back to your place, Toots, where I can assess the situation." Without another word, Phil scooped up the ten-pound dog and gently cradled him against his shoulder.

Toots was outraged. "I cannot believe no one bothered to take poor Frankie. Why didn't someone say something? Jamie is here. She would've taken him in."

Bernice gave her a dirty look. "Think maybe this is why I was sent back here?"

"No, I don't, but whatever you were doing over here, I'm glad you were here. I know you weren't sitting on the back stoop, because I just had a cigarette out there two minutes before you called. We can talk about your sneaking off later."

By that time, they were back at the house. Phil put on his physician's hat. "Is there someplace where I can put him? Somewhere soft?"

"Follow me," Toots said.

In the formal living room, Toots told Dr. Becker to place Frankie on the sofa. Who cared that she'd paid thousands to have it reupholstered?

Phil put the little dog on the sofa, careful not to make him hurt any more than he did already. He ran his fingertips along the base of his spine, then helped Frankie into a standing position. As soon as the dog stood, his hind legs collapsed.

"Just what I thought. If no one wants this little guy, which from the looks of it, they don't, I'll take him. I have a friend in Naples, Florida, who specializes in neurological injuries. Since we don't know how long he's been in this shape, time is of the essence. Toots, let's take a rain check on dinner and take a quick trip to Naples to see if we can try to save this little guy. What do you say?"

Toots looked down at her clothes. "Give me two minutes to change." She left them in the formal living room and returned in two minutes with Sophie, Ida, and Mavis trailing behind. Mavis had Coco in her arms, and as soon as the little dog saw Frankie, she started whining, like she was crying.

"Oh my! What's happened to this animal? Coco senses when another animal is hurt. That's why she's making this noise," Mavis said.

"He has a back injury," Toots explained. "Dr. Becker and I are going to Naples, Florida, to a specialist." She turned to the doctor. "Right?"

"Yes, and I'll need to borrow a crate if you have one," he said to Mavis. "We want to keep him as still as we can. Now, I need to make a phone call."

Phil left the room, leaving the three g's and Toots with the dog. Bernice sat on the sofa next to him. "Mavis, get Coco's carrier, a water dish, and a blanket. I know I can't go with Dr. Becker, but I want Frankie to be comfortable," Bernice said.

"Sure, Bernice. I've got everything you need. Be right back." Mavis raced out of the room so fast, she created a breeze.

Ten minutes later, Frankie had been given a dish of water, which he lapped up greedily. Mavis had given him a small plate of turkey breast, which he gobbled up so fast, they all teared up.

"Who knows when he had his last meal?" Toots said. "This really pisses me off. Those Realtors who put up that FOR SALE sign must have known he was there. I'll have their license before this is over with. I hate anyone who is cruel and negligent to an animal."

"We don't know that for sure, Toots. But I get where you're coming from, even though I think Coco is a royal pain in the ass," Sophie said, then bit her tongue, remembering that Mavis was in the room. "I meant that in a good way, Mavis. I love Coco almost as much as you do."

They all knew that was a humongous lie, but like Toots, Sophie did have a soft spot for animals in general, no matter how much Coco in particular annoyed her.

Changing the subject, Toots asked, "Will we need a ride to the airport?"

"No, we can take my car. I have a buddy with a Learjet. He's waiting for us now. Shouldn't take more than a couple of hours to get to Naples. I've called Dr. Carnes, and she said she would be waiting for me."

She? Toots wondered if Dr. Carnes was a former love interest, but now wasn't the time or place. And he had asked her to fly to Florida with him.

Add another point to Dr. Becker's growing list of excellent attributes.

"I assume this Dr. Carnes is one of the best if you're willing to travel to Florida with a stray dog," Mavis said in a serious tone.

"She is. I went to medical school with her father," Phil explained to them. "She runs a place called the Animal Specialty Hospital. Does nothing but emergency medical treatment. No vaccines or nail clipping. She's top of the line, trust me."

Toots breathed such a deep sigh of relief that they all turned to look at her. "What?" she asked when they wouldn't stop staring.

"You sounded like a big gush of hot air just blew out of your mouth," Sophie said.

Everyone laughed except Phil Becker. He looked at his watch. "Let's get to the airport. Time is really important in cases like this. It'll determine whether this little man walks in the future." Being as careful as he could, he lifted the crate off the floor.

Bernice, Sophie, Ida, and Mavis followed them to the front door.

"Call us as soon as you know anything, okay?" Mavis called out as Toots and Dr. Becker walked down the front steps.

"I will," Toots said. "You girls try to stay out of trouble while I'm gone. Bernice, if I hear of you snooping at the Patterson place, I'm going to personally slice your tits off."

With that, Toots climbed inside Dr. Becker's minivan.

As they drove through the gates, Toots had a terrible thought: if they spent the night in Florida, would Phil expect her to sleep with him?

A delightful chill shivered down her spine at the thought.

Chapter 11

Thousands of people were clustered behind portable barricades along Hollywood Boulevard as the limo came to a stop in front of the famous Grauman's Chinese Theatre for the premiere of *As Time Goes By.*

As per Chris's instructions, the limousine driver, dressed to the nines in black, gold brocade, and shiny black shoes, opened the door. Chris stepped out of the sleek limo and offered his hand to Abby. As soon as they turned away from the limo, there were hundreds of bright flashes from the paparazzi snapping their photograph. Chris smiled and took Abby by the hand, as though this were an everyday event. She'd been to a few premieres in her days in LA, but never as a guest. She'd always been one of the outsiders, shouting out at any star whose attention she had a chance of getting. This time it was different. She was being watched like a specimen on a slide.

She leaned close to Chris and whispered in his ear, "I really do not like this."

He smiled, waved at someone, then leaned down, his lips close to her ear. "Honey, you're the one that's in love with Hollywood. This is it in its truest form."

"I still hate it," Abby mumbled between clenched teeth, managing to keep smiling as the flashes of dozens of cameras continued to dazzle the eyes.

Chris led her down the red carpet, his hand cupping her elbow, guiding her through the maze of television personalities with microphones in their hands. Gayle King was there on behalf of her new show, now being aired on OWN, the Oprah Winfrey Network, run by the media giant herself. *Entertainment Tonight*'s Nancy O'Dell was making her way over to Sandra

Bullock, and Giuliana Rancic from *E!* was trying to corner George Clooney.

"Wonder where Joan Rivers is tonight?" Chris asked, a teasing glint in his eyes.

"Maybe she decided to go trick-or-treating instead," Abby shot back, deliberately reminding Chris of his earlier remark.

"It's not time for Halloween, just in case you didn't know," Chris said, then added, "Though after tonight, I might just have a change of heart."

Chris continued to guide her through the crowds of stars, producers, and well-known directors. When they reached the end of the red carpet, where the line to enter had slowed to a virtual crawl, someone in the crowd shouted, "You better watch out, Abby Simpson!"

At the sound of her name, Abby whirled around, searching for a face to put to the voice. She felt as though she'd heard the voice before, like maybe whoever it was had tried to disguise it.

"Abby, stay calm. It's probably just some jerk out there wanting to yank your chain." Chris placed a protective arm around her waist.

Abby scanned the crowds. "I've heard that voice before, Chris. I know I have."

The line moved forward a few more feet.

"It's probably some nutcase who reads *The Informer* and wants his five minutes of fame. And he'll get it if you don't keep quiet."

The words were no sooner out of his mouth when the voice from the crowd yelled, "You're a bitch, Abby Simpson."

Anger made her flush. She peered into the throngs of people behind the barricades, hoping to see a face, someone she might recognize. Abby knew she'd made enemies. In her line of work, it was a given. Whoever it was, for him to go as far as following her and making a public spectacle of himself, this had to be more than an angry reader or a former coworker.

"Let's get inside and enjoy the evening. We've both been looking forward to tonight. Don't let this asshole ruin it for us," Chris said. He kept his hand on her waist the entire time, leading her closer to the theater's entrance. Abby could get used to this.

She took a deep breath and scanned the crowd one more time. No one caught her eye. As she was about to brush the entire incident aside, she saw a man dressed in an out-of-style tuxedo, shoving and pushing his way through the crowd. Several people in the crowd were shouting profanities at him as he bumped through the herd of looky-loos.

Her heart slammed into her chest. "Wait!" she called out. She tried to jerk away from Chris, but he wrapped both arms around her, preventing her from moving away from him.

"Shhh, you don't want to make a scene. Let the wannabes do that," he whispered in her ear.

Abby turned around, her eyes level with his chest. Knowing that Chris was right, she looked up into his eyes as though they were the only two in existence. "Do you know who that was running through the crowd?" she asked, a smile on her face all the while blood rushed to her head. Her hands were shaking so badly that if she let go of Chris, she was sure that they would rival the blades of an electric fan.

Gazing down into her baby blues, he teased, "No, I didn't get a good look. An old boyfriend maybe?"

She rolled her eyes. "I don't have any old boyfriends in LA. And for your information, that idiot running through the crowd was none other than Rodwell Archibald Godfrey, *Rag!* Does that refresh your memory?"

Suddenly, Chris's face went grim. He dropped his arms to his sides, pulling her inside the theater. "You're sure?"

No longer the least bit excited about seeing what was being touted as the next Oscar winner, Abby was suddenly anxious to escape. She had to get out of there.

"Chris, let's just go. I know you went to a lot of trouble tonight, hiring a limo and wearing that sexy tux, but I won't enjoy myself for one second knowing that bastard might be on the loose. Who knows? He might end up trying to trash the offices at *The Informer*. Remember, his pal tried to burn the place down right before Rag disappeared?" Abby felt bad, but she didn't have a lot of time to consider her decision. "I'm going, Chris. With or without you."

"With," he said and led her back outside, where the crowd was getting bigger by the minute. It would be near impossible to find anyone there without a GPS attached to their ass, but Chris wasn't going to say this to Abby. He knew that when she made up her mind to do something, there was no stopping her.

They backtracked over the red carpet, not bothering to respond to the paparazzi calling out to them. It wasn't like they were celebrities. A dark-haired guy, tall and with a beard to his chest, raced alongside them as they tried to make an exit. Chris was one second away from telling the photographer to fuck off when he spoke.

"Abby Simpson!"

They both stopped, turning to look at the bearded guy. Chris wrapped a protective arm around Abby's shoulders and guided them closer to the guy so they could talk without being overheard.

"Oh shit," Abby said. "What are you doing here? And what's with the beard?"

"You know this guy?" Chris asked.

She nodded, then moved away from Chris and leaned over the barricade. With her right hand, she reached up to tug on the extra-long beard. It moved, but the guy didn't seem to feel an ounce of pain. "I hope you have a good explanation, *Josh,* because you're supposed to be working." Abby turned to Chris. "He works at *The Informer.* He's my computer geek."

"Gee, thanks, Abs," Josh replied.

"Don't call me Abs, either. Now, tell me why you're here, before I fire your ass." She was beyond ticked. Josh was the second in command, or at least he had been. Not only had he ruined her evening, but he hadn't followed her orders. Not that she ordered him around, but she'd counted on him to direct *The Informer*'s reporters to the right places. Tonight was a big night in Hollywood. Not only was there tonight's premiere, but there were also a couple of celebrity weddings, and they were trying to find the locations.

Josh leaned across the barricade, then turned around. "I got a tip, Abs. I mean Abby. You know I wouldn't intentionally do anything to cause problems at the paper. I received a phone call a couple of hours ago. Whoever it was said that Godfrey was attending tonight's premiere. I figured given all the grief he's caused you in the past, I'd show up, see if I could spot him, then call the police. Of course, I would've called you first." Josh scratched at the fake beard and raised his eyes, as though asking for mercy.

"Okay, you did the right thing, but you should have called me *first*. And your tip was on the money. He was here. I saw him, and he saw me. He actually called out to me. I was about to try to chase him down when *someone* shouted my name! So for what it's worth, I'm wasting my time standing here explaining this to you. Now, head back to the office. If you hear anything, you call me first. Do not leave the office, is that clear?"

Josh had the grace to blush. "I thought I was doing what you would do. I know how important tonight is . . . *was*. Sorry, Abby."

Damn! This wasn't Josh's fault. He'd tried to do the right thing. She would've done the exact same thing had she been in his position. Minus the beard.

She took a deep breath. "Forget what I said. Just get back to the paper. I'll see you later. And if you get any more suspicious calls, you call me right away. Is that understood?"

"Yes, Abby. I understand you loud and

clear." Josh saluted her, then backed away from the barricade. "I'll call you if I hear anything."

Abby waved, but Josh turned around before he could see.

She looked at Chris. "Let's get out of here. Maybe I can find that jerk before he has a chance to get away again. He's been on the run for over two years now. I think it's high time he paid his dues."

"If you insist, but I doubt we're going to find him in this crowd. Just look. It's tripled since we've been here. The fans are out tonight," Chris said.

Abby looked at the throngs of excited people, all there hoping to catch a glimpse of a movie star. Suddenly, it all seemed silly and meaningless to her. Who really cared? This wasn't reality; it was the land of make-believe. And she'd spent the better part of her adult life actively pursuing these people as though doing so truly mattered. Abby knew she'd just had a major epiphany. Tabloid reporting was her life. Now was not the time for such a revelation; she had to find Rodwell Archibald Godfrey first. Then, and only then, would she think about her future.

"Yes, and we're just standing here wasting time. Come on, let's get out of here." Abby pulled Chris by the arm. Several flashes of light went off in her face. She didn't bother trying to avoid them; she couldn't. As her mother always said, "It is what it is."

Chris removed his cell phone from his pocket. He spoke; then a few minutes later the sleek limousine, which he had hired to drive them to one of the hottest tickets in Hollywood, pulled alongside the curb, where several other limos were parked.

Neither spoke as they drove away from the fans hoping to catch a look at the stars and wondering who was driving away from the premiere even before it began.

Chapter 12

Toots was no stranger to flying in a private aircraft. As the Learjet rolled into the FBO—fixed base operator—at Naples, KAPF Auxiliary Page Field, they were met by the usual red carpet, as the line crew had been alerted to their medical emergency.

After they whisked Frankie quickly into the courtesy car provided by the airport, it was a quick drive down Radio Road to the Animal Specialty Hospital, where Dr. Carnes waited for their arrival.

Pulling into A.S.H., they were met by Dr. Carnes and her assistant, Daphne.

Dr. Becker hadn't seen Michelle since

she was a little girl with red hair and freckles. He'd read in a medical journal that she had earned the distinction of being one of only 160 animal neurologists in the United States.

Dr. Carnes wore teal green scrubs and looked nothing like the little girl he remembered. "I can't believe you're a full-fledged doctor now. I hear you're one of the best in the country. Your dad must be very proud of you," Phil said.

She gave him a huge smile and a hug. "Yes, he is. Now, let me look at this little guy here and see what we can do for him." There would be time for pleasantries after Dr. Carnes performed her magic.

Having made a quick assessment of Frankie's condition, Dr. Carnes explained her treatment plan. "The herniated disk can cause something known as deep pain, causing permanent damage to the spinal cord. If it's been more than twenty-four hours since he suffered the injury, he could be left permanently disabled. We'll need to do an MRI, and if it's as I suspect, we'll need to immediately begin preparations for Frankie's emergency surgery. Since we're looking at several hours, give your contact information to Daphne while I take care of Frankie."

As soon as they gave Daphne Dr. Becker's contact information, he called the airport and arranged to keep the courtesy car overnight. Once that was completed, he turned to Toots and asked, "Is it too late for that date I promised you?"

Toots smiled as they got into the car. "I'm game if you are." The evening was turning into something she had never experienced. The excitement of the unknown gave her the same giddy feelings she'd experienced in her teens when she'd prepared for a date.

Who would've thought poor Frankie's misfortune could be the start of yet another love interest? She couldn't think of number nine and what it would imply.

Dr. Becker was no stranger to the many places and things to do in the Naples area, and told her so. There was Fifth Avenue South, with many fine restaurants and nighttime entertainment. But he remembered Fort Myers Beach and how he used to enjoy walks in the cool evening breeze on his many trips here in the wintertime. It was only a short drive north on Highway

41, then left on Vanderbilt Beach Road, which would take them along the shoreline of the Gulf of Mexico to some of his favorite hangouts. And after an evening out, there was always DiamondHead, the resort where they could spend the night. The thought excited him, but he didn't want to get ahead of himself.

"I've vacationed here for years. There's lots to do during the daytime hours, but I'm positive we can find someplace that's still open for dinner. Then we could take a walk on the beach if you want."

Toots found the prospect of a romantic stroll on the beach more exciting than she would admit. "That sounds nice." *God,* she thought. She was about as exciting as a pig in a mudslide. She'd all but forgotten proper dating etiquette. She was used to being the one in control, even in some of her marriages. Hell, what she was thinking? She was *always* in control. But she kind of liked letting someone else make the decisions for a change.

"Just nice?" Phil asked as he reached across the console for her hand.

Toots felt a shudder in places that hadn't shuddered in a very long time.

"Actually, I feel more than nice. I haven't felt this way for many years."

Had she revealed too much too soon?

He squeezed her hand. "I know the feeling. How do you feel about raw oysters? I know a place that serves the best on the beach, Snug Harbor. It's on the water, and the view is out of this world. The fishing boats come and go in and out of the inlet. It's quite a sight."

Raw oysters? An aphrodisiac, one of nature's gifts to the pleasures of mankind. Toots wondered about the rest of his plans for the evening.

"I love raw oysters. Nothing like an oyster on a fresh saltine cracker piled high with horseradish, lemon juice, and a bit of salt. So yes, Snug Harbor sounds good to me. Are they open late?" Toots asked, grinning to beat the band.

"They're always open till the wee hours of the morning," Phil informed her as they swung into the parking lot.

Because it was so late, the parking lot was nearly empty. As they got out of the car, loud music from a bar across the street blasted away the tranquillity of the evening. The night air was thick with humidity.

The scent of fish and salt water filled the air. Seagulls dipped into the gulf in hopes of catching their next meal.

"This is nothing like California, though it does remind me of Charleston, what with this humidity." Toots waved her hand in front of her face as they walked down the small pier leading to the restaurant's entrance.

"The heat is treacherous here in the summer, but it's great in the wintertime. Mid- to low eighties, with no humidity."

When they reached the door to the restaurant, Phil was informed by a waiter dressed in a crisp white shirt and black slacks that they were no longer serving dinner but offered an after-hours menu in the lounge.

"Is that okay with you?" he asked Toots.

Hell, she would've enjoyed McDonald's as long as he was with her. "It's perfect. I don't like to eat late at night, anyway." Toots knew that wasn't the full truth, but he already knew about her sugar addiction. She didn't need to tell him about her nighttime forages in the freezer for ice cream. Besides, she wasn't sure she could eat a full meal, anyway. She was too excited.

And not once had she craved a cigarette. Phil Becker was good for her.

Faded pictures of locals with giant fish twice their size still hung on the walls. The nautical theme hadn't changed since he had been there the previous time. Fishing nets filled with seashells, starfish, and sea sponges decorated the walls. The view he'd wanted to share with Toots was un- available in the bar area, but there would be other times, he hoped.

They sat at a tall table, where a cocktail waitress took their drink order. Both de- clined alcohol because of the late hour; plus, Phil was driving. He ordered two dozen raw oysters with all the extras Toots had asked for. Ten minutes later, a platter covered with ice and the creamy gray oys- ters was placed between them. A basket of saltines, a dish of lemons, and a cup of horseradish filled the table. There was barely enough room for their Cokes.

Between bites, they made small talk.

"So what do you do when you're not saving lives?" Toots asked.

"I fish when I have time off. I have a place in Myrtle Beach, where I've been playing around with the idea of writing a novel. Work consumes a big part of my life. I haven't had a lot of free time to pursue anything more than that."

Toots was intrigued. She loved reading the tabloids; hell, she owned one. To learn that he was interested in writing a novel was just another plus in Dr. Becker's list of many admirable qualities, as far as she was concerned. "What, all work and no play? I thought doctors lived on the golf course and flew around the world when they were not saving lives."

"Not me. I've devoted my life to medicine, which is why I've never married. Didn't want to commit to a relationship when I took the Hippocratic oath. Looking back, I'm sorry I didn't marry and have a family. Now that I'm slowing down and thinking about retirement, meeting someone as fascinating as you has made me realize just how much I've missed. Enough about me. I know you're dedicated to your friends, and that you have that fancy house in Malibu, but there has to be more. What about Abby's father? Is he still around?"

Toots had dreaded this moment ever since she realized that Phil was interested in her. What would he think when he learned of her past? Would he think her a tramp or some floozy who married for money, as all her husbands, except her first, Abby's father, had been very well to do? How did she go about explaining this to a man with a blank past in the marriage department? *Oh my God, where do I start?* With number one. John Simpson, Abby's father and the first love of her life.

"Abby's father died in a car accident when she was five. Lucky for me and Abby, John had a huge life insurance policy. With the help of a good friend who's a banker, we relocated from New Jersey to South Carolina, and he made some very wise investments for us. One of the companies was a fledgling computer company now known as Apple. Then there was Wal-Mart, and after that, Amazon. So, I was lucky. I hired Bernice right before I decided to move, and she's been with me ever since. I've been married and widowed a couple times since, but life has been good to me. I have my health and a daughter I adore, plus the three women you met tonight, all of whom just happen to be my daughter's godmothers. We've been friends since seventh grade."

Toots hoped that was enough information about her past to satisfy his curiosity. She'd done a few things she wasn't proud of, like the time she and the g's broke into that warehouse in Charleston to get material for Mavis's line of clothing for the dearly departed. Then there were the séances. That was not something she could reveal on a first date to a renowned cardiologist. He would run as fast as that Learjet could return him to Charleston. Fearing another question, she wanted to give a sigh of relief when she heard the bartender shout, "Last call."

Chapter 13

A fugitive known to Venezuelan authorities as Richard Allen Goodwin, known in Los Angeles as Rodwell Archibald Godfrey, former owner of *The Informer,* hid in the crowd of fans as he watched Abby Simpson and her date race back to the limousine.

Sure that she'd recognized him, but just in case, he'd called *The Informer*'s office beforehand in hopes of luring that idiot who manned the computers out to the premiere to warn Abby. He'd made it perfectly clear to the stupid kid just exactly who he was. He laughed when he recalled the conversation.

"Tell me where Abby Simpson is to-night, or she dies."

"Who is this?" Josh asked.

"Your old boss, the rightful owner of The Informer. *Do as I say, and Abby won't get hurt."*

"Rag!" Josh exclaimed. "What . . . Where are you?"

"It doesn't matter where I am. Give me her location."

Then he'd hung up, knowing that the kid would rush out to wherever Abby was. From there, all he had to do was follow the geek. He'd stationed himself among the crowd of fans in front of Grauman's Chinese Theatre. Lady Luck was in his pocket that night. He'd seen Abby almost immediately. And the geek had led him right to her, just as he'd known he would. He'd even gone to the trouble to disguise himself with that fake beard.

Phase one. Complete.

After two years spent on the run in the Dominican Republic and Venezuela, his luck had run out when the husband of his last lover discovered he'd swindled her out of his entire fortune.

He'd gradually changed his appearance throughout the years. First, he'd gone to a well-known plastic surgeon, where he'd used part of the fifty grand he'd ripped off Micky Constantine to pay for the hair plugs he'd wanted for the past twenty years. Then he'd lost forty pounds and spent weeks working out, trying to rid himself of his pudgy gut. When working out no longer seemed to be doing the job, he'd taken the last of his ill-gotten funds and had liposuction. As dark as the natives from the sun, he no longer looked like the man who'd left LA two years ago.

But some things never changed. Abby Simpson still had her reporter's instinct, just as he knew she would, and she'd recognized his voice and his face in spite of the changes he'd made. And that was what he'd hoped for. This time around, he had a surefire plan, and part of that plan was that he would not get caught. This time, he would walk away with the ten million dollars that in his mind rightfully belonged to him.

He was sure Abby would show up at *The Informer* after she'd had a chance to change into her street clothes. He'd give her an hour, which would give him just enough time to hide out in a place where he knew he'd have instant access to Abby.

A secret place that he, and he alone, knew about.

On the drive back to Brentwood, Abby and Chris barely spoke a word to one another for fear the damned limo was bugged. Once the driver dropped them off, and they were safely ensconced inside Abby's house, she let loose.

"That son of a bitch! I can't believe after all this time he's back! I can't wait to get my hands around his neck!"

Chester ran around in circles, trying to get her attention. She leaned down for a doggy kiss, then headed for her bedroom. "I'm going to change. Then I'm going to the office."

She made fast work of slipping off the designer dress that only hours ago had excited her. She threw on a pair of jeans with a black T-shirt and a pair of sneakers. Something told her she might need them tonight, just in case she had to run after that sneaky piece of garbage.

Back in the living room, Abby filled Chester's food bowl and refreshed his water. Chris sat on the sofa, unusually quiet.

"Abby, you need to calm down. Let's call the police. Remember, he's wanted by the Feds. Let them do their job. You're not equipped for this kind of stuff. And I don't want you to, either," Chris said, his tone serious.

"I remember after the fire, I took all of Rag's old files to the basement. Maybe I can find old addresses, contacts, or maybe some old IRS tax files. Maybe I can find an old contact, something that will give me an idea of where he's hanging out. He's on the run, but knowing him, there's probably a woman involved, even if it's unknowingly. I might find an address for one of his old girlfriends."

Chris had seen that look in Abby's eyes before and knew there was nothing he could say that would stop her.

"I'll stay here with Chester. Call me when you get there and before you leave, okay?" Chris said.

"Sure," Abby replied as she grabbed her keys and headed out.

The best he could hope for was that she would somehow stay out of trouble. He'd do whatever he could, but without her knowledge.

Maybe it was time to place a call to Toots.

Chapter 14

It was 11:30 by the time Abby arrived at the office. As promised, she called Chris to let him know that she was there. *The Informer* was quiet at that time of night as most of the reporters were out searching for the next big story.

The stairs leading down to the basement were dark and dirty, as they were seldom ever used anymore. The old printing press was still there. It reminded her of the days after the fire, when they'd had to use it as backup until the new operating system was installed and they were back online.

She was on a mission that night and was going to find where that son of a bitch was staying. With luck, she would manage to find him. After she had him cornered, she would let the authorities take over. She just wanted five minutes alone with him. With all the grief he'd caused, the suffering the staff had gone through, he owed her that much.

Yes, she wanted her five minutes alone with the worthless piece of garbage. Images of him locked in a five-by-seven cell made her smile.

The air in the basement was musty, and she detected a slight scent of mold. As she felt around, searching for the old-fashioned chain to switch the overhead light on, she paused, swearing that she detected a movement out of the corner of her eye. She hoped like hell there weren't rats in the basement. Knowing her mother was the face of LAT Enterprise, she knew the place had been treated for any infestation. She raised her hand above her head, feeling for the chain again. Finding it, she breathed a sigh of relief. She yanked on the chain as hard as she could.

Nothing.

She tried it again, expecting a dim ray of light, and again there was nothing.

She knew where the file cabinets were located. She was down in the basement and was not going upstairs empty-handed.

After her eyes had adjusted to the darkness, Abby spied the filing cabinets, which had been shoved against the old wooden door that had remained closed for as long as she'd worked for *The Informer.* Probably just an unused storage room.

The streetlight outside that shone in through the single basement window afforded her just enough light to guide her to the filing cabinets.

As she felt her way toward the set of file cabinets, she stopped dead in her tracks when she noticed they had been pushed away from their original position. Abby found it beyond strange that the old door, normally locked, was ajar.

Wanting to get this over with as quickly as possible, and now motivated by fear, Abby yanked the top drawer open. Using both hands, she reached inside, grabbing a stack of manila folders. Once she was back upstairs, she'd look through them, and if she didn't find anything, she'd come back downstairs with a flashlight.

But before she knew what was happening, a cloth with a chemical odor was shoved over her mouth and nose.

"I told you I would get you, bitch."

Abby's world went black.

Chris was startled awake when Chester barked in his ear. He bolted off the sofa, stunned that he'd actually fallen asleep. He'd tossed his tuxedo jacket over the sofa and kicked off his shoes, relaxing while he waited for Abby's second phone call. He looked at his watch. She'd had more than enough time at *The Informer* to do what she needed and head back home. It'd been almost two hours since she called to tell him she'd arrived at the paper. He'd give her five more minutes, and if she hadn't called by then, he would try to call her. He didn't want to appear as though he was checking up on her.

"Come on, Chester, I bet you need to go outside." Chris walked through the kitchen, opened the back door, and the big shepherd ran outside. Chris waited at the back door while Chester marked every shrub in the backyard. He looked at his watch again. It had only been two minutes.

The hell with calling Abby. He was going down there.

"Come on, Chester, we are going for a ride."

Hearing the word *ride,* Chester raced back inside the kitchen. Chris located his shoes in the living room and quickly stepped into them. He found the keys to his Toyota Camry in his pocket. Glancing around the house, he locked the back door and left through the front, with Chester at his side. Abby had given him a set of keys to her house a few weeks ago. That night was the first time he'd needed to use them. As he locked the door behind him, suddenly a feeling of doom, like a heavy shroud, embraced him.

Maybe Sophie's psychic powers were beginning to rub off on him.

He sensed Abby was in trouble.

Chapter 15

Toots couldn't recall when she'd had a more pleasant evening. Phil was charming, intelligent, had a wonderful sense of humor, not to mention that he was kind to animals. She'd never felt as blissfully happy on a first date, and she'd had more than her share.

The shrill ringing of a cell phone ended her euphoric reminiscing about the evening.

Phil answered on the second ring. "Dr. Becker," he replied in what Toots now thought of as his doctor voice.

"Yes, Michelle. Wonderful. I can't thank

you enough. I'll see you first thing in the morning." He hit the END button and tossed the phone on the seat.

"Frankie made it through the surgery just fine. Michelle seems to think he'll be okay."

"Super! We did the right thing, then. I'll have to call the girls and tell them," Toots said, then paused. What would she tell them if they asked where she planned to spend the night? Should she even mention it? No, she wouldn't have to, because Sophie would ask. And what would she say when she did?

"Frankie will be in recovery for another four or five hours. Given how late it is, why don't I give Mary Ann a call at Diamond-Head and see if my time-share is available?"

"What? You have a time-share here?" Toots asked, wondering how many girls he had brought here in the past.

"It's just an investment thing Mary Ann conned me into several years ago, along with several of my colleagues. We all thought we'd hit pay dirt, and for a few years we successfully rented them out at a decent profit. Then the real-estate bubble collapsed, and now I'm stuck. Actually, this will be the first time I've stayed here since I bought the place."

Toots gave a mental sigh of relief. At least he hadn't used the place as a social screwing joint. Sophie would want to know that, too. She was sure of it.

Phil hung up the phone. "We're in luck. The place is empty, as is quite common this time of the year, you know, the off-season in Florida. Mary Ann said she would have the night staff prepare the condo."

Ten minutes later, they pulled into a huge parking garage. It was nearly empty. The entrance to the lobby was well lit and clearly well maintained, flanked by giant urns of bright blooming hibiscus.

A gush of icy cold air greeted them as soon as Phil opened the door. One more point in his favor. He opened doors for women. She added this to his growing list of quality characteristics.

The night staff greeted them as though they were welcoming home a family member. The bellman brought a brass rolling cart to retrieve their luggage.

For a moment, Toots was embarrassed.

She didn't want the staff to think she was a one-night stand, but then who cared? She was sixty-six years old. She could do as she damn well pleased.

Sensing the awkwardness of the moment, Phil spoke up. "I'm Dr. Becker. We came here to secure emergency medical treatment for a patient, and neither of us had time to pack a bag. I hope there's some of those fluffy terry-cloth robes in the condo. I don't know about you, Toots, but I could use a warm shower."

The night clerk immediately called housekeeping to ensure they wouldn't lack any of the amenities they provided to all their guests. After giving him a key card, she directed them to a bank of elevators. Once inside, neither Toots nor Phil spoke. As soon as the doors swished open, they revealed a walkway made of solid concrete that traversed the entire tenth floor.

Toots walked alongside Phil, remarking, "This is very . . . sturdy-looking."

"Yes, they haven't done much with exterior decorating since hurricanes Charlie, Francis, Ivan, and Jean." He laughed.

"Sounds like the name of a hit song,"

Toots replied, "'hit' being the key word. This place can withstand category five hurricanes, and that's why there aren't a lot of extras. The foundation and building are as solid as the Rock of Gibraltar. Most of my rentals are locals here, to ride out the storms. Even though their homes might not survive hurricane-force winds, at least while they're here, they know that they're safe. Many people who had to evacuate weren't allowed back on Estero Island after the last hurricane came through a few years ago."

Toots hadn't expected an entire history of the island and its past, but she realized that Phil was as nervous as she was. It'd been a long time since either had spent the night with someone of the opposite sex. Phil told her it'd been years since he'd been on a date.

When they reached the condo, Phil slipped the key card into the lock and pushed the heavy steel door open, allowing Toots to enter first. She mentally chalked up another point in his favor.

Upon entering the room, Toots saw floor-to-ceiling sliding glass doors facing the Gulf of Mexico. She hurried through the small living and kitchen area to admire the view.

At high tide, the rush of the gulf water caressed the shoreline, leaving behind clumps of seaweed. Toots peered over the edge of the railing, spying the scattering of white dots sprinkled along the beach. Seashells. Hundreds of them, just waiting to be collected and given a place of importance on some vacationer's coffee table. Could the evening be more perfect? Minus Frankie's misfortune, tonight was turning out to include some of the most memorable moments from the hundreds of trips she'd taken. Or was it just the company?

She sensed Phil's presence as he stood behind her. She drew in a deep breath when he gently placed his hands on her shoulders. "Thanks for going with me tonight. It means more than you know. I've never taken a woman to a veterinarian's office on a first date, or any other time, for that matter."

"It's a first for me, too," she whispered, thinking that at her age she shouldn't be having any more *first* anything.

Continuing to gently massage her shoulders, their bodies touching, he brushed a light kiss in the sensitive hollow area between her neck and shoulder. A jolt of raw desire rushed through her, and she knew this was *not* a hot flash. He pulled her closer, and she felt what she knew was not a set of keys in his pocket.

Suddenly, Phil stepped back and said, "Why don't we get a shower?" At that point he was thinking of a cold one. "You take the master bath, and I'll use the guest bath. Then let's meet here"—he nodded at the chairs on the balcony—"for a second date, and while we're sitting out here and admiring the view, we can talk about what we're going to do on our third date."

Chapter 16

Chris had tried Abby's cell numerous times, and there was still no answer. He'd called the paper's main line, where they put him through to the security office.

Toots had spared no expense on security. After the fire, she'd remodeled *The Informer*'s offices and hired the best security team available.

Upon arriving at the newspaper, Chris and Chester were greeted by security chief Dave Thompson. "Mr. Clay, I can assure you this building is as secure as Fort Knox. Miss Simpson has not left the building,

according to our computer. We'll find her."
Dave spoke into the radio attached to his
shirt collar. "This is Chief Thompson. All
security personnel report immediately to
the main lobby."

A team of three smartly uniformed guards
assembled in the lobby. Dave barked instructions in the manner of a drill sergeant.
But they all knew that this was no drill.

"George, you secure the outside perimeter. Mike, you and Ed take the second,
third, fourth, and fifth floors. I'll check the
first floor."

Wanting to assist, Chris said, "Do you
mind if Chester and I tag along?"

"Of course not. Follow me."

They began their search in the most
obvious place, Abby's office. Her custom-
made desk sat in the middle of the room.
On top were three iMac computers, turned
off. Chris thought this extremely unusual.

"Wouldn't these computers be on if she
was here?" Chris asked.

"She has access to all the computers in
the office, so no, this doesn't really mean
anything." Dave thoroughly searched Abby's office. "She's probably upstairs in
the pressroom." Hitting his mike button,

he asked, "Mike, you or Ed see anything yet?"

A crackling response emanated from the speaker. "Nothing on either floor, Dave."

"Okay, continue the search. Check under all desks, anywhere someone could hide. Check the restrooms. I want no stone left unturned."

"Has anyone checked her car?" Chris asked.

Pressing his mike once again, Dave spoke into the small black square on his shoulder. "George, you still outside?"

"Yeah, nothing so far."

"Check the yellow MINI Cooper in the parking lot and get back to me ASAP."

Seconds later, George radioed back. "The car is locked up. No sign of Miss Simpson."

"Roger that," Dave said.

Chris noticed that Chester was missing. "Chester, here, boy," Chris called, then placed his pinkies to his lips and whistled as loudly as possible.

Still, no Chester.

"Something is wrong. He always comes when I call him."

"He can't be far," Dave said.

After a quick search, they found Chester lying in front of the door leading to the basement.

"Where does that door lead?" Chris asked.

"Oh, that door is never unlocked. It leads down to the basement, where the old printing press is."

Before the words were even out of the security chief's mouth, Chester stood on his hind legs, pushed the unlocked door open, and raced down the stairs.

"This is the door that's always locked?" Chris asked, his tone slightly condescending.

Dave Thompson, a man who was always used to being in control, was at a loss for words.

Without waiting for Dave, Chris followed Chester downstairs to the dark basement.

"Wait, Chris. We keep the power shut off down there," Dave called out as he made his way to the basement. "We pull the breaker here so no one can start up the machinery. The last thing *The Informer* needs is another scandal." Dave switched on the breaker. The basement was instantly flooded with light.

"Chester," Chris called, and he got no response.

Damn, he was really starting to worry. First Abby, and now Chester.

"What is this?" Dave asked out loud.

A deep growl, coming from somewhere behind the filing cabinets, sent both men to investigate.

Dave had been in the basement several times. Not once had he noticed the filing cabinets having been pushed away from the wall.

In an instant, they discovered where the low growls were coming from. A small wooden door behind the filing cabinets revealed a passageway that led out of the building, where they both heard Chester frantically barking.

Both Chris and Dave stopped dead in their tracks when they spied a single slip of white paper, which read, *Are you looking for Abby?*

Chapter 17

If she weren't there to experience it herself, Toots would never believe that she would be sitting on a tenth-floor balcony over-looking the Gulf of Mexico, wearing a plush robe and nothing else. Add that a hand-some doctor sat beside her in the same attire, and she could only assume that he, too, was nude beneath his robe, and that excited her more than she cared to admit. She'd made a promise to herself after Le-land that she would never get involved with another man. But sometimes prom-ises were meant to be broken.

As the staff had assured, a large basket containing several kinds of gourmet cheeses and crackers sat atop the small kitchen table. A plate of fresh fruit and chocolates, accompanied by two large bottles of chilled sparkling water, waited to be consumed. Taking it upon herself, Toots fixed a plate for each of them and brought them out to the balcony since she was the first out of the shower.

Now, according to Phil, they were on their second date. Toots was totally relaxed for the first time since arriving at the condo. It might also have something to do with the fact that she felt super refreshed from her shower and comfortable without her clothes. Again, she would never have imagined herself in such a scenario. If only the girls could see her now. She smiled, just thinking of all the sly comments Sophie would be sure to make. And Ida, too. Mavis might even toss in a word or two herself. Bernice, on the other hand, would not like the fact that Toots was sitting in the buff with her friend's cardiologist.

Neither spoke, and Toots felt the mood turn in another direction, meaning romantic, and she wasn't sure that she was ready for that. She opted for small talk instead.

"You think Frankie will make it? I still can't believe no one from the Patterson family took that poor little dog."

"If no one claims him, I'll adopt him. And yes, I think he'll be just fine. It's just going to take some time. Michelle studied with some of the best neurosurgeons in the country. Her father is a brilliant cardiologist. She's as bright as he is."

"That makes me happy, and I know that wherever Mrs. Patterson is, she's smiling down on you."

Phil grinned.

Laughing, Toots asked, "So, what are the doctor's orders for the rest of the morning?"

Before Phil could answer, Toots's cell phone rang. Alarmed, she raced inside to answer the phone. Phone calls in the wee hours of the morning always brought bad news.

OMG, what if it's Bernice? Here I am, naked, contemplating seducing her cardiologist!

She found her purse in the master bedroom and answered the phone. "Hello?"

"Toots, it's Chris."

Her heart pounded in her chest like an

air-powered jackhammer. This was definitely not good. "What? Chris, where are you? Where is Abby?"

Phil stepped inside the master bedroom, knowing instinctively that something was up.

"He's . . . he's got her, Toots. She's gone," Chris said, his voice breaking.

"Who, Chris? Who is he? I don't understand," Toots said, fear racing through her veins.

"That Rag son of a bitch who used to own *The Informer*. He's taken Abby."

"Where? When? How?" Toots asked.

"While we were attending the premiere at Grauman's Chinese Theatre, someone was heckling Abby from the crowd. Josh had disguised himself as one of the paparazzi. He had come to warn Abby that Rag was back in town and had called the paper, making threats. We left immediately and returned to Abby's house. But she left me with Chester and raced off to the office."

"Are you telling me that with all that security at that paper, someone got in and abducted Abby?" Toots cried out. "I will have Dave Thompson's ass sliced up and served on a platter. Have you called the police?"

"Yes, Dave notified the police, and they're here now."

"I'll be there as fast as I can," Toots said, then tossed her cell phone on the bed.

With all thoughts of modesty tossed aside, Toots yanked off her robe, not caring that Phil was in the room. She frantically searched for her clothes.

"I have got to get to LA now! My daughter has been abducted. . . . I . . . have to get to an airport!"

Phil gathered Toots in his arms. "Don't worry. I will take care of everything. Get dressed and meet me at the car in five minutes."

Stunned, since Toots was always in control, she was grateful for Phil's take-charge attitude. Abby was her life. If something were to happen to Abby, Toots would simply die.

Three minutes later, Toots met Phil at the car. He helped her in, slammed the passenger door, and raced around to the driver's side. Sliding behind the wheel, he left only burnt rubber in his wake as he exited the parking garage.

"Okay, we are going to the airport in Fort Myers. I have booked us two first-class seats on American Airlines flight seven twenty-eight. It departs at six in the morning, and thanks to the change in time zones, we'll arrive at LAX at eight."

In a shaky voice, Toots asked, "It's already five o'clock. How long does it take to drive to the airport?"

"Normally from here about forty minutes, but we're going to do it in twenty."

Phil was a doctor. If stopped, he would simply say there was a medical emergency and he had to get to the airport immediately. Given the early-morning hour, there was virtually no traffic. Most likely, the cops were in search of their morning doughnut fix.

They arrived at Southwest Regional Airport with time to spare. Phil parked the car at the Enterprise rental lot. He explained to the rental agent that this car was from their Naples airport location. The attendant assured him that he would see to it that it was returned.

Having no baggage and given the early hour, they breezed through security just as the final boarding call was announced.

Phil grinned at Toots. "We're gonna make it."

Once airborne, having finally caught his breath, Phil asked, "What's going on?"

Toots sighed and said, "It's a long story."

Phil looked at his watch and replied, "You've only got five hours to tell me."

For the first time in her life, Toots was at the complete mercy of a practical stranger. A man she barely knew, yet she'd allowed him to take charge of her life as though it were his responsibility. And that was when the thought hit her; she hadn't even called Sophie. Her face must have shown the shock at this thought, because Phil spoke to her as if she were a child.

"Toots, I know you're not okay, but what's going on in that head of yours? You just turned as white as a sheet."

Dreading what lay ahead, and fearing the unknown, she knew Phil was about to play an important role in her life. After all he'd done in the past ten hours, she owed him an explanation.

Keeping it simple, she briefed him on the last two years of her life, minus a few husbands.

"So what you're saying is, you think this

Rag guy, the former owner of the newspaper you now own, who disappeared two years ago and almost took you for ten million dollars, now has your daughter?"

"If what Chris told me is correct, then that's exactly what's happened." Just saying the words out loud frightened her more than ever. Losing eight husbands didn't even begin to compare to the loss of a daughter.

No! She would not go there! *Please, God, don't let anything happen to Abby.* She would do anything to keep her daughter safe. She'd say a million Hail Marys every day for the rest of her life, anything. All she wanted was for her daughter to be returned, unharmed.

The five-hour plane ride seemed to take fifty. Their plane arrived on time, and Chris was there waiting. Hadn't it only been a few months ago that she and Abby had been in an airport, waiting for Chris to return from his nightmare with Laura Leighton? It seemed like a lifetime ago.

She made quick introductions, then asked Chris, "Has there been any news? I am about to lose it. I don't know what to do. Damn, I haven't even called Sophie and the others. I need to call Goebel, too. If anyone can find her, he can." Sophie could help find her, too, but she didn't want to mention that in front of Phil just yet. She'd already told him enough about her life. Explaining Sophie's psychic abilities would have to wait.

"I've already called them, Toots. Goebel, too. They're all on their way here as we speak. Sophie asked me to tell you not to worry about Bernice, that Jamie would stay at the house with her."

Toots breathed a sigh of relief, however temporary. "Thanks. I am not thinking straight."

Once they were out of the airport and inside Chris's car, he filled her in on what had happened.

"The son of a bitch actually left a note. On one side of the paper he wrote, 'Are you looking for Abby?' On the back were instructions. The police have the original, but I made a copy at the paper before they arrived. I was careful not to leave any of my prints on the paper."

"Do you have it with you?" Toots asked.

"I knew you'd want to see it. Of course I brought it with me." He reached into the glove compartment and removed a single sheet of plain white copy paper.

To Whom It May Concern:

I have your editor in chief, Abby Simpson. Do not contact the police or the FBI. I will call The Informer *tomorrow at noon with further instructions. No harm will come to her if my demands are met.*

"That's today! What are we going to do? It says right here no police. I can't do anything to jeopardize my daughter's safety."

Phil, having been silent for most of the ride, spoke up. "I'm sure the police know how to deal with situations like this. It's probably in your daughter's best interest to let the authorities handle things."

Chris thought to himself, *He really doesn't know the power of Toots and Abby's godmothers. Add Goebel into the scheme of things, and Rag doesn't stand a chance.* He couldn't tell this to Phil, though. Chris was an attorney, and he had many contacts in the Los Angeles Police Department. As did Abby. He'd already contacted them, and they were in the process of setting up their trace equipment in the basement.

"Bullshit! I'm going to the paper. When I get finished with Dave Thompson and his crew of misfits, he'll wish he'd chosen to work for the sanitation department."

This sounded more like the Toots he knew and loved. "Hang on, old girl. Dave and his crew did an excellent job securing the building. No one could have known that there was a secret passage behind the filing cabinets. Remember, this building was built in nineteen twenty. Wasn't that around the time of Prohibition? Who knows what that passage was used for? It ends in an abandoned building across the street. Not even Abby knew of it. So don't be too hard on them. If it hadn't been for Chester, we wouldn't even know about the door."

"One would think, when they did the original security assessment of the building, someone would've noticed a wooden door and might've taken the time to check it out. Never mind. It doesn't matter now. What time are the girls expected to arrive?"

"They should be in around ten thirty, about an hour from now. I've arranged for a car to bring them to *The Informer.* I knew you'd want them there with you when Rag calls."

They were silent for the remainder of the ride. Once they arrived at the paper, Toots was out of the car in a flash. Phil and Chris raced to catch up with her.

Chapter 18

Still groggy from what she assumed was chloroform, Abby blinked her eyes several times, trying to clear her blurred vision. Her mouth was covered with duct tape. Her arms were pulled behind her back, tied together with something plastic that was cutting into her wrists. Zip ties, she guessed, like those that the police force used. Carefully, she gazed down at the floor and saw that her sneaker-clad feet were tied securely to the front legs of a chair. Panic rose in her when she realized she was completely immobilized. Her vision clearing somewhat, she searched the area around her.

Puke green walls, gray marble-colored linoleum, and a stench that would rival a decomposing body permeated the air. Straining to peer out of the single-pane window, Abby didn't recognize any landmarks that would give a clue to her location, but judging from the smog she could see with her limited view, she was pretty sure that she was still in Los Angeles. Telephone lines crisscrossed in every direction. She strained to hear and was able to make out the sounds of racing engines, the *boom bada boom* of rap music, and the muffled sound of . . . an *auctioneer?* No, it was hagglers. Maybe she was close to a flea market?

Since she knew the low-life bastard who had brought her there, it was probably close to the seedy South Central neighborhood where the LA riots had taken place years ago.

With each passing minute, Abby was becoming more focused, the cobwebs from the drug fading fast. She could hear movement of some kind in the next room and tried to call out for help, but with the tape securely placed over her mouth, a low muffle was the best she could manage.

She almost jumped out of her skin when the door burst open and her captor, the SOB himself, came into the room.

"Good. You're awake," Rag said. "If you keep your voice down and promise not to scream, I'll remove the tape from your mouth, you bitch."

Abby nodded in agreement, and he yanked the silver tape from her mouth. She licked her lips and wanted to spit on the son of a bitch, but caution won out and she refrained. She had to play by his rules, at least for now.

"I don't want to hurt you, but what I do want is the ten million dollars your boss stole from me when he bought the paper."

"My boss?" Abby said, her voice barely a whisper.

He doesn't have a clue that Mom owns the paper.

"Yeah, the bastard that owns LAT Enterprise."

She could use this to her advantage if she played her cards right.

Hoarse, she answered, "I've never met the people who own it. Rag, get me a god-damn glass of water."

"Oh, I see you're getting back to normal. I always hated you, but you wouldn't re-member. You were too damned busy try-ing to get my job."

WTF? Abby thought. Had Rag suffered a brain injury? *No,* she thought. He was just an asshole. But she'd play his game a while longer.

"Please, my throat hurts."

"All right, but if you make a sound, I will stuff my *dirty* underwear down your throat."

The image forced hot bile to spew in the back of her throat.

"Just a drink, please." She forced her-self to act meek and intimidated.

He disappeared for a few seconds, re-turning with a bottle of water. He removed the cap and held the bottle to her lips. "Drink," he said, shoving the bottle hard against her teeth.

He is going to be so frigging sorry.

Abby managed to swallow a few sips of water before choking. She turned her head away, letting him know that she was fin-ished.

He capped the bottle of water and tossed it on the floor.

"So, Rag, why do you think you were cheated out of ten million dollars?"

"It's simple, actually. I arranged to have all that money transferred to a bank in the Bahamas, where I could live out the rest of my life in comfort. But no, some asshole banker reversed the transfer before I could get my hands on the money, and gave it to a bunch of jerks who claimed I owed them money."

Abby pulled at her restraints, then stopped when she felt the plastic dig deeper into her wrists. "So let me see if I have this right. You owed people more than the paper was worth, and that's my fault, how?"

Rag kicked the bottle of water across the room. "No, you little bitch. I didn't say it was your fault. You're just the tool I need to get my money back."

"What makes you think my boss would pay ten million dollars for me? I have never met him. He doesn't even know me."

"For your sake, I hope you're wrong about how he'll react to your situation."

"Tell me, just exactly how do you plan to execute this master scheme of yours?"

"I am not going to do a thing, Abby dear. You're going to do it for me."

"I am?"

He stood in front of her and leaned so close to her that their noses touched. The scent of old sweat clung to his clothing, and his breath reeked of garlic. Again, Abby fought back the bile that threatened to spill forth from her mouth.

"Yes, you are. In exactly"—he looked at the cheap gold wristwatch given to him by the woman he'd just screwed over—"fifty-six minutes, you're going to read a little speech I've prepared for you. If my writing skills are as good as they once were, I'll get my money, and you will have your freedom. Doesn't that sound like a fair trade to you?"

She wanted to kick him in the balls and spit in his face, after she clawed his eyes out, but she'd wait.

"Sure, Rag. It sounds good. I can't wait to read your little speech. And just for the record, your writing always sucked. I never told you, for obvious reasons, you being my boss and all, but let me say it now. Your fucking stories sucked, and I've seen better writing from preschoolers. So, if this speech is as good as you say it is, let's just get it over with."

Abby didn't see Rag's backhand. Before she knew what hit her, blood oozed from her nose and mouth. A tinge of fear trickled down her spine as she realized she really did not know this man at all, didn't know what he was truly capable of. Maybe she shouldn't have been so quick to lash out, so quick to reveal her lack of fear.

"I see you're having a change of heart. That's a good thing. Now, we're wasting time. Read this." He removed a piece of folded paper from his pants pocket. "Let's make sure your reading skills are still up to par. Reading and writing all that Hollywood gossip tends to dull one's literary abilities. Not that you have any, but let's give this a trial run. You know what they say—"

"No, I don't. Why don't you tell me?" Abby interjected. She just couldn't help it. This overage, too-tanned idiot was out of his mind. Yes, he'd been a total ass when she worked for him, but this . . . this was *insanity.* He was a loose cannon ready to go off at any time.

Another slap, only this time she'd anticipated it. She turned her head so his hand couldn't make full contact with her cheek, and he barely managed to graze her this time.

She licked her lips, tasting the salty blood that pooled on her upper lip. "I never took you for an abuser, Rag. Thanks for proving me wrong. Now I don't feel so bad knowing what a true asshole you are."

"You're a real bitch, Abby, but I've already told you that. If you can't keep your trap shut, I might decide to close it permanently. You catching my drift? Don't answer that. Here, read this."

The last thing she wanted to do was submit to the bastard, but resisting him was proving to be futile. Her next thought: she'd try to play up to his sense of humanity, decency. But that ploy would prove to be a nonstarter, she realized, since he had none. She nodded at the paper in his hand. "I'll read it."

"'Please follow these instructions to the letter. Any deviation from them, and Abby Simpson will suffer the consequences. At precisely five o'clock, be at the Santa Monica Pier, at the Marine Science Center, under the carousel building. I want a carry-on suitcase with one million dollars in cash placed next to the men's room. An additional nine million dollars is to be wired to an account. The numbers will be in a red envelope taped to the top of the garbage can in the men's room at the drop-off point. I'll be watching. At the first sign of police or the Feds, you will never see Miss Simpson alive again. Once I am safely on board a plane of my choosing, I will call back with the location of your editor in chief.'"

Abby looked up from the paper he held in front of her. "Five o'clock? Do you really believe the powers that be can come up with that much cash in such a short time?"

For a moment, Rag seemed to actually consider the validity of her question. "Shut up! Now, read this again."

Abby read through the ridiculous ransom note a second time, but she couldn't help herself when a sheer wave of black fright swept through her.

Chapter 19

Toots hurried inside, Chris and Phil Becker following closely at her heels as she entered the offices at *The Informer.* This was the first time Toots had been there without her daughter running the show. They didn't bother with niceties when they were greeted by the paper's three main reporters. Goebel had advised them not to say anything to anyone until he arrived.

Not caring that she was inside, or that Phil Becker was a cardiologist, Toots reached inside her purse for the unopened pack of Marlboro Lights. She tore the cellophane wrapper off and placed a cigarette between her lips. "Don't either of you dare say anything. I'm nervous, and I own the damned building." She lit the smoke and took three puffs before crushing it out in an empty soda can. Tears filled her eyes. This was Abby's office, and more than likely, that soda can was hers. Toots felt a pang of remorse at dropping her cigarette inside but knew it really wasn't important now.

"Chris, what time is it?" Toots asked for the tenth time.

"We've got about forty-five minutes, Toots. Try to stay calm. The police are in the basement. The phones are tapped, for whatever good it will do. I suspect Rag knows phone calls can be traced, though hopefully he thinks we haven't called the police. I've pulled every string I know and called in every favor I'm owed to keep this as hush-hush as possible. If this Rag is as stupid as he acts, we'll have Abby back in no time, and his ass safely behind bars, where he should've been for the past two years," Chris said, hoping to reassure Toots. He was beyond worried, but he knew he needed to stay focused, for Abby and Toots.

Later, he could fantasize about what he planned to do to that low-life son of a bitch.

"I know it's not my business, but I'm concerned about you, Toots. What can I do to help?" Phil asked, even though he was out of his element inside a tabloid paper.

"Phil, you've been a godsend. Just having you near is enough." Toots hoped she hadn't overstepped an emotional boundary, but Phil had held her in his arms while she was totally nude, he'd seen her fully exposed physically. He had done exactly what needed to be done, taken control without expecting anything in return.

Toots knew right then that something magical was happening between them. Even though she felt more fearful than she ever had in her entire life, it comforted her to know that Dr. Phil Becker had her back.

"Oh, Phil! I just remembered. What about your patients? If you need to get back, I'll hire a private jet. It's the least I can do."

They stood in the center of Abby's office. If observed, their attraction would be quite obvious. Circumstances being what they were, Toots was beyond grateful that

Phil had stayed by her side. There was something about him that reminded her of John, her first husband and Abby's father. This could be trouble for her, but she'd worry about it another time. When Abby was safely home.

Phil motioned for Toots to sit in the chair next to him. "I'm just a doctor, Toots. Not God. I've plenty of partners who will cover for me. I took care of it before we left DiamondHead."

"Thank you, Phil. I hate dragging you into my personal problems, but I'm really glad you came with me."

Toots saw Chris watching them and knew what he was thinking. He had a slight smile on his face, so whatever it was, it couldn't be too bad. Right at that exact moment, the only thing that really mattered was Abby's safe return.

Several loud voices could be heard from outside Abby's office. Toots raced through the doorway. The sight of Sophie, Goebel, Ida, and Mavis was the most welcome vision she'd had all morning.

"Oh, Toots," Mavis cried, "what has happened?" They embraced; then Sophie wrapped her arms around the two of them.

Never one to be left out, Ida wrapped her arms around the other three.

Goebel watched, waiting for his turn. He gave her a quick hug. "Toots, we're going to find her. I promise you. If you don't mind, I am going downstairs with the guys and will monitor the call when it comes through." He looked at his watch. "It's almost time. Are you sure you can handle this? If not, I'll take the phone. This idiot doesn't have a clue who he's dealing with. As far as he knows, it's some corporate giant that he believes is willing to just hand him ten million dollars like it's peanuts."

"Goebel, if that's what I have to do to get Abby, I will," Toots informed him. "My daughter's life is worth whatever he asks for. Just so you know, I've contacted Henry Whitmore, my banker in Charleston. It won't be easy to come up with that much money in cash, but it's doable." Toots sounded more like her old self. In control. "I want all of you to know, we can't risk doing anything that will harm Abby. Sophie, what's your . . . you know, what are your thoughts about this?" Toots directed her gaze to Phil. She hadn't told him about Sophie's psychic abilities. Another secret.

"This is her office, right?" Sophie walked around the room, touching things, then closing her eyes. When she spied Chester curled up in his old blue recliner, Sophie stooped down to scratch the dog between the ears. She'd learned through her many readings that often it wasn't unusual for an animal to pick up on its owner's psyche. Chester leapt out of the chair and ran to the door.

"Woof! Woof!" His barking was strong, persistent.

Sophie followed him to the door. "I want to see where he goes, what he does. We have a few more minutes, right?"

"Go, Sophie, but hurry back. I need you here with me when that phone rings," Toots stated. "You understand?"

She nodded, then followed Chester out the door.

From his expression, Toots knew that Phil had questions, but they'd keep. She wasn't sure she wanted to explain Sophie's abilities just yet. She'd play it by ear.

"Phil, you know Mavis and Ida. And that burly guy who was just here is Goebel. He runs a private detective agency. He and Sophie are—"

"Sleeping together," Ida filled in. "I caught them in the shower together this morning." Ida grinned, but it didn't reach her eyes. She was trying to lighten the mood. Poor Ida, she was human, after all.

"I think that's fantastic! Nothing like finding your one true love at our age, is there?" Phil asked, staring at Toots as he spoke.

Toots blushed. Was he trying to tell her something? Surely not!

"It is. You know I met a wonderful man, George, who owned a string of dry cleaners all along the West Coast, but he needed a . . ." Mavis realized what she had almost said and caught herself. "He had a medical issue, and it didn't work out."

Toots suddenly realized something was missing. "Mavis, where is Coco?"

"Jamie is taking care of her for me. Coco loves her, so I thought that, under the circumstances, it might be best if I left her behind."

"Coco is Mavis's Chihuahua," Toots informed Phil.

"Maybe we can introduce her to Frankie when he's back on his feet again," Phil said.

"How is that poor little wiener?" Mavis asked. "I wish I had known he was at that old house. I would have taken him in an instant, but I had no idea he had been left behind."

For the zillionth time, Toots asked, "What time is it?"

"Two minutes," Chris said.

Right on time, the phone rang, sending a chill down Toots's spine, along with a fury that only an enraged mother could experience.

Toots picked up the phone immediately. *"The Informer."*

Chapter 20

Abby was shocked when she heard her mother's voice. Knowing that her mother would have called in all the troops, she felt an instant sense of hope.

"This is Abby Simpson. I need to speak to the CEO of LAT Enterprise."

Rag stood in front of her, holding the single white sheet of paper. "Read."

"'Please follow these instructions to the letter. Any deviation from them, and Abby Simpson will suffer the consequences. At precisely five o'clock, be at the Santa Monica Pier, at the Marine Science Center, under the carousel building. I want a carry-on suitcase with one million dollars in cash placed next to the men's room. An additional nine million dollars is to be wired to an account. The numbers will be in a red envelope taped to the top of the garbage can in the men's room at the drop-off point. I'll be watching. At the first sign of police or the Feds, you will never see Miss Simpson alive again. Once I am safely on board a plane of my choosing, I will call back with the location of your editor in chief.'"

Toots was taken aback when she heard Abby's voice, but was grateful to know she was still alive and, hopefully, unharmed. She knew the conversation was being recorded by the police, and no doubt Rag would be listening as well. Toots would get the details from them later. Now she needed to quickly figure out a way to get a message to Abby before she hung up.

"Miss Simpson," Toots said in as firm a voice as she could muster. "This is Ms. Loudenberry. We have never met, but I have the independent members of the board of directors, Mr. Clay and Mr. Goebel, here with me. We are prepared to do whatever is necessary to ensure your safe return. After all, where would I find an editor of your caliber?" Toots's voice broke on the last word.

"South Central LA, I would guess."

Rag instantly ripped the phone from her hand. "Listen, whoever you are. I am serious. If my demands are not met by five o'clock, this bitch of an editor is history." On that threat, he hung up the phone.

Toots could no longer hold back her tears. This was a nightmare, but at least Abby was alive. Phil was immediately at her side. He handed her a wad of tissues from the box on Abby's desk.

"Sophie, did you get anything from that?" Toots asked while drying her tears.

Chris gave a halfhearted grin, and Phil looked puzzled.

"Does Sophie have supersonic hearing?" Phil asked, hoping to lighten the atmosphere, if only a little.

"My gut feelings are good, Toots. Let's leave it at that for now."

Toots nodded her understanding.

Before they could explain Sophie's . . . *abilities,* Goebel's and Chris's police connections returned to Abby's office.

"Were you able to pick up on anything?"

Toots asked anxiously. "I think Abby was trying to give me a clue to her location."

"We got that, and we were also able to get the number of the cell phone they used. It'll take a little doing, as this is off the record, but I'm sure we can get a general location via the pings from a cell tower. I have a couple of guys on duty who can take care of it for me right away," Chris's friend, the self-appointed officer in charge, explained.

Goebel spoke next. "We have less than five hours to get the money and put everyone into position. Toots, have you made arrangements to get a large sum of cash?"

"Yes. I called Henry Whitmore at the bank in Charleston. He's contacted the local branch here. The cash is available now."

"Good. Now, we'll need some transportation."

"I have two perfectly good vehicles at the beach house," Toots said. "Chris, I know we can't all fit in your car. Any suggestions?"

"I have a spare set of keys to Abby's MINI. I'll take Chester. Ida and Mavis, you can ride with me. Goebel, you, Toots, Sophie, and Phil can follow me in my car," Chris said.

"Once we get to the beach house, then, Toots, you and Phil can go to the bank and get the cash. Ida, you and Mavis find suitable luggage to transport all that money. Chris, stay in contact with your police buddies, and if you hear anything before we arrive at the beach, call my cell phone. Sophie, you're with me," Goebel said firmly.

"Rag, I've been here for hours. I don't know about you, but my kidneys are working just fine. I need to pee," Abby complained. And she did, but maybe if he cut her loose, she might figure a way out of there.

"I wondered when this was gonna happen. You damn women are worse than a baby. You have to piss every time you turn around. Since phase two of my plans seems to be working out well, I suppose I can let you loose long enough to take a piss."

Rag left the room, returning with a hunting knife. "Don't get any ideas, or I'll do more than cut you loose."

Ordinarily, she would've told him to kiss off, but remembering that he had had no qualms about hitting her, she kept her mouth shut. The troops were out; that much she knew. But if she saw an opportunity to make a break, she sure as hell was going to give it her best shot.

None too careful, Rag cut the duct tape from around her ankles, then stared at her squarely in the face. "I mean it. I will hurt you, so forget whatever you're thinking."

Abby wanted to kick the old son of a bitch right in the nuts, but with her hands still tied behind her, she couldn't.

He yanked her up with her hands still tied behind her. "This way," he directed and shoved her down a short hallway to a filthy bathroom.

"I can't use the bathroom without my hands untied."

"Oh yes, you can," he said as he reached for the zipper on her jeans. In an instant, her jeans and panties were bunched around her ankles.

"You perverted son of a bitch!" For the first time since being taken, tears of anger filled Abby's eyes. She was humiliated when Rag yanked her jeans down.

"Just piss, Abby."

Her bladder was about to explode, yet when she looked at the filthy toilet, she was afraid to sit down on it, and there was no way in hell she was going to straddle the seat with her pants at her ankles. "Can you at least put some tissue on the toilet seat?"

"You damn well amaze me! Who do you think you are? The queen of England? Next you'll want a bidet. Sit down, piss, and shut the hell up."

"Could you at least give me a minute of privacy?" She looked at the small bathroom window with bars covering it. What kind of a place had steel bars on the bathroom window? She cringed just thinking of it. "It's not like I'm going anywhere."

Rag looked at the window. With her arms tied behind, he knew there was no escape. Deciding to play nice guy, he said, "One minute." He stepped out of the smelly bathroom into the hall.

Figuring she'd scrub herself raw later, Abby dropped down onto the toilet seat and relieved herself. She looked around for something to wipe with and realized she couldn't use her hands, but there was a small dingy hand towel dangling from a rusty hook. Leaning against the wall, she backed up to the towel and wiggled in a way that allowed her to wipe herself somewhat. She could only hope that Rag would use this to wipe his face. She grinned.

"Potty time is over."

Abby squatted down quickly to the point where she was able to maneuver her hands around the back waistband of her panties and pull them up enough to cover herself. That asshole wasn't going to get another free shot at her.

"Okay, pervert, I'm finished."

He kicked the door open. "I see you were able to pull your little pink panties up. Were you afraid I was going to try to do something nasty to you?"

She clenched her teeth, rage filling her. "What? Were you planning on adding rape to your repertoire? Let me see, we have kidnapping, extortion, and physical abuse, not to mention all the charges the FBI has against you. Have I missed anything?"

"Go ahead, joke about it. I am about to become a very wealthy man. And you, my dear, will be returning to your silly little life."

With that, Rag jerked up her jeans, not

bothering to fasten them, and led her back to the chair in the center of the room. He proceeded to duct tape her ankles around the chair legs a second time. And just because he could, he wrapped three layers of duct tape around her mouth and hair, too.

"Let's see you make a smart-ass comment now, bitch. I don't want you screaming while I go relieve your boss of ten million smackeroos."

In just a few short hours, he crowed to himself, *I will be on my way to a life of leisure.*

Chapter 21

They made the drive from *The Informer* to Toots's beach house in Malibu in record-breaking time. Once they'd parked Abby's MINI and Chris's Camry, they gathered at the front entrance while Toots unlocked the door.

Toots led them to the kitchen, which had always operated as a command central of sorts. The white cabinets, blue granite countertops, and chrome appliances sparkled like they were brand-new.

"Nice," Phil commented.

"It used to look like a whorehouse be-fore it was remodeled, right, Toots?" Sophie said to Phil. "A pop star lived here before she bought the place. She was overly fond of purple and hot pink."

"Now isn't the time, Sophia," Ida admonished. "We're here for Abby."

For once, Sophie actually kept quiet.

Goebel sat down at the table, motioning for the others to sit, too. "We don't have a lot of time. It's after one already. There is no room for screwups. We get only one shot, and it has to be perfect. Chris, you're sure that your off-duty buddies can be trusted?"

"I'd trust them with my life, and Abby's, too. And I guess I have, haven't I?"

"Good. I've pulled up a map of the Santa Monica Pier here." Goebel turned his iPhone so the others could view the map. "The Marine Science Center is located here." With a few taps of his index finger, he enlarged the map to indicate the area where Rag wanted them to drop off the ransom. Goebel glanced at Toots to see how she was holding up. This wasn't a stranger they were talking about. "I've asked Dave Thompson to head out there now, just in case."

"That idiot can't even keep Abby safe at

the paper!" Toots charged. "Damn, Goebel, I'm surprised at you." Her hands shook as she fiddled with the top button on her sheer black blouse. Had it only been yesterday that she and Sophie had cackled with laughter over what to wear on her date with Phil? It seemed a lifetime ago.

"I understand where you're coming from, Toots, but let's face it. The building is old. There may be even more secret tunnels and passageways. Dave is good at what he does. You said yourself, you hired the best security team money could buy. And he's the best. Dave took an early retirement ten years ago. He was with the Secret Service."

Dave hadn't wanted to disclose that tidbit of information but felt he had no choice. When they were downstairs at *The Informer,* Goebel had grilled him like a suspect, and that was when Dave told him about his past. He'd made a couple of hasty phone calls to confirm Dave's background. And he really was one of the best.

"So what you're telling me is a former member of the Secret Service didn't know what lay behind that door?" Toots echoed.

Goebel nodded. "I think it's safe to say

we can trust him to monitor the comings and goings at the Marine Science Center."

"I trust Goebel," Sophie added. "Remember, I've seen him in action."

"Yes, we know," Ida smirked. "In more ways than one."

Sophie, being Sophie, gave Ida the finger.

Toots just shook her head. "Come on, you two. Ida, you said it yourself. Now isn't the time. Once Abby's home safe and sound, then I don't care what you two do to each other."

Goebel waited for them to stop talking before he continued. "Toots, you and Phil need to leave now. Mavis, can you or Ida locate luggage for them?"

Without being told further, Ida and Mavis raced upstairs as though they were in a race for their lives, and in a sense they were, as Abby belonged to them, too.

Ida went to her bedroom and came out within seconds. Mavis hadn't even entered her room yet. "I left this behind. It should work."

"That was fast. Good. Let's give this to Toots," Mavis raved.

Ida pulled the Louis Vuitton suitcase

behind her, and with Mavis in the lead, they practically flew back down the stairs.

"Is this big enough?" Ida asked.

All eyes focused on the designer piece of luggage.

"I don't know. I've never had a million in cash," Sophie said. "And certainly not in a Louis Vuitton suitcase."

Goebel spoke up. "It'll do. Toots, you and Phil go now. Don't waste a minute. This LA traffic is awful. Once you have the money in the luggage, I want you both to be at the entrance to Bubba Gump's at the pier at exactly four o'clock." Quickly, he homed in on the map again, pointing to the restaurant's location.

"Phil, you can back out now," Toots blurted out. "I can't imagine what you're thinking."

"I'm thinking we need to get our asses out of here, just like Goebel said."

"Then we'll take the Thunderbird. It's fast, and I'm a damn good driver." Toots headed to the door leading to the garage, then stopped. "Goebel, you have my cell number and Phil's, too, right?"

Goebel nodded. "If there's any news, I'll call you first. Now, get out of here. When you arrive at the pier, park in the public parking lot. I'll find you."

Toots nodded. She and Phil left without saying another word.

"Chris, you and Chester are coming with me. We might use this old boy to sniff out Abby if we have to. He's already proved that he can detect her. Shepherds are smart dogs," Goebel commented.

"And what about us? What are we supposed to do? Sit here and twiddle our thumbs?" Sophie declared as she fiddled with a pack of matches.

"No, I want you with me. All of you. We'll all pile into Toots's Escalade. Now let's go. We're wasting time."

Chapter 22

Toots swerved to avoid a head-on collision in the parking lot of the bank.

Phil placed a hand on her arm. "Careful. We don't want to get in an accident. We've got to find Abby," he said, gasping.

"Sorry. I just . . . I want this over with as soon as possible." Toots pulled into the first empty parking space she saw. "You want to come inside with me?" she asked as she shifted the red sports car into park.

"I wouldn't be here if I didn't. Stop worrying about what I want, Toots. Let's find your girl. I'm not going anywhere." He grabbed the Louis Vuitton luggage off the floor of the car.

Without another word between them, they entered the People's Bank, where the president personally escorted them to his office. "Ms. Loudenberry, I am terribly sorry for your daughter. Henry Whitmore explained your circumstances." A large black duffel bag stood out like a sore thumb in the center of his desk. "Take this and good luck."

Phil grabbed the duffel bag and stuffed it inside the designer luggage. Within minutes, they were in the red Thunderbird and heading directly toward the beach.

Once they arrived at the Santa Monica Pier, Toots parked in the public parking lot, just as Goebel had instructed. There was still plenty of time before they were all to meet at Bubba Gump's. Toots's nerves felt as if they were tied up in knots.

The two of them sat in the car, the silence thick between them. She had never been in this kind of predicament and didn't have a clue if she should even try to have a conversation with Phil.

"We can't drag this luggage around just

yet. You okay staying in the car for a while? I could go find us a soda or something," Phil suggested.

Toots realized that she hadn't had anything to eat or drink since their abbreviated stay at Phil's condo on Estero Island, and she hadn't had a cigarette since she'd lit up in Abby's office. "Yes. I could use something to drink. And a smoke, too." She removed her cigarettes from her purse, opened the door, and got out of the cramped car. She lit up, not caring that Phil was a cardiologist, not caring if her lungs were as black as the tires on her car. All she really cared about was Abby.

How in the hell had this happened? Had the authorities put forth much effort when that scumbag disappeared two years ago? The world was not that big, she knew. She'd been around it a time or two. When Chris and Henry Whitmore stopped that ten-million-dollar wire transfer, had she unknowingly placed a bull's-eye on her daughter's head? She should have hired Goebel to track down the son of a bitch. Had she known then what she knew now, he wouldn't be running around, abducting innocent women. *But, as the old saying goes, hind-sight is twenty-twenty.*

Phil returned with two Styrofoam cups. "I thought you might like an iced tea. I brought extra sugar if you want some. I can't drink the stuff unless it's syrupy sweet."

Just one more thing they had in common.

"I don't drink anything unless it's laced with sugar." She took the packets from him, dumping them in her cup. She used the straw to mix up the sugar crystals in the bottom of the cup. She took a long drink. "Thanks."

Toots leaned against the car, gazing at the scene before her. The afternoon sun had burned off the morning mist, for which the Santa Monica Bay was so well known. Somehow Toots remembered that the locals referred to the foggy beach days as May Gray and June Gloom. That day was definitely gloomy, the sun having yet to make an appearance on this side of the city, even though it had been bright and sunny at the beach house. Everything around her seemed so normal. In the distance, she could see the old Ferris wheel, the bright colors distinguishable even at this distance. The pier jutted out into the ocean and was loaded with fishermen casting their poles in hopes of catching something they could brag about later.

Leaning on the car beside her, Phil said, "I'll give you five bucks for your thoughts."

"You can have them for free." Toots lit another cigarette and took a long pull of her iced tea. "It's my fault Abby's been abducted, or kidnapped, or whatever the hell they call it these days. I could have stopped this had I been more grounded. I've always had a nose for the tabloids. Abby has, too. That's why she chose this field as a career. I'm sure it doesn't sound like much of a career to you, but we have always loved Hollywood, and the behind-the-scenes gossip. When Abby was younger, she always talked about coming to Hollywood. For a while, I thought she might have had aspirations of becoming an actress, but she squelched that idea real fast. She was never a prissy girl."

Toots stopped. She couldn't take it any longer. Tears gushed down her face, and she didn't care what Phil Becker thought. She'd just caught herself referring to her daughter in the past tense. *No! No! No! Abby is fine. If she isn't, Sophie would know and would have told me so.* She trusted Sophie's psychic abilities as much as she trusted herself.

Phil produced a handkerchief from out of nowhere. He stood in front of her and gently blotted her eyes, wiping the salty tears from her cheeks. "Abby's going to be just fine, Toots, especially with you watching out for her. Plus Goebel. I realize I just met the man, but if I were in trouble, I'd want him to have my back. And that Secret Service guy, too. You're doing everything humanly possible, sweets."

Sweets? Had she heard him correctly?

Toots took the hankie from Phil and blew her nose, then folded it in half and used the other side to blot her eyes. "You're a nice man, Phil Becker."

"Not always," he said.

"I find that hard to believe. You just flew an abandoned dachshund to Florida for back surgery, and you hopped on a plane and flew across the country with me. Plus, you haven't said one nasty word about my love of tabloids. That all fits under the 'nice' category to me. And this is just our first date," Toots said. "Or is it our second date, which got so rudely interrupted?" Without waiting for an answer, she glanced at her watch and saw that there was still plenty of time. If she could just get through the next few hours without losing it, she might be okay. Well, no, she would not be okay until her daughter was found safe and sound.

Phil casually draped an arm around her neck as they stood side by side. Seagulls flew high in the air, then dipped low in the water, searching for their next meal. Waves crashed against the shore, and a slight wind had picked up. Without any sunlight, the afternoon air held a trace of a chill. If the situation were different, he would take her in his arms and kiss her, but he knew that it wasn't the right time. When her daughter was found safely, then . . . Well, he knew exactly what he wanted to do.

"I'm about to tell you something that I've never told a single, solitary soul in the world," he said out of the blue.

"Wait. If it's something really juicy, I'll probably tell Sophia. We tell one another almost everything," Toots said. She felt a tiny bit better just because Phil was standing next to her. This wasn't a good sign given her history with men, but just then she really didn't care. She needed all the moral support she could find.

Phil laughed. "I'll let you determine if it's juicy or not. Being single and of a certain age, well, let's just say I don't have women lining up on Friday nights, waiting to make me dinner. So"—he stopped, scratched the top of his head, then went on—"unless I'm at the hospital on Friday nights, I usually spend the evening reading every single tabloid printed. Hell, I've even started to read the ones online. So there. You tell me if that's juicy or not."

Toots wanted to kiss him. She wanted to wrap her arms around him and plaster her lips directly on his.

Oh, hell, she thought. *You only live once.*

Without giving it a second thought, Toots turned to face Phil Becker, then placed her hands on either side of his face and brought his mouth to hers.

Sparks flew, blood pounded in her head, her heart felt as though it were about to explode from her chest, and her knees trembled so badly, she wasn't sure she could stand. She hadn't experienced a kiss like this since . . . ever. Knowing she had to break away from him before they made complete and total fools of themselves for all to see, Toots stepped out of Phil's arms and instantly felt a fleeting sense of loss.

"Hot damn!" Phil said as he released her.

"Yeah. Hot damn," Toots parroted. Tears filled her eyes again. "Phil, I . . . this is . . . Shit, I don't know what to say." That moment was definitely not the time to fall in love. Her daughter was missing, her life was hanging in the balance, albeit *figuratively,* and here she was, making out on the beach. Maybe she was in the early stages of dementia, because there couldn't be a more inopportune time for something like that to happen.

"Then don't say anything," he said as he took her in his arms again.

Chapter 23

Rodwell Archibald Godfrey, or Rag, as he was used to being addressed and referred to by this bitch and her coworkers at *The Informer*, paced the small living area. He'd been living in the two-dollar dump for four weeks. Steve, the owner of Steve's Pawnshop, had given him a deal on the place because they'd done business together in the past. When Rag had spent every dime he had gambling in Vegas, Steve had always been there to lend him a few bucks for whatever piece of junk he dragged in. Looking at the place through the eyes of his captive, he truly saw what a shit hole it was. There he was, living on top of a pawn-shop, about to pawn Miss Simpson off to some big-deal corporation for ten million bucks. The irony of the situation made him smile.

He was actually surprised and, of course, delighted that in this day and age, LAT Enterprise, the faceless corporation that apparently had no face-to-face relation-ship with Abby Simpson, hadn't told him to go to hell. No reporter was worth that kind of money. Hell, no editor in chief was worth that kind of money. He knew damn well that he would not have paid a single dime if one of his employees had been taken for ransom.

He felt her eyes as she followed his every move. "What? You think I'm enjoying this?" Actually, he was, but he didn't want Abby to know. "Don't bother answering. Oops, I forgot, you can't talk. Your big mouth is taped shut. It's hard, huh?"

He looked at her and could see the venom that shot from her eyes. For a brief second, he almost felt a pang of pity for her, but it passed as quickly as it came. Rag was not the kind to feel pity for any-one other than himself.

He looked at the cheap gold watch on his wrist. It would be one of the first things he replaced once he had all those millions. Every time he looked at it, he thought about that cheap old floozy in Venezuela. He'd milked her out of most of her husband's fortune, and she'd given him this watch on their one-year anniversary. *The cheap bitch.* She had enough money. She could've bought him a Rolex.

Once he had that money, he would get himself a Patek Philippe World Time Automatic Platinum. Only the very best from then on. He wouldn't have to depend on anyone ever again. He'd travel the world, stay in the finest hotels, eat delicacies, and if the urge hit him, and it did often, he would buy beautiful women who would do anything he wanted.

He looked at the watch again, only this time, he actually looked at the time. He had less than two hours until he hit the lottery. Rag walked across the living room to the one lone window. Scanning the parking lot and the surrounding street, he didn't see anything or anyone that looked out of place.

Wait.

What was that?

Pushing his face against the grimy window for a better look, he couldn't help but notice an extraordinarily shiny black Lexus, with tinted windows to match, parked in front of the shit hole across the street. Who would own a fifty-thousand-dollar car and live in a dump that even the rats had vacated? The neighborhood hadn't improved much since the Watts riots took place all those years ago.

He squinted. *Wait a minute. This doesn't look right. What if it's the police, and they've figured out where I am?* No, they weren't that smart. And if they were, they weren't so dumb that they would use a car that would stand out the way the Lexus did.

Besides, he'd covered his tracks. Hell, no one knew what he looked like anymore. He barely recognized himself. He'd watch that car, just to be on the safe side. He'd come this far, and the last thing he wanted was someone trying to horn in on his master plan.

Enough.

Time to start phase three.

Abby watched Rag as he paced back and forth, stopping to stare out the window.

Something was about to take place. Nervous energy flowed from him like water from a spigot.

Had Goebel found her already?

No, it was too soon. Abby wasn't sure if her mother or Goebel had picked up on her clue when she'd been forced to read Rag's demands. She had stared out the window for so long, and something had kept nagging at her. That was when she saw the world-famous Watts Towers in the distance, and she tried to tell them that she was in South Central LA.

Abby passed the time by imagining what she would do to this slimy excuse for a human being. First, she would yank those kinky hair plugs out of his head one at a time, but maybe not. She wasn't sure where they came from. It really looked like pubic hair. Abby grinned in spite of the tape covering her mouth. Knowing Rag, he would've shopped around for a bargain, and it was quite obvious he'd found it. She wondered if it was donor hair, or leftovers from a Brazilian wax job. She couldn't imagine a better home for all those lost hairs, considering he was a true dickhead.

After that, she'd go for public humiliation.

Her episode in the bathroom would be mild compared to what she'd inflict on him. Maybe she could have Sophie perform a séance and literally scare the shit out of him. He was terrified of the unknown and had always avoided talking about the after-life or anything related to the paranormal. *What a work of art,* Abby thought. And to think, he was once her boss.

Chester. She would sic Chester on him, and he'd chew his ass like a piece of gum. She smiled again, but this time she felt the tape as it tugged against her skin. She was quickly reminded of the seriousness of her situation. This wasn't a game. This was real, and she'd already been hurt. But it was nice to think about what she would do, if she could.

"Well, sweet cheeks, as they say, parting is such sweet sorrow, and it's time for me to get the hell out of Dodge." He walked over to the metal chair; Abby followed him with her eyes. "Relax. I'm just going to drag you to that closet over there." He nodded toward a door that she hadn't paid much attention to.

Until then. Garbled sounds came from her.

"Shut up and quit your whining. As long as Ms. LAT Enterprise doesn't try to double-cross me, you'll be home in time to catch the ten o'clock news. Maybe you can use this as your lead story. I can see it all now, 'Previous Owner Found and Lost.' I'm going to buy a private island for myself. Maybe I'll even build a casino. You, of all people, know how much I like to gamble. It doesn't really matter. I won't be here, and you will."

He opened the closet door, then tilted the chair on its two back legs and slid it through the doorway. Once he had repositioned the chair, he spoke. "Yes, yes, I know it's hot in there. I'm sweating, too. Now I'm going to close this door, and you . . . Well, try to relax. Someone will find you, I'm sure. And if they don't, Mr. Steve will notice the stench eventually. Sooner or later." He slammed the door shut and, for added measure, took another metal chair and shoved it beneath the doorknob.

Abby Simpson wasn't going anywhere.

He removed the red envelope from the kitchen drawer, checking the numbers one last time. He wouldn't want them to transfer all those pretty millions to the wrong account. Then he walked through the

three-room dump one last time to gather
his things. In the bedroom, he grabbed the
leather satchel emblazoned with his ini-
tials. He stuffed a few dirty shirts and a
change of underwear inside. In the bathroom, he took his razor and toothbrush
and jammed them in, too.

Well, that was it. Once again, he was
running from Los Angeles. But this time,
he wasn't leaving empty-handed. This
time, he'd leave a very, *very* rich man.

Not wanting to attract any unnecessary
attention to himself, he left through the back
door and used the fire exit, which would
take him to an alley behind the pawnshop,
where he'd parked his newly purchased
wheels from a "buy here, pay here" car lot.
His hair plugs had cost more than the car
did. It didn't matter, because he was planning on ditching the piece of garbage at
the airport. The repo man would find it
soon enough, and it would be up for sale
once again.

Inside the car, he adjusted the rearview
mirror. When he saw that the black Lexus
hadn't moved, a trickle of alarm caused him
to press down hard on the accelerator. He
made a quick turn onto South Central Ave-

nue, then another onto West Century Boulevard, which would lead him to the Pacific Coast Highway. From there, it was just a hop, skip, and a jump to the pier, a quick walk to the Marine Science Center, and with luck, he'd be on his way to the airport no later than six o'clock. He'd hired a private jet to take him to an undisclosed destination.

Money talks and bullshit walks, he thought as he drove along the coast. He'd spent most of his life looking at others from the sidelines. The rich, the famous. It was his turn now. He didn't care about the famous, but the rich, well, he figured that spoke for itself.

Traffic was still relatively light as the five o'clock rush hour was still an hour and a half away. He would arrive at the pier in plenty of time to plant his little envelope and blend in with the crowd. He might even have a bite to eat while he waited for the money to be dropped off.

That would complete phase three of the plan to change his life from Rag's to riches.

Chapter 24

At precisely four o'clock, Goebel told the hostess at Bubba Gump's he'd like a table facing the pier for a party of eleven. Since it wasn't yet dinnertime, she was able to show them to a table for large parties immediately.

Once they were seated and had placed an obligatory drink order, Goebel produced a small black pouch. He looked from side to side, making sure that no one was paying attention. "This is how we'll communicate." He removed several mini two-way radios with earpieces from the pouch and handed one each to his and Chris's three buddies from the police department, whom they knew as Ron, Keith, and Jeff. "I'm sure you guys know how to use these, but let's check and make sure they work." Goebel had every kind of surveillance equipment commercially available and some that wasn't.

Trying not to attract too much attention, each man slipped the earpiece in.

"Dave, you hear this?" Goebel asked as he squeezed the TALK button.

Dave replied, "Loud and clear."

"Ron, Keith, Jeff?"

All three men nodded in the affirmative.

"Dave, I want you to be the one who puts the money inside the garbage can," Goebel said.

"I checked out the place as soon as we arrived. The can is against the wall to the right of the door. You can't miss it," Dave informed him.

"Keith, you're going to have a bad case of the squirts. I'll need someone inside the stall across from the trash can."

"Figures, I always get the shitty jobs."

"This isn't the time for jokes, my man. A woman's life is at stake," Goebel admonished.

"Sorry," Keith said. "Just cop talk."

"Jeff, you and Ron blend in with the crowd. Wait for my signal to move in. After Rag retrieves the luggage containing the money, we'll grab him."

Toots and Phil listened intently as Goebel orchestrated his plan.

"How do you plan to get him to talk? I want to know Abby's whereabouts the second you nab him."

"Don't worry, Ms. Loudenberry. I've done this before. I promise we'll get him to talk," Dave said.

The waitress arrived, carrying a large tray full of drinks. They'd all ordered Cokes to make it easy. This was anything but a social gathering.

Sophie spoke to the waitress. "Is there a Ping-Pong table nearby?"

The young girl, wearing denim shorts and a bright red T-shirt, laughed. "No Ping-Pong tables here. Did you ever see the movie *Forrest Gump?* Tom Hanks's character became a famous Ping-Pong player in the movie and started the Bubba Gump Shrimp Company. We use the paddles here for you to signal us if you need something. Red is for stop, and green is for go."

Perplexed, Sophie said, "So what you're telling me is if we *don't* need anything, we still have to hold up the green paddle, telling you to keep going because we *don't* need anything?"

Toots was about to lose it. "Sophia Manchester, could you shut the fuck up?" She yanked the green paddle from Sophie's hand and placed it at the end of the table, so they wouldn't be disturbed.

Apparently embarrassed, the waitress hurried away.

"Sophie, I know you mean well, but please let's get Abby home. Then you can do whatever you want. You can play with all the Ping-Pong paddles you want."

"And balls, too," Sophie couldn't help but add.

Toots had to laugh. She knew her dearest friend was as concerned about Abby as she was. She just hid behind her humor even more so when times were rough. It was how she'd managed to survive her abusive marriage as well as she had.

Ida and Mavis, on the other hand, had yet to utter a word.

Ida couldn't seem to take her eyes away from Dave Thompson. *Well,* Toots thought,

I'm just as bad, because it was only a short while ago that I was making out in the parking lot with Phil.

"I want the rest of you to wait here. Phil, Chris, make sure they don't go anywhere. I'm going to get Chester out of the car now so we can get into position. You guys ready?"

Toots's hands were shaking like dry leaves in a fall breeze. "Goebel, please, whatever you do, find out where Abby is. I don't care what it takes. You know what I mean? I've got zillions of dollars and a stepson who just happens to be an attorney. You get my drift?" Toots didn't know any other way to say it. If it meant finding Abby, no cost was too high.

Not even the life of the perverted little son of a bitch who took her.

Chapter 25

Rag arrived at the Santa Monica Pier with plenty of time to spare. He saw that there were still open parking spots on the pier itself. Lady Luck was in his hip pocket that day. A spot at the end of the parking area was open. Planning his escape, he backed the hunk of junk into the open spot. Grabbing his bag, he removed the red envelope and tucked it in his back pocket. He didn't want to be rummaging through his satchel inside the restroom. He planned to be in and out as quickly as possible.

The faded, uneven boards on the pier made it difficult to walk. He wondered just how heavy a suitcase containing one million dollars was. If he was lucky, maybe the suitcase would have wheels. Damn, he should've demanded that in his note. *Too late now,* he thought as he walked as quickly as he could toward the Marine Science Center.

As usual, the pier was crowded. People from all over the world could be found there. It was one of the reasons why he'd chosen the place. He wouldn't stand out among the crowd of bums, surfers, bikers, even Goth freaks, you name it, who could be found at the pier any time of day or night. Sometimes his genius amazed him.

Casually strolling past the pier, Rag almost tripped over the uneven boards when he spied the Santa Monica substation on the entrance side that led to the men's room in which he planned to pick up the first part of his winnings. Trying not to be too obvious, Rag scoped out the police officers promenading up and down and around the pier. *WTF? Have I been double-crossed somehow? If I have,* he thought, *prissy Miss Abby Simpson can kiss her ass good-bye.* Giving himself time to consider the matter, he continued walking toward the Marine Science Center. *Nice and easy, like you don't have a care in the world. Just out for an afternoon walk on the beach, like everyone else.* Rag crammed his hands in his pockets. Damn, the men and women in blue were all over the place!

Forcing himself to calm down, he reasoned that if the cops were here for him, they sure as hell wouldn't be wearing uniforms. Nope, they'd have the plainclothes crew out for him. He felt a burst of pride. They'd need the big guns to take him down. This was nothing more than a slight oversight on his part.

A minor flaw in phase three.

Once he'd located the men's room, as a precaution, he lingered outside the entrance for a couple of minutes just to make certain he wasn't being watched. The coast was clear. Rag went inside.

Continuing along in his mode of just a guy taking a stroll, now about to take a piss, by all appearances he was doing just that. Glancing over his shoulder, he saw a father and son exit one of the three closed stalls. A pair of boot-clad feet in a second stall across from the garbage can was positioned in such a way that Rag knew the guy was going to be there for a while taking care of business, and doubted he'd even know anyone else was in the restroom, let alone someone in the midst of collecting the ransom from a kidnapping. Groans and grunts from the stall assured him that whoever was in there, he was concentrating on only one thing.

Quickly, before anyone else came inside, Rag removed the dark green plastic lid on the trash can, took the red envelope out of his back pocket, and inserted the corner of the envelope's edge at a seam along the base of the lid. Tape would've helped, he thought, but this would work. Placing the lid back on the can, he peered down and looked inside, just to make sure the envelope remained intact. It would totally ruin his day if LAT Enterprise, whoever the hell "they" were, failed to locate the note with the information about his offshore bank account.

Yep, it was exactly where it belonged. He quickly exited the bathroom, glad for the breath of fresh air. As he walked away from the stench, he briefly wondered if the guy wearing the boots had ever heard of a courtesy flush, because it smelled like something had crawled up his ass and died.

A short walk across the pier was an arcade that afforded him a bird's-eye view of the men's room. Looking at the carnival-style arcade, with all its noise, kids running around in circles, parents tossing away hundreds for two-dollar toys, Rag thought he couldn't have picked a more perfect location to monitor the comings and goings of those in need of a place to relieve themselves.

While Rag was positioning himself, Goebel, with Chester at his side, was meeting Dave and the three cops at the base of the pier. The dog was beyond well disciplined, and for that he was thankful. He had his master's scent from a T-shirt Chris had found in the trunk of Abby's car. He hoped it wasn't necessary to use the dog's olfactory skills, but just in case, he was prepared. Something he'd learned after spending more than thirty years in the NYPD: never, *ever* enter into a situation unprepared.

All eyes were on the Louis Vuitton luggage containing one million dollars in cash. Goebel had removed it from Toots's

Thunderbird when he took Chester out of the Escalade. Now it was their main focus.

He removed a small box about the size of a pack of cigarettes from his shirt pocket. "Dave, you know what this is, don't you?"

"Yes, it's an ink bomb," Dave said.

"This one is motion activated with a three-minute delay. This'll give him time to exit the bathroom and be out in the open when the device explodes. Hopefully, in all the confusion the Santa Monica police officers will be focused on crowd control, so we can jump in, grab the bastard, and whisk him away."

"What if he suspects something and doesn't take the luggage?" Keith asked.

"Then it's going to be up to the rest of us to catch him. Remember, you're going to be inside, on the john, while all this is going down," Goebel explained. "If you see anything, you'll radio us so we can surround the bathroom."

The atmosphere pulsed with testosterone, each man more than willing to do his part, whatever it took, to capture the son of a bitch responsible for taking Abby.

"Keith, make sure you're in the stall before Dave goes in. We don't want anyone else to get his hands on that luggage," Goebel said. "And we don't want anyone to spot it in the trash and report an abandoned suitcase to the authorities."

"Dave, once he's inside, wait two minutes. Then put the luggage in the trash can. We know he's going to be watching for someone to come in there with a suitcase and leave empty-handed. It's imperative that you leave the area as fast as you can, so he feels secure enough to make the pickup."

"Will do," Dave responded.

"Have I left anything out?" Goebel asked, aware that he was human and knowing full well that there were times when input from someone else could point out omissions. No one said a word. Goebel looked at his watch. Four thirty-one. They had twenty-nine minutes before showtime. They scattered like ants to their designated positions.

"Good luck," Goebel called out. They were going to need all the luck they could muster, and then some.

Abby's life was in their hands.

Chapter 26

Abby struggled to contain her fear. She tried counting to one hundred, then a thousand. Nothing.

Panic-stricken, she counted seconds, then minutes, in order to calculate how long she'd been locked inside the small, sweltering closet. Guessing she'd been in the closet for about half an hour before she began counting, Abby tried inhaling through her nose, then slowly exhaling through her mouth. It was difficult given the three layers of duct tape around her mouth, but she managed to use her tongue to maneuver the tape away from her lips in order for a pocket of air to escape. It was just enough to keep her anxiety from overwhelming her. Never having suffered from claustrophobia, Abby felt a new sense of empathy for those who did.

Sweat trickled down her back, settling at the base of her spine. The skin around her wrists and ankles felt raw and bruised. She tried to kick off her shoes by ramming the heels of her sneakers against the legs of the chair and pushing up. Nothing. She wished now that she'd thought to wear socks as they would have helped to absorb some of the perspiration. She wiggled her toes every once in a while to keep her feet from falling asleep. She had to do something to get the hell out of this heat box, or else she would completely lose it.

Turning her neck from left to right, she managed to use the elasticity of the tape to force it away from her mouth. Finally, she could actually touch her top lip with her tongue. That gave her hope and reduced her anxiety to a manageable level.

Knowing that Goebel, her mother, and her godmothers were aware of her abduction, she realized that it could only be a matter of time before they found her. And her mother wouldn't stop until she did. Abby tried to keep the thought uppermost in her mind. Soon, she'd be out of this two-by-two closet, and home. Anywhere but here. Chester. He would wonder what had happened to her. They'd been together for five years. Poor thing, but again she assured herself that he was being well taken care of by someone in the family.

Then she thought about Chris and the time they had spent together.

Their last date.

Had it really only been a few hours ago that they'd walked the red carpet together? They'd both decked themselves out for the event just because Abby, as editor in chief of *The Informer,* which was close to overtaking the *National Enquirer* as the leading tabloid, had received an invitation for a stupid movie premiere! Just thinking about the senselessness and stupidity of the powers that be in Hollywood caused her stomach to churn. As much as she'd enjoyed all the fanfare and hoopla that went along with her job, and her lifestyle, she was absolutely ready to consider a new career. And it would definitely not be in Hollywood.

Wet with perspiration, Abby tried once again to find a position that didn't deaden her nerve endings any more than they were already. Shifting from one side of her butt to the other, hoping to relieve the numbness, she squeezed her glutes just the way she did at the gym. If anything, when she was found, she'd be able to get up and walk without assistance.

Abby tried to stretch the muscles in her lower back and felt a tinge of relief.

Hope, that was what she had to cling to. If not, she didn't even want to imagine how this nightmare would end.

Toots and Phil hadn't said much since Goebel and Dave left Bubba Gump's to drop the luggage off at the arranged spot. Sophie chattered enough to keep them all entertained.

"Toots, have faith. Remember, Goebel is one of the best in the business. Like you, Phil, you're one of the best cardiologists in Charleston. We're going to find Abby, and when we do, we're all going to party like it's nineteen ninety-nine."

"Please, Sophie. That is so yesterday," Ida informed her. "We're going to thank the big man upstairs. Then we're going to party. Then we're all going to become movie stars."

Toots looked at Ida like she had little green men coming out of her ears. "No thanks. This Hollywood stuff is going to be my downfall. When Abby is home, I plan to have a serious discussion with her about *The Informer.* I want to get rid of it, sell it to anyone who wants it for whatever they are willing to pay. I'll take a loss. I don't care. It's the root of all my troubles now." Again, for the hundredth time, tears pooled in Toots's eyes as she thought of all the trouble owning the paper had brought her. It just wasn't worth it.

"I'm not so sure Abby will agree with that, and maybe she can buy the paper herself. It's been her baby for the past two years now," Chris said, but he didn't sound convinced.

"No matter what we do, we'll all do it together. Toots, you can always join Ida and me. We could teach you how to dress the dead and make their final journey as pleasant as possible," Mavis said, though Toots knew that dear old Mavis was just trying to cheer her up.

"What did you just say that you do?" Phil asked, doubting that he could have heard what he thought he had and suddenly more curious than ever about this group of women.

"They lay out dead people, and Ida paints their faces. Mavis dresses them and also sells a line of clothing called Good Mourning for the living. It's her philosophy that you should be able to wear mourning clothes to other places besides funerals. Toots has buried so many—"

"Not now, Sophia!" Toots warned her.

"Sorry. Anyway, we all started new careers when Toots sent for us two years ago."

Phil smiled. "And you can fill me in on the details as soon as Abby is home. I can't wait to hear them."

Toots asked, "What time is it now?"

"It's four fifty-five," Chris said.

"That son of a bitch is here somewhere now, and I don't even know what he looked like when this all started, much less now. Maybe we should go outside and look, see if we spot anyone who looks suspicious."

"No, Toots, that is the very last thing you need to do. Let Goebel and Dave, and my buddies on the LAPD handle this. They know what they're doing. Besides, if Rag spotted people searching the crowd, who knows what he might do? Let's wait here a little. It's going to be over soon, I promise," Chris said, praying that his words were true.

"I'd just like to have five minutes with him. I guarantee you it would be the most memorable of what's left of his worthless life."

"Toots," Sophie said, "I tell you what. If I have the chance, I personally will whack that bastard's dick off, stuff it down his throat while Mavis shoves a bouquet of flowers up his ass, and Ida can tattoo his forehead with the word 'useless' with her permanent makeup kit. He ain't gonna be anything to look at when we're finished with him." Sophie grinned, but Toots knew she was simply blabbering, saying anything to pass the time until they received word from Goebel that he'd found Abby's location.

Toots looked out the large window. Her heart did a double beat. "Oh my God, game's on. There go Goebel and Chester!"

Chapter 27

Goebel held tightly to Chester's leash as he walked along the pier, trying to look as though he was just another old guy out for a walk with his best friend. He looked at his watch. Keying the mic, he asked, "Is everyone ready? It's showtime."

"Roger," Keith confirmed.

"All set," Dave added.

"LA's finest ready," Jeff said.

"Ditto," Ron concurred.

"Okay, Dave, Keith's in position. Make the drop." Goebel focused his binoculars on the Marine Science Center, trying to appear as though he was searching the ocean for dolphin activity.

Dave was amazed at how heavy the suitcase was. Lucky for him, it had wheels. It was difficult to make it appear lighter than it really was, and he didn't miss the few stares from passersby who noticed he was pulling a three-thousand-dollar piece of luggage along like it was nothing out of the ordinary. It would be tempting to some to take the money and just keep right on walking, but he wasn't that kind of guy. His integrity was on the line. Abby had been abducted on his watch. He took his duties seriously and wasn't about to screw this up.

People of all shapes, sizes, and colors walked the boardwalk and bought treats from many vendors. Children laden with stuffed animals and big, fluffy pink balls of cotton candy were oblivious to what was about to go down. Dave could only hope the operation went as smoothly as Goebel had planned. The last thing any of them needed was innocent bystanders getting hurt. For a moment, he almost radioed Goebel, to say there were children everywhere. But they were professionals, and a woman's life was on the line.

It was now or never.

The steel door to the men's room looked as if it had twenty-five coats of paint on it and still needed a few more. Dave wondered how many thousands of people came in and out of the area every day of the year. He wanted to search for the son of a bitch who was about to take a fortune and run with it, but there was no time.

Seeing that Keith was in the stall, he went into the stall next to him, where he hoisted the luggage across the toilet seat. Quickly, he opened the suitcase and placed the ink bomb in the middle of the stacks of hundred-dollar bills. It had been quite a while since he'd seen so much cash in one place. During his years with the Secret Service, he had occasionally worked at the United States Mint, where he'd had quite a few opportunities to see such large sums of money. Now, *that* was a place for cash. He closed the luggage, then carefully lifted it so as not to arm the motion detector, and quickly glanced over the top of the closed stall door just to make sure there wasn't anyone watching.

When he saw it was clear, he exited the stall and yanked the green plastic lid off the garbage can, saw the red envelope, then carefully placed the money inside the can. Just for good measure, he tore several towels from the dispenser and placed them on top of the luggage so that the can would appear to be filled with trash.

"The package is in place. I'm exiting the building," Dave said into the small microphone hidden under his collar.

Once outside, Dave hurried toward the end of the pier like a football safety prepared to jump on anyone who got free from the cornerbacks.

Rag watched the tall man enter the men's room with a medium-sized suitcase. About three minutes later, he came out, walking at an unusually fast pace. Rag tried to follow him with his gaze, but he disappeared too quickly into the throngs of people. If the guy was smart, he'd get the hell out of there.

Rag had hit pay dirt this time around. Heart racing, he glanced around the arcade to make sure that no one leapt out of the corners to grab him. When he saw that all was clear, he left the arcade and casually walked across the pier to the men's room.

As luck would have it, there were three people inside the men's room. Someone was taking a dump in the first stall, and two men were standing at the urinals, their backs to him. Should he wait? Yes, he had no choice. He hoped that dude in the stall wasn't as smelly as that last asshole, because he was going to have to loiter inside for a few minutes, until the other two guys finished.

Impatiently, he drummed his fingers against his side. Damn, what the hell were those two guys doing? Were they taking a piss or jerking off?

Okay, come on, motherfuckers. You don't need to wash your hands. Get out, and don't come back.

He quickly peered out the door to see if anyone else was about to enter. Nothing. *So far so good.*

Finally, the two jack-off artists washed and dried their hands and left. *Never mind the guy in the stall.* It was time to collect his prize.

When he removed the lid, he nearly

crapped himself. All he saw were wads of wet paper towels. Reaching inside, he realized that the paper towels had been purposely placed on top of the luggage. *Pretty smart.* He lifted the designer suitcase out of the large can and said, "Yes! Wheels! This is my lucky day!"

He was almost home free. He could taste a fine bottle of wine and a sexy young girl. It was within his reach. Placing the luggage on the floor, he extended the handle and, using his back, pushed open the two-way door.

Suddenly, the weight of the door was gone.

"I see you've packed, motherfucker! Don't move."

Rag felt cold, icy steel as the barrel of a gun was jammed into the middle of his back. "You'll never see Abby again if you don't let me go!" He heard the fear in his voice.

"Who the fuck is Abby?" the man with the gun asked.

"Who the fuck are you?" Rag demanded.

"Who we are is not important. What we want is your sorry ass to carefully walk away from the building and down the pier to the black Lexus waiting in the parking lot."

"What?" It was then he recalled seeing a black Lexus parked across the street from his apartment.

The man shoved the gun harder against his back. "Let's just say you have a friend in Venezuela who wants to have a chat with you about his wife and some missing money."

Rag felt his bowels loosen. "Wait! I can explain. How much are you being paid? I'll double it."

The man with the gun leaned over his shoulder, his warm, foul breath blowing in Rag's ear. "The only money you ever had is what you stole from our boss. Move now, and don't try anything funny. Joey here has an itchy trigger finger. It's been a while since he's blown someone away."

Rag could handle this. Once these assholes saw the pile of money he had, he'd be out of there. Leading the thugs toward the end of the pier with the nose of a gun to his back, he dragged the suitcase alongside as they walked toward the parking lot. "You know there are cops everywhere.

You'll draw attention to us with that gun poking in my back," Rag said.

"You make a wrong move, and the cops will be the least of your worries. What you'll need is a coroner. Keep walking, mother-fucker."

Damn, Goebel thought, *this is not going down as I'd planned.* "Keith," he said into his mic, "what's happening down there? Who are those two guys with Rag? Buddies of yours?"

Keith peered out the door. "I heard them come in but didn't want to make myself known. I think they're hoods. They sure as hell aren't cops. No one knows we're here. This is off the record, remember?"

"Stand by," Goebel said. "That case is gonna blow any minute."

The words were barely out of his mouth when a muffled explosion that sounded like a giant firecracker filled the air. Hundreds of black-inked bills exploded like confetti from the suitcase.

Rag's body went limp, and he dropped to the ground in a heap.

The two thugs, covered in ink and dazed, fell a few feet away from him.

"What the fuck did you do?"

"The gun went off, man. I didn't mean to shoot the asshole!"

Thundering footsteps approached from every direction.

"Freeze! Drop that gun now! Put your hands on your head! Now!" a police officer called out to the two thugs, spread-eagled on the ground.

"Okay, okay, man! Don't shoot!"

Looking through the binoculars, Goebel knew immediately that something had gone terribly wrong. "Move in. Rag is down." With Chester running alongside him, Goebel ran as fast as he could. He had to get to Rag before anyone else did. As soon as he arrived at the scene, he saw Rag lying facedown on the ground. Blood streamed out of his back, and when Goebel rolled him over, he saw what was probably an exit wound on the side of his neck. Not caring, he yanked his collar, screaming, "Where is Abby? What did you do with her?"

Pinkish bubbles gurgled from Rag's mouth, but no audible sound came out.

"Where is she, you son of a bitch!"

Goebel continued to scream at Rag, hoping against hope for an answer.

Before he knew what was happening, Goebel felt a heavy hand slam down hard on his back. "Freeze. You're under arrest!"

Racing footsteps broke through the crowd that had gathered at the scene. Keith, Ron, and Jeff, with badges out in front of them, shouted, "LAPD!"

Sweat dripped from the three guys as they pushed their way toward the gaggle of cops surrounding Goebel, Rag, and the two thugs.

"This man is working undercover. Let him go," Keith said.

"The injured man is wanted in connection with a kidnapping that took place last night. We need him to talk."

Sirens blazed as an ambulance drove up to the scene. The crowd parted to make room for the EMTs as they raced to the fallen man with a gurney between them.

The uniformed cop lowered his gun and said, "I don't think this guy is gonna be talking to anyone anytime soon, if at all."

The EMTs quickly placed a backboard under Rag, carefully lifting him onto the gurney. "Start an IV. This guy's losing blood fast."

"Wait," Goebel shouted to the EMTs, who were lifting Rag into the back of the ambulance. "This man is wanted for kidnapping. I need to talk to him now!"

"Sorry, but if we don't get him to the hospital ASAP, he ain't gonna be talking to anyone but St. Peter."

Chapter 28

Every patron at Bubba Gump's gathered at the window to stare at the growing crowd on the boardwalk end of the pier.

"What's going on?" Sophie asked their waitress.

"The manager said someone was shot. Probably a gang thing or something," she said as she strained to see out the window.

Toots sprang out of her chair. "Shot! Who? Chris, let's get out of here now." Not waiting for the others, Toots raced out of the restaurant, fearing the worst.

An ambulance passed Toots as she

raced toward the Marine Science Center, where a huge crowd stood, surrounded by dozens of police officers. Toots looked behind her, seeing Chris, Phil, and the godmothers.

"Goebel! Where is he?" Toots screamed into the crowd, as if someone had an answer.

"Wait, Toots!" Phil shouted from behind.

She turned around when she heard his voice. Chris was right beside him.

"Wait here, Tootsie. Let me see what's going on," Chris said.

"No way! I'm coming with you," Toots shouted.

Chris spied Keith talking to one of the uniformed officers. He hurried to his side. "What happened, and where in the hell is Goebel?"

"He's right there," Keith said, pointing in the opposite direction.

"Oh my God, he's been shot," Sophie cried out as she saw Goebel before Toots had a chance to turn around and see him covered in blood. "Quick, someone get Phil," Sophie shouted.

Keith walked over to the hysterical Sophie. He placed a comforting hand on her shoulder. "Calm down, ma'am. That's not his blood. He's fine. He's just answering a few questions."

"About what?" Sophie asked.

"Just calm down," he said, before walking away to join Ron and Jeff.

Seconds later, Toots and Phil were at Goebel's side. Phil reached out to check the source of the blood that covered Goebel's shirt.

"Oh my God," Toots cried. "What happened? Where is Abby? Did you find her? Please tell me she isn't hurt!"

"Rag was shot. This is his blood, Toots. He's in bad shape. I tried to get him to tell me where Abby was, but the bastard's lost so much blood, he's unconscious. He can't speak."

Toots drew in a breath, then let it out in one giant swoosh. "Goebel, we have to make him tell us where she is. Let's go to the hospital now."

Calmly, Goebel took Toots off to the side. "Listen, Abby is fine. I'm going to the hospital, and I'll wait until the son of a bitch wakes up, and I promise you, he'll tell me where she's at before the night is over. Trust me, Toots."

About that time, Dave inserted himself into the conversation. "I still have a few connections, Goebel. I can have someone posted at the hospital to keep us updated. I'll tell them he's got a kidnap victim in an undisclosed location, and we need to know where to find her as soon as possible."

"Good. Do it," Goebel said succinctly.

By this time, Chris's buddies had gathered around Goebel. They talked among themselves for a few minutes; then Goebel filled Toots and the others in on what they'd just relayed to him.

"Apparently, we weren't the only ones looking for Rag. He was shot accidentally by one of the two hoods who were sent from Venezuela to get him. It seems Rag ripped off the husband of some broad he was having an affair with, and said husband wasn't too pleased. He sent his henchmen to bring him back. Jeff said they had narrowed those cell-phone pings down to an area in South Central LA, what used to be called Watts."

Toots perked up at that news. "Abby told me that! She said something on the phone, remember? We've got to find her, Goebel. I will absolutely move heaven and earth, whatever it takes, to get her home safely. This can't end like all those stories we hear on the news. She has to be all right."

"I'm familiar with the area. Not a place you'd want to be after dark, or during the day, for that matter, but remember, Abby is tough as nails," Chris said.

Upon hearing his mistress's name, Chester made himself known. He'd lingered where Rag's body lay.

"Hey, boy, come over here," Mavis called. She and Ida had remained totally silent throughout the entire episode. Chester trotted over to Mavis. She scratched between his ears and leaned down so he could lick her face. "I'll keep him with me."

"Thanks, Mavis. In all the commotion, I didn't think about him," Toots said. "Abby would have wanted us to take good care of him." Toots teared up again as she caught herself thinking again of her daughter in the past tense.

"Jeff, how much of an area are we talking about with those pings? Can we cover the area on foot? Can we go door to door?" Chris asked, more worried than he let on. Toots was one hair from losing it. Someone had to remain calm in order to see this through to the end, meaning finding Abby. That night.

Goebel cleared a path, motioning for everyone to gather around. "We're not accomplishing anything here. Let's get back to the beach house, where we can regroup. Dave's buddy is already headed to the hospital. He'll keep us posted. The second Rag talks, we'll know."

None of them had slept, eaten, or showered since the day before. They agreed and returned to their vehicles for a traffic-jammed drive back to Malibu.

An hour later, they were assembled at the beach house. Mavis made coffee, heated up some frozen pastries, while the rest took showers in the four bathrooms.

When they were all seated around the kitchen table, refreshed and caffeinated, Goebel's cell phone startled them all. He answered, and they watched and listened.

"I see. Okay. Let me know if there's any change." Goebel clicked the END button on his cell and looked at Toots. "That was Dave's buddy calling from the hospital. Rag is in recovery but has slipped into a coma. They're not sure of anything now. It could be days. I'm so sorry, Toots. I wish I had better news."

Toots looked at Sophie; then tears gushed from her eyes. Sophie sobbed, Mavis struggled to remain calm, and Ida wept uncontrollably.

"Now there is no one who can help us find Abby," she said in a defeated voice.

Sophie grabbed a napkin from the holder in the middle of the table. She dried her eyes, then cleared her throat. "I know someone who can help us."

"Who?" Toots asked.

"Abby's father," Sophie said, a smile lifting the corners of her mouth.

"But I thought he was dead?" Phil asked, puzzled.

"He is, but that's never stopped us before," Toots replied.

Chapter 29

"What exactly does that mean? I thought you were a widow," Phil said to Toots.

Out of her mind with worry for Abby, the last thing she wanted to do was explain Sophie's paranormal abilities to him. He was a doctor. A man who lived by the rules of science. She didn't want to scare him away. So far, he'd been a great rock to lean on. If she told him about the events that took place in the dining room, he might suffer from a heart attack himself, and then what would she do?

"She is. A few times over," Sophie interjected.

Toots shook her head. "Please, Sophia, not now. It's . . . The timing is all wrong, please. Let's not talk about this. All I'm concerned with now is Abby." She gazed at Phil. "Maybe you should just head back to Charleston. You have done enough, and I appreciate it, but your patients must need you much more than I do." Toots didn't want to sound ungrateful, but she couldn't see dragging Phil into this part of her life. Eight dead husbands, a best friend who just so happened to speak to dead people. And now a daughter missing. It was simply too much to ask of him.

"My patients are just fine, and if they're not, there are other cardiologists to cover for me. I'm not going anywhere until we find Abby. And don't tell me what I should and shouldn't do. I want to be here, Toots. No one is holding a gun to my head. Okay?" He reached for her hand, and once again she began to cry, her tears flowing as freely as a baby's.

"Toots, we're all here for you, no matter what you say," Mavis said in a soft voice. "I believe Dr. Becker . . . uh, Phil is trying to say he cares about you." Mavis blushed, but she wasn't usually so forthright around strangers.

"Thank you, Mavis. That's exactly how I feel. I don't care what you or your friends have done in the past. I care about the future. Our future. Abby is a part of your future, so she's going to be part of mine as well. Now, Sophie, can you please explain to me what you meant when you said Abby's father could help us find her?"

Everyone gathered around the kitchen table focused their attention on Sophie, then Toots. Several seconds passed. Toots took a deep breath, then nodded at Sophie, giving her permission to reveal her psychic abilities.

"Where should I start?" Sophie asked.

Toots, Mavis, and Ida all gaped at Sophie.

"The beginning is always a good place," Phil said. "Is this something illegal? Because if it is, don't worry. I go through traffic lights all the time. I'm sure someday I'll have my driver's license taken away."

Sophie's eyes twinkled. "Uh, no, there's nothing illegal about it. At least I don't think there is. If it is, the wife of our former governor wouldn't have requested my services. If only I'd known then, I could have told her what a . . . cheating scumbag he is."

"Sophie, please," Mavis said. "Now isn't the time."

"Okay. Toots purchased this dump about a year ago. It had formerly been owned by Desi Arnaz and Lucille Ball, before they divorced. A young pop star rented it for a number of years from the estate that owned it, and redecorated the place. Toots got it for a song, or so she said"— Sophie raised her eyebrows—"but she had to practically gut the inside and start from scratch. Well, and here's where it gets a little . . . sticky. We were staying here in the early stages of the remodeling. My bedroom started out as Toots's until . . . she had a very traumatic experience, and we switched rooms." Sophie paused suddenly, not sure where to go from there, then decided she might as well get it out in the open. If she was going to make contact with the dead tonight, Dr. Phil Becker needed to know immediately.

All eyes were focused on her.

"So, with all the remodeling, tearing down walls, we must have disturbed the spirits. Toots woke up and found these shadow-like images floating around her bed. They were like clouds, but inside were the faces of Bing Crosby and Aaron Spelling, the actor and the movie mogul. I'm sure you've heard of him. He had several successful sitcoms in the seventies and eighties."

The old proverbial "you could hear a pin drop" applied to that moment in the kitchen. No one uttered a single, solitary word.

Sophie went on. "To make a very long story short, this dump was haunted, and it still is, because we hold our séances here now. I've been quite successful reaching the dead, so I guess you could say I'm more than a little bit psychic, and a medium to boot. That's why Toots always asks me how I feel when things are . . . well, like they are now. I haven't had a bad feeling about Abby yet, but if I can contact her father, it's possible he can guide us to her location before those cell pings do. Now, it's not one hundred percent, but I've helped quite a few celebrities. I even located Chris and that stupid actress a few months ago, when they disappeared. So, basically, that's it."

"Now, let me get this straight. Is it your intention to have some sort of séance and basically ask Abby's father to guide you to where she is?" Phil asked, seemingly unshaken.

"Well, yes, that is the general idea," Sophie quipped. "So, you don't think I'm crazy?"

Phil shook his head. "Remember where I'm from? I was born and raised in Charleston, so the supernatural, or paranormal activities, is something I'm not a stranger to. I've even been on a few ghost tours in my day." He rubbed his hands together. "So, what are we waiting for?"

Toots's, Ida's, and Mavis's jaws dropped to their chests. Goebel gave a wry smile, and Chris just shook his head. Toots spoke first.

"You can't be serious?"

"Why not? Don't I sound serious? Not all doctors believe science and medical books have all the answers. I've seen patients die on the operating table and come back and tell me things that happened thousands of miles away, as if they were there when the events took place. A lot of it was backed up by family members. People have told me about events that would take place in the future more than enough times. The most memorable was a young man who'd suffered a heart attack and was clinically dead for five minutes. We were able to bring him back, and he told me he had seen an apple sitting on a desk next to a ruler, and an explosion in the sky. It was three weeks later when Christa McAuliffe was killed in the space shuttle. So, I guess you could call me a believer. Every day we see and hear things and dismiss them. Not many of my colleagues believe this, but I've heard too much not to know there is another plane of existence out there."

"Then let's get started. Does everyone want to attend? If not, say so now. I don't want any disturbances, unless they're from the other side."

No one said a word.

"Okay. Mavis, you know what your job is. Toots, are you up to this?"

"Yes, let's hurry. I want to find Abby tonight. I don't think I can go another night not knowing where she is," Toots said.

"Follow me." Sophie led them all to the dining room, where they'd performed many séances in the past. Even though Toots had remodeled the entire house, they'd left this one room alone since it was where Sophie made contact with the other side.

Once they were in the dining room, Mavis placed several candles around the room, quickly lighting them. Sophie pulled the heavy drapes aside. Toots found the purple silk sheet they used as a tablecloth and spread it across the table. On the floor, in the corner, was a box of rocks glasses they used as a tool for communication should a spirit decide to join them. Ida placed one of the glasses in the center of the table.

"Let's all take our places. Chris, you can sit where Abby normally sits. Goebel, you sit next to Ida, and, Ida, keep your hands off. Mavis and Toots, I want you two on either side of me. Phil, if you're sure you want to involve yourself in this, have a seat next to Chris."

Once they were all seated, with candles flickering, the purple silk sheet atop the table, Sophie began the séance as she always did.

As always, when Sophie prepared to make contact with the other side, her voice changed to one that was soft, almost seductive. "Now, if everyone is ready, let's begin. First, I always start with a prayer. Please bow your heads," Sophie instructed.

They all bowed their heads.

"Oh, great one, bless this dump and those who may inhabit it, living or dead. We wish to make contact tonight with John Simpson. Let's all join hands."

One by one, they reached for the hand next to them. When Toots took Sophie's hand, she gave it a little extra squeeze.

"Let's close our eyes," Sophie said.

Again, the group did as told.

They remained that way for several minutes; then Sophie spoke again. "Let's all place our fingertips on the glass in the center of the table."

They did.

"Tonight we would be greatly pleased if John Simpson could come through. Abby is in trouble, and we here on earth cannot find her." She closed her eyes, took a deep breath, then relaxed, her body almost limp.

No air circulated in the room, yet the candles flickered as though a slight breeze had passed over them. Hundreds of tiny white lights began to fill the room.

There were several gasps from those in the room.

"Don't let this frighten you. These are *orbs*." She closed her eyes again, then opened them. "John, are you here with us?"

Suddenly, the room was filled with a noise that sounded like thousands of bees. Bright orbs began to whirl around the room, and a cool blast of air settled around the table.

"This is quite normal," Sophie explained, as she knew that Phil and Goebel were experiencing supernatural contact with the dead for the first time. She didn't want them to be frightened, even though it was a bit scary, even to her at times.

Suddenly, Sophie's head dropped to her chest. She appeared to be unconscious; then, seconds later, in a voice that did not belong to her, she spoke. *"I don't recognize you anymore. You've lost weight."*

Mavis looked at Sophie as though she'd seen a ghost. Well, of course, she had.

"Herbert?" Mavis whispered. In all the séances they'd held, Herbert had never made himself known.

"Mavis, I am so proud of you. Find someone else. Be happy."

The air in the room dropped several more degrees; then the orbs began to swirl around the room, dancing like fairies. The candles flickered again. Then, as fast as it happened, the room became warm again. The orbs disappeared, and the temperature returned to normal, yet Sophie still remained in her trancelike state.

"John," Sophie called, her voice her own, yet soft and low. "Can you make your presence known? Your daughter needs you."

The room was still as night, the occupants motionless.

For the second time that night, the temperature in the room dropped precipitously. And from nowhere, a translucent cloud suddenly appeared, hovering above the center of the table.

"Let's move our hands away from the glass and join hands," Sophie instructed.

Toots stared at the glowing image inside the cloud. "Oh my God!" she said out loud. "John!"

"John Simpson, if this is you, whirl around the room," Sophie requested.

The cloud sprang around the room, stopping to hover above Toots.

"Where is Abby?" Sophie asked in a whisper.

"Mr. Steve. Hot. Dark. Riots. Hurry."

Again, the room returned to its normal temperature. The candles stopped wavering, and Sophie's head jerked up. "Toots?" she asked when she saw the look of shock on her friend's face. "Are you all right?"

Inhaling and exhaling, Toots nodded, but her hands were shaking so badly, she couldn't control them.

"Was that John?" Phil asked.

"Yes, yes, it was," Toots answered. "He was so young when he died. But I don't understand what his message was." Defeated, Toots appeared to age right before their eyes.

"I remember what he said," Chris told her. "Remember the riots in South Central LA? Watts? Wherever Abby is, she's in the area where they took place. I don't know who Mr. Steve is or how he is relevant, but I would bet everything I own that Abby was taken and left in one of those run-down apartments there."

Ida switched the lights on and blew out the candles.

"Call the hospital, Goebel, and see if Rag is awake. Maybe the son of a bitch can tell us what this means," Chris said. "Meanwhile, I'm going to call Jeff to see if he's homed in any closer on those pings. Maybe he can tell us more."

Toots stood up, shaking but a bit more in control of herself. "We need to get to South Central LA, and we need to do it now. Mother's instinct tells me we don't have a lot of time."

Chapter 30

"They're not sure he'll make it through the night," Goebel said as they gathered in the kitchen before leaving.

"That son of a bitch," Chris said. "I would love to choke the life out of him myself, but it may be too late for that. Jeff said the pings were close to South Central Avenue. That's in the heart of South Central."

"Then what are we waiting for? Let's go to South Central and start looking," Toots said, already grabbing her purse and racing to the door. "I don't think we should all go. Someone should stay here, just in case, by some fluke, Abby calls. We'll bring

Chester with us. If she's close, he could help find her."

"I'll call Jeff back and have him meet us there. He's as committed to finding Abby as we are." Chris called him back. "He'll meet us in the McDonald's parking lot on South Central Avenue in thirty minutes. Ron and Keith are coming with him."

"I'll stay here. I have a few phone calls to make," Ida said. "I'm going to postpone our Home Shopping Club debut. This is way more important."

"I agree with Ida. I'll notify all the funeral homes that Ida and I won't be available for any services until further notice," Mavis added.

"Let's take the Escalade. It's got a GPS, so we can put that street in and go directly to the McDonald's," Goebel said.

Within minutes, Goebel, Sophie, Toots, Phil, Chris, and Chester piled into the Cadillac SUV. Goebel punched in the street name, and they took off.

Once they were on the Pacific Coast Highway, Toots, somewhat calm since the séance, spoke. "Chris, does 'Mr. Steve' mean anything to you? Or would it mean anything to Abby? I don't have any idea what John meant. What about it, Sophie? Do you have any explanation?"

Sophie, seated in front with Goebel, turned around to look at Toots in the middle seat, with Phil's arm draped around her shoulders. "I don't have a clue. I'm just the medium. I have never made contact that fast. Did you happen to think of that? This is a good sign. It makes me think John is with Abby wherever she is, watching over her until we find her. I know all of this sounds crazy, but I just know these things. Don't ask me how. I just do."

"Then he said, 'Dark and hot,'" Chris offered. "I would think wherever Rag is holding her, that it's in a place that's hot and dark. Maybe a basement. Or an old wine cellar. They're still around—I don't know if South Central has any—but at this point, I'm willing to look in every possible nook and cranny."

No one said anything for a while. The buildings they passed were shoddier, older, and many were boarded up. The local economy hadn't recovered since the Rodney King incident all those years ago.

A mechanical female voice spoke. "Destination on the right in three miles."

"Almost there, Toots," Goebel said. "Okay, there's the McDonald's. I see Jeff and the others are there."

Goebel pulled up next to Jeff's vehicle. He pushed the DOWN button for the electric window. "Let me fill you in on what we know. No news from Rag, he's in a coma, and they don't know if he is going to make it through the night. I can't reveal my source, but we're looking for a place that's dark and hot, one where you could hide someone. Also something to do with Mr. Steve. We're not sure if this is a place or a person. Does it mean anything to you guys?"

"Doesn't ring a bell for me," Jeff said. Turning to his right, he asked Ron and Keith. "How about you guys?"

"This is nowhere near our precinct. But I know a guy I can call who patrols this area. Let me give him a call real quick," Ron said and took his cell phone from his pocket. "Hey, Frank. It's me, Ron. You on duty tonight? Good. I need some help. I'm working a case for a friend right now. It's off the record, but nothing illegal. I need some information. We're here on Central Avenue in South Central, looking for a young woman who's been kidnapped. I can't say who my source is, but does the name Mr. Steve mean anything to you? What? No shit. Thanks, man. I owe you one." Ron clicked the END button on the phone.

"What?" Goebel asked. "Did you learn anything?"

Ron rolled the window down and spoke to Goebel. "You're not going to believe this, but apparently Mr. Steve's is a big-time pawnshop in the area. He owns several apartments that he rents out, some by the hour, if you know what I mean."

"Follow me," Jeff said. "It's right around the corner."

Ten o'clock was early by South Central standards. The streets were crowded with gang members shouting obscenities to one another. Loud music blared from a souped-up Dodge Neon with a muffler that resembled a megaphone, and an older-model Cadillac with four-thousand-dollar wheels bounced along the street, stopping at a traffic light. The driver of the Neon pulled up beside the Caddy, revved its four-cylinder engine, and looked at the traffic light as though it were the Christmas tree light on a drag strip. The second the light turned green, engines raced, tires squealed, and both cars sped to the next traffic light.

"God, if Abby is here, I pray she is safe. This is worse than a third-world country," Toots said.

"It's not one of LA's hottest nightspots, that's for sure," Chris agreed.

"Look! There it is, Mr. Steve's Pawnshop," Goebel said, slowing down to get a closer look at the place. Neon lights of every color in the rainbow glistened from the three-story building. Old, probably from the early sixties, the bright neon signs read WE BUY GOLD; BUY, TRADE, OR SELL; and BEST PRICES IN TOWN.

Keith, Ron, and Jeff parked in front of a fire hydrant and entered the building.

"Toots, you and Sophie wait here with Phil. Chris and I will go inside with the guys. If I suspect there's anything connected to Abby here, I'll come and get you. Now, roll up the windows and lock the doors." Goebel and Chris followed the cops inside the building.

Inside the pawnshop Keith, Ron, and

Jeff flashed their badges at a young punk sitting behind the counter, sending text messages on a cell phone.

"Whatcha need?" he asked, then noticed their badges. "Hey, man, I just work here. I didn't do anything," the kid said defensively.

"I need to see the owner. Now," Keith said in his cop voice.

The kid looked behind him, where a curtain separated him from whatever lay behind it. "Steve," he called out. "We got the cops here. Probably bought some stolen shit from somebody."

The kid resumed texting at such a fast pace, he would rival Evelyn Wood.

From behind the dark curtain, a heavyset man with a too-tight shirt that revealed a fat, hairy stomach waddled his way to the counter. "What'sa problem?"

"You know a guy named Rodwell Archibald Godfrey?" Keith asked.

With an accent that sounded like it came from the latest gangster movie, "Do I look like someone who would know some prissy ass named Rodwell?" Steve replied.

Goebel stepped up to the counter. "He goes by Rag. Does that ring a bell?"

Laughing, Steve said, "Rodwell Archibald Godfrey! You mean Rag? That's his name? What's that piece of shit done now?"

"That doesn't concern you. Tell me what you know about him," Keith demanded. "When was the last time you saw him?"

Before Steve could answer, Chester leaped through the door, with Toots trying her best to contain him. Phil raced in behind her.

"He went crazy. He was clawing at the window. He always does this when Abby's around," Toots said.

Growling, hackles raised, tail stiff at attention, Chester snarled, every tooth in his mouth ready to chomp a few inches from the pawnshop owner's ass.

Steve jumped back. "Hey, get that dog outta here!"

"Never mind the dog. When did you last see him?" Keith asked.

Chester continued to growl.

"The last time I saw that little bastard, he was sneaking out of the apartment I let him have for next to nothing. He's probably trying to skip out on the rent again this week."

At that moment, Chester jumped up,

placing his front paws on the glass counter-top.

He began to bark excessively.

"Down, Chester," Toots shouted. The shepherd jumped back from the counter but continued to growl ominously.

"Where is this apartment? We have reason to believe he's kidnapped a woman. She could be there right now, and unless you want to be held as an accessory to kidnapping, I suggest you tell me now!" Keith shouted. "Now, man. I'm not gonna ask you again!"

"Okay, jeez! Give me a minute. I gotta get the keys." Steve disappeared behind the curtain, returning with a giant ring of keys. "There's a back entrance. There is a set of stairs here that leads to the apartment. Let me unlock the door."

Chester sprang from behind, knocking over several stacks of DVDs and passing everyone as he raced up the flight of stairs and entered the apartment. The big canine raced over to a door with a chair wedged against the handle. He began to scratch at the dark chair and bark wildly.

Seconds later, the others entered the

apartment, where they saw the chair and Chester. It was then Toots knew that they had found her daughter.

"Abby!" she screamed as she yanked the chair away from the doorknob and pulled the door open. What she saw brought tears of joy to her eyes. "Oh my God, Phil, come quick!"

Immediately in physician mode, Phil placed his hand on Abby's neck to check for a pulse. "She's alive but barely conscious. Someone call an ambulance." He pulled the chair out of the closet into the center of the room. "A knife," he shouted.

Goebel whipped out a pocketknife and sliced the tape from her legs, cut the zip ties from her hands, then gently removed the tape from her mouth but left the tape on the back of her hair. They could remove that later. Phil laid her down on the hard floor.

Toots dropped down on her knees beside her limp daughter. "Abby, can you hear me?"

Her eyes fluttered, and she tried to speak, but Toots couldn't make out what she said. It didn't matter. She was alive.

Chester, seeing his mistress lying on the floor, dropped down beside her and began to lick her face like he always did.

Abby's eyes opened again, only this time they could hear her words clearly.

"I knew you would find me."

Chapter 31

The smell of antiseptic assaulted her nostrils. Bright fluorescent lights above her forced her eyes shut. Hushed voices spoke softly around the perimeter of her bed. Abby thought she had to be dreaming, because when she licked her lips, there was nothing to bind them, no sticky residue. Fleetingly, she dared to open her eyes just enough for her to view her surroundings. When she saw her mother standing next to her, her eyes instantly opened all the way.

"Mom?" Abby asked, her voice scratchy,

her throat raw and dry. "Where am I? What time is it?"

"Shhh, you're going to be just fine, Abby. It's a little past seven in the morning. You've been out most of the night," her mother told her. "Try to relax. We're all here for you."

Suddenly, the events of the past thirty-six hours filled her head like a heavy fog. "How did you—"

"It doesn't matter. Relax. We can talk later," Toots assured her as she brushed Abby's damp hair away from her fore-head.

Abby tried to push herself up into a sitting position, but her wrists were both wrapped in heavy gauze, both sore. "Why are my hands . . ."

Her mother stepped away from the bed, Chris taking her place. "You're going to be fine, Abby." Gently, he patted her arm.

"Did you find—"

"Rag? He's in the hospital. I don't think he's going to be leaving anytime soon. At least not without the assistance of a gur-ney, or, if we're lucky, a frigging casket!"

By now Abby had managed to push herself into a sitting position despite the large bandages on her hands. "What do you mean? Is he here in this hospital, too? What happened to him, the slimy son of a bitch!"

Everyone in the room who knew Abby smiled. She was going to be absolutely fine.

"Let's just say Chester can smell shit from a mile away," Chris teased. "Your old boss isn't going to be going anywhere for a long time, if at all. He was shot at the ransom drop-off point, though I'm not sure of the details at this point. After they saved his life at the hospital in Santa Monica, he was transferred here after we found you. We've got a former member of the Secret Service, your director of security, outside his room. If he blinks, we'll know about it before he can do it again. Now, tell me exactly what happened?"

Abby repeated her story for Chris and her mother. Goebel and Sophie, and some man she didn't know, listened intently while she told of her trip to the basement, searching for Rag's old files, thinking she might find a clue, something, anything that would lead to him.

"And I found more than I expected,"

Abby concluded. "It's hard to believe no
one ever noticed where that door led. I've
been in that basement dozens of times. I
thought it was just an old storage closet.
Unreal." She shook her head, then lay back
against the starched pillow. "How long was
I in that closet, anyway?"

"Too long as far as I'm concerned,"
Toots said. "Thirty-six hours ago, I was in
Naples, Florida, worried about a dog."

"What dog? Chester?" Abby inquired. "Is
he okay?"

"No, it was Frankie," Toots said. "It's a
long story and . . ."

Phil stepped in again to rescue Toots.

"Abby, we have never met. I'm a friend
of your mom's. Phil Becker. Bernice is my
patient. She found a little dachshund right
next door to your mom's place in Charleston."

"You mean Mrs. Patterson's little dog,
Frankie?" Abby asked.

"The one and only," Phil said. "He suffered a spinal injury, and I knew a neurolo-
gist who specializes in back injuries to
animals. As luck would have it, I was about
to take your mother out to dinner when
Bernice found the little guy."

Abby looked at her mother, then again at the doctor. She raised her brow in question. "Oh, I see." In spite of all that had taken place in the past thirty-six hours, Abby grinned. *Uh-oh,* she thought. *Phil better watch out.* She studied her mother's face and saw something in it she hadn't witnessed before.

"No, you don't," her mother said quickly. Toots looked at Phil.

"Your mother and I have become friends. We met when Bernice was brought to the hospital for surgery." He didn't expound any further. He didn't have to. Abby could see he was as smitten with her mother as she was with him.

"Amazing," Abby said, then spied Sophie wearing a huge grin. "Sophie, you're just dying to tell me a secret, aren't you? I've seen that look on your face before."

Sophie walked across the room and stood at Abby's bedside. "No, no, I'll leave that to your mother. I'm just grateful we found you." Sophie turned to Toots. "Should we tell her *how* we found her?"

Toots rolled her eyes. "You're going to tell her no matter what I say, so you might as well."

With a grin, Chris added, "Tell the whole story, Sophie."

Sophie flipped Chris the bird, and he flipped one right back. The entire room filled with laughter.

"Before you start, remember, Sophie, I've accumulated quite the arsenal of ammo throughout the years. Don't make me trigger-happy," Toots added.

"I'm talking about how we found Abby. Nothing more. You don't have to worry," Sophie informed Toots.

Abby raised a bandaged hand to move her hair away from her face. When she did, she felt a sharp twinge of pain on her cheekbone, and that was when she remembered Rag slapping her across the face. "Wait, Sophie. Don't tell me anything yet. You said that son of a bitch is here, right?"

Abby sat up, shoved the sheet off herself, then swung her legs over the side of the bed and stood. Dizzy but determined, she held on to the guardrail to steady herself. Chris was at her side instantly.

"Abby, this isn't a good idea. He isn't going anywhere, except maybe to hell. Get back in the bed, or I'll have Dr. Becker order a sedative." He laughed when he said this, but he was serious. Abby could tell by the expression on his face.

"See these bruises on my face? I owe him. Big-time, and I always pay my debts." Abby leaned against the bed. Another wave of dizziness hit her, but she remained standing.

"There will be time for that later," Toots told her. "Right now you're more important than that waste of humanity. He'll get his, Abby, if not here, then in the afterlife. If we're lucky, we can have Sophie torment him while he roasts in hell."

Abby knew that her mother was right, but her desire for revenge was strong. However, she knew that this time around, Rag would get the punishment he so deserved. Thanks to Charles Lindbergh, kidnapping was a felony, and the Feds would have a nice place waiting for him to stay if he survived. And truthfully, Abby did not want him to die. She just wanted justice, and more than anything, she wanted to see him suffer and think about all the people he'd hurt.

Toots's cell phone broke the silence. She looked at the caller ID. "Oh my God! It's Bernice!"

"Yes, Bernice. I know I said I would call. Abby is fine. Yes. Sophie found her. Well, sort of. Yes, I will tell her. Okay." Toots clicked the END button. "I can't believe I didn't call Bernice. In all the confusion, it was the last thing on my mind. She will never forgive me for this," Toots said.

"How did she sound?" Phil asked, in physician mode once again.

"Bitchy as ever. She's fine. Jamie is with her, and we know she adores her. Hopefully, Jamie will keep her busy in the kitchen until we return."

"That's what I like to hear. My patients bitching. Always a good sign," he joked.

"Speaking of patients," Abby said, "how long do I have to stay here?"

"Dr. Mason says you can leave when you can keep a full meal down and you're not dizzy anymore. You were badly dehydrated when we found you," her mother said.

"I feel fine now, and I'm getting better by the minute. As a matter of fact, I'm starving. Can you guys get me something from the cafeteria?"

"I'll take care of it," Chris said. "Toots, why don't you all head back to the beach house, get a little rest, and clean up? I'll stay here, and when she's ready to be released, I'll call you."

"If Abby's okay with that," Toots said, regarding her daughter, "then I am. I could use a shower and a cigarette myself."

"Mother! You and Sophie need to stop that nasty habit, or you'll be lying in a hospital bed yourself."

"I've told your mom that, but she has a mind of her own," Phil said. "I would hate to see her wind up on my operating table."

"We have hardly smoked," Sophie added. "We're down to just a few a day, right, Goebel?" Sophie said.

"Yep, that's right," Goebel said. Then he rubbed a band across his now-slim stomach. "After all, I lost that spare tire when Mavis put me on that diet. I think we can figure out a way for the two old coots to give up the habit," Goebel said in jest.

Toots stood beside Abby's bedside. "You're right, and you know I will try. One thing at a time. Chris, you call me the second you know when my daughter can come home. I think the two of us have some very important business that we need to discuss."

Abby nodded at her mother. "Yes, Mom, we most certainly do."

"Then let's go so we can be ready to return for Abby. Even though I'm not the attending doctor, I would imagine they'll let this little lady go home before the sun sets. We all have a lot of catching up to do," Phil said.

If a stranger had been observing them, they would never have guessed that this was Phil and Abby's first meeting.

After many hugs and well wishes from all, Abby and Chris were finally alone.

Chapter 32

Mavis, anticipating their arrival, had prepared a healthy breakfast fit for a king, to
be served as soon as they arrived. After
Toots filled her and Ida in on the previous
night's events and assured them both that
Abby wasn't seriously injured, telling them
it was highly likely she would be released
from the hospital within a matter of hours,
they sat down to a breakfast of homemade
blueberry pancakes covered with fresh
strawberry topping, sliced honeydew melon,
and several cups of coffee. When everyone had satisfied their hunger, it was

decided they'd all take showers, then rest until they heard from Chris.

"Phil, you want to take a shower first?" Toots asked when they were alone in the kitchen, everyone else having dispersed. "I've just got to have a couple of drags off a smoke. And before you remind me, yes, I know they're killers. Maybe you can give Sophie and me a few pointers on quitting."

"A shower sounds good. I can write you a prescription for a medication to wean you off the cigarettes, but it's been my experience in my practice, most of my patients do better just going cold turkey," Phil said. "If you'd like, you could join me in that shower. We could finish the evening we were about to have at DiamondHead."

"I don't recall that part of the evening," Toots said, blushing.

"Well," he teased, "you can't blame a guy for trying."

"Just get your shower, Romeo," Toots said, wanting to wring his neck. But at the same time, a little thrill raced up her spine at the prospect.

There would be time for those thoughts later. Now that she knew Abby was safe, all she wanted to do was relax. Sophie,

Ida, and Mavis were all outside on the deck, while Goebel and Phil took their showers.

It seemed like it had been forever since the four of them had spent some time alone.

Sophie slid open the glass door and poked her head in. "Toots, get your ass out here and join me. I feel like I've got something contagious. Ida and Mavis won't come near me."

Toots stepped outside to the deck that faced the Pacific Ocean. Seagulls cawed, and waves swept against the oyster-colored sand. The voices of morning beachcombers could be heard coming from below. Toots thought that while the beach was nothing like the one she encountered on the Gulf of Mexico, each was unique in its own right.

Sophie handed her a lit cigarette, which Toots gratefully accepted. After taking a hefty drag, she sat down in her favorite deck chair, next to Sophie. Ida and Mavis took their usual positions at the outdoor table.

"I can't tell you how much it means that you're here. I don't know what I'd do without you girls. Abby's thrilled you're here, too," Toots said, besieged by a moment of sentimentality.

"Did you think we'd sit around in Charleston, waiting?" Ida said. "I know I haven't been much help, but Abby is my godchild, and I love her as much as the rest of you do."

Mavis smiled, her sweet voice projecting her happiness. "Yes, since we never had children of our own, we love that young lady as much as you do, Toots. I'm just thankful we were able to make contact with John." She paused, then went on. "Do you think this psychic stuff will scare Phil away? He certainly seems to have it bad for you."

Toots took a long draw from her cigarette. "Nah. If this were going to scare him off, he would have left last night, before the séance. You heard what he said. He's a good guy, and no, Sophie, I have not slept with him, and when and if I do, it's none of your business."

Ida piped up. "Well, I certainly recall you and Sophie sticking your noses where they didn't belong when I was involved with Patel. Of course, that was a good thing, but nonetheless, I think our private lives should remain private."

"Oh bullshit, Ida. You can't wait to let us know when you're getting some. You might not come right out and say so, but we know you like the attention," Sophie declared in her usual inimical style.

"Girls! Please, let's not fuss," Mavis urged. "We should be celebrating. Abby has been returned relatively unharmed, and that nasty old Rag isn't going to get away this time. If he lives and is prosecuted, he'll be going away for a very long time. Abby will never have to worry about his showing up in that old tunnel again."

Toots crushed her cigarette out in the giant seashell they'd been using as an ashtray since she bought the place. "I'm glad you brought this up, Mavis. I'm going to make arrangements to have that damn thing filled in or something. At this point, I'm not so sure I want to keep *The Informer.* It has caused too much harm for both Abby and Chris. I'm considering putting it up for sale."

There, she'd said it. Now all she had to do was figure out a way to tell this to Abby without pulling the rug out from beneath her. This was her daughter's passion, her livelihood. If Abby wanted the paper, she would simply sign it over to her. Toots could only hope that Abby saw things her way.

All three women focused on Toots.

"You can't do that! That paper is Abby's life," Sophie proclaimed.

"And it just about cost her her life, Soph. Don't forget, Abby's a smart woman. I don't think the paper is her top priority, the way it once was. Have you seen the way she and Chris look at each other? It's way beyond what it was when he got back from that ill-starred fiasco with that two-bit actress. Something important has changed between them, and I, for one, couldn't be happier. I'm guessing, and keep in mind it's only a guess, but I believe Abby and Chris are about to become a complete couple, if you know what I mean," Toots predicted.

"You mean as in getting married?" Ida asked.

"Something like that. Chris told me he's all but given up entertainment law. I wouldn't be surprised if he made a career change. He's certainly young enough. Remember, he also owns that big plantation house in Charleston. It's where he was living when

I married his father. It was left to me in the will, but I signed it over to Chris years ago. I figured that when the time was right, he'd take over the house himself. And now I'm wondering if it's time. No, he hasn't said anything, but though I am only his step-mother, he and I have always been close. I know how he thinks," Toots explained. "Now, how Abby would feel about that, I'm not sure, but I plan to discuss all of this with her as soon as she's out of the hospital."

Upon hearing Abby's name, Chester flew out the doggy door onto the deck. He raced over to Mavis and started whining.

"He misses Coco," Mavis said, petting the big German shepherd.

"Yes, but we'll have them back together soon," Toots said. "I'd like to stay here with Abby until I am sure she is okay."

Before they could even finish their con-versation, Toots felt her cell phone vibrate in her pocket.

"Toots, Abby's doctor just left. They're releasing her this afternoon. They're giv-ing her an IV now, something about extra glucose. Anyway, as soon as it's finished, she can go home. I just wanted to give you a heads-up," Chris said.

"Wonderful! I'll tell the others, and, Chris, tell Abby I love her."

She relayed the news to the godmothers. They all agreed that it was the best news they'd heard all that day.

Phil chose that moment to poke his head out the door. "Hey, I just got a call from one of my partners. It seems I'm needed back in Charleston, ASAP. I booked a flight for later this afternoon. Think someone can give me a ride to LAX?"

Toots's heart sunk. She'd wanted Phil to meet Abby, the real Abby, when she wasn't lying in a hospital bed with revenge on her mind. *But, it is what it is,* she thought. "Of course we'll give you a ride. I just spoke to Chris, and Abby's being released this afternoon. We can take you when we head to the hospital."

Toots had a brief thought: Was this his way of backing away from her and a possible relationship and the insanity that seemed so normal to her?

She didn't know. What she did know was, she missed him already, and he hadn't even left.

Chapter 33

Bernice peered through the newly purchased set of binoculars she'd ordered from a catalogue she'd read while she was on the treadmill. She scanned the front yard again and again. Still, there was no sign of that giant FOR SALE sign that had been there when she found Frankie and brought him home, just two days ago.

With a renewed sense of purpose, she again thought of her reason for being here. She didn't give a hoot what Dr. Becker or anyone else who had been with her in that operating room said. She *had* died. She remembered hovering above her body, looking down, and seeing her own heart as it was pumped by a mechanical contraption that looked like something out of an old Frankenstein movie. Knowing she'd helped save Frankie was something to claim, but she knew she'd been sent back to earth for another important purpose. Not that saving little Frankie wasn't important; it was. But her gut told her there was something more about to take place at the old Patterson place, and now, with the FOR SALE sign gone, she had a funny feeling that it was about to happen.

One last time, before Jamie caught her spying with her binoculars, she scoped out the house. It wouldn't do for Jamie to see her, as she would be on the phone to Toots so fast, it would make her heart race faster than that of a horse in the Kentucky Derby coming down the stretch and straining to reach the tape first.

Tucking the binoculars in the bushes so they would be there when she returned, she hurried back inside. Jamie was baking sugar-free brownies this afternoon, since Bernice hadn't indulged in anything remotely sweet since her bypass surgery. She felt better than she had in years, and she didn't want to do anything to mess it up. She was seventy-two and in remarkably decent shape. Who knew? Maybe she would live long enough to see her wandering son again. She cleared those thoughts from her head, because they would only depress her. As she was about to go back inside, she heard voices. Quickly, she stepped back to the bushes, spreading them apart just enough so that she could see where the voices were coming from.

Two men, one of whom was probably close to her in age. One was carrying boxes and placing them on the large wraparound porch. They sounded like they were arguing. She strained to make out their words.

"Look, Robert, you can kiss my old ass, okay? I got the place for a steal. If you think you're not going to be happy living here in Charleston, then I will be more than glad to return you to that nursing home in Atlanta I just dragged you away from."

Bernice was enthralled! Someone else telling someone to kiss their old ass! Her favorite words! Maybe this was a sign; maybe these two new neighbors were the reason she'd been allowed to live. Wanting to find out as much as she could, simply because she was nosy and admitted to it, she was suddenly grateful for Jamie's brownies. She was going to bring her new neighbors a nice little treat and introduce herself. From there, well, she'd play it by ear.

Hurrying back inside, but using the front door just in case, she called out to Jamie. "Looks as though someone has purchased the place next door. That FOR SALE sign is gone."

Jamie was in the kitchen, slicing her healthy version of brownies, and had just started a pot of decaf when she heard Bernice come in through the front door. Knowing that Bernice was nosier than most, she almost pitied whoever the new neighbors were. Unbeknownst to the little old woman, Jamie knew that she'd been spying on the old Patterson place, but didn't say a word. Bernice needed something to do that didn't involve Jamie.

Bernice sat down at the kitchen table. "I've decided I don't want those brownies. If I can't have the real thing, there's really no point. I don't want to see them go to waste, so I had an idea. I'm sure we have new people next door. I saw them carrying in boxes as I was . . . checking the mail. They look like two old men who would really appreciate a sweet treat. Would you be greatly offended if I took those brownies over there? With that pot of coffee I smell, and maybe you could make a tray of sandwiches or something?"

The words were no sooner out of Bernice's mouth than they heard a loud banging on the back door. Jamie placed the plate of brownies in the center of the kitchen table, then hurried to get the door before Bernice.

What she saw brought a huge grin to her face. Possibly this was Bernice's find.

"Hi," she said as she opened the screen door. "Can I help you?"

A tall, slender man who appeared to be anywhere from his mid-sixties, with a full head of black hair and a warm, friendly smile, nodded. "I'm Wade Powell. I just bought the place next door. I was wondering if I could borrow your phone? The utilities aren't on yet, and they were supposed to be on this morning, before my brother and I arrived from Atlanta. My cell phone is dead, and I can't even plug it in to charge it."

Jamie, sensing the older man's embarrassment at having to ask, spoke in as friendly a voice as possible. She wanted to convey to him right away that he was more than welcome to use the phone. "Of course. Come on in. Bernice and I were just getting ready to have a snack. Would you care to join us?"

"Sure smells good, but I wouldn't want to leave Robert too long. He gets antsy when he's alone."

"Well, why don't you make your phone call, then go back and get Robert? Bernice and I would love to meet him," Jamie announced as she handed him the portable phone and the phone book.

"You know what, young lady? I am going to take you up on your offer. It's been a long drive today, and we didn't bother to stop. Robert hates eating out."

Bernice was seated at the table, with a bird's-eye view of the man she'd seen carrying the boxes in next door, but before Jamie took it upon herself to introduce him, she raced out of the kitchen into the small powder room at the end of the hall. She looked at her reflection in the mirror. Shit, she looked like hell. Quickly, she twisted her loose hair into a French twist, splashed cold water on her face, then pinched her cheeks so hard she almost screamed, but she achieved the desired effect. A rosy glow.

Minutes later, she seated herself at the table again. Jamie was still speaking to the man she now knew was Wade, who had an older brother who didn't like to eat out. Amazing what you could learn when you were as nosy as she was. Bernice smiled.

Jamie brought a stack of dessert plates to the table, allowing her neighbor a few minutes of privacy in which to make his phone call. "Why, Bernice, you look . . . so different from the way you did minutes ago. I'm honored that you're cleaning up before our little afternoon snack. My grandmother was always big on coming to the table well groomed."

Bernice rolled her eyes. "Can't a woman brush her hair without a fuss being made? I just went to the bathroom and saw how wild I looked, that's all. Now, where are those brownies? I'm famished all of a sudden."

"I thought you wanted to give these to our

new neighbors over at the old Patterson place? What made you change your mind?" Jamie asked, knowing the answer, but loving to mess with dear old Bernice.

Jamie and Bernice couldn't help but overhear Wade as he raised his voice. "Are you serious? I was told they would be turned on first thing today. Tomorrow afternoon is the earliest you can turn the power on? Yes, yes, of course I know I'm not the only newcomer in Charleston. A storm? No, I didn't know that. Well, then I suppose I'll see you tomorrow."

Wade cleared his throat, his way of letting the girl know he was finished with the phone. She had disappeared for a minute, and he didn't want to leave without thanking her, and hopefully, she'd remember that she'd just invited him and Robert to join her for whatever the delectable smell was wafting throughout the kitchen.

"We're over here," Jamie said. A two-sided fireplace separated the kitchen from the large dining table.

"Well, it looks as though I won't have power until later tomorrow. Apparently, there is a hurricane headed up the East Coast, and the power company is preparing for massive outages. They said it was headed as far north as New York City. Can you believe that? A hurricane in New York. Beats anything I've ever heard."

"Yes, I've been listening to the weather reports. It doesn't look good," Jamie said.

Before Jamie had a chance to utter another word, Bernice stood and said, "Oh, hello. I heard someone talking, but I didn't know who it was. I see you've met my granddaughter. I'm Bernice, and you are?" She held her hand out as though she were the queen.

"Wade Powell." He held out his hand and shook hers. "I was just telling your granddaughter we're without power. Seems this big hurricane has delayed the power company a bit. I guess we'll have to dig through all those boxes we have. I'm sure there's a stray flashlight and a candle or two in them somewhere," Wade said.

"Well, Granny," Jamie said, looking at Bernice, "I think we probably have a flashlight or two we could lend them."

"Nonsense!" Bernice said. "They'll come and stay with us until their power is on. I insist. We have plenty of extra room here. Plus, we have power."

"Oh no, I couldn't impose like that, Bernice. But I will take your granddaughter up on that little snack. If the offer still stands, I'll just run home and get Robert. Like I said, he doesn't like to be left alone for very long."

"Granny, why don't we ask Wade and Robert to stay in *your* guesthouse? The last time I checked, it was fully stocked with everything one would need, and then some. And please, Wade, do run along and get your brother. I won't pour the coffee until you have returned," Jamie added.

As soon as Wade left, Jamie turned to Bernice. *"Granddaughter?* Why in the name of all that's holy did you tell that poor man I was your granddaughter? Not that I mind. You know how much I love you, but isn't that . . . dishonest?" Jamie asked, obviously confused.

Bernice felt her face turn red, but Jamie would understand. "Listen, I know you and the others don't believe me when I tell you I was allowed to live so that I could find out what, if anything, is going to happen next door. I just thought it would appear . . . proper if they thought I was the home owner, instead of some old housekeeper who should have been put out to pasture a long time ago." Bernice knew she sounded like a crazy old woman, but what the heck? She wasn't out to harm anyone. Toots and the godmothers were in Los Angeles. Who knew when they'd return? And by then, Bernice was sure she could come up with some story as to why she'd lied. But for the moment, well, she just wanted to be queen for a day. Or two.

"Oh, Bernie, you know better. No one feels that way about you. You're family. But I'll cover you for now. Your secret is safe, at least for a little while."

Bernice didn't know what had come over her. She normally wasn't one to fabricate things. That was more along Sophie's line. However, it was already too late to take it back. Later, if she got to know Wade better, she'd tell him the truth.

Ten minutes later, there was another knock on the back door. Wade and Robert stood on the back stoop, looking like two mischievous boys.

"This is Robert, my older brother. Robert, this is Jamie."

"Come in. It's nice to meet you, Robert. Please make yourselves at home while I get the coffee. My granny is over there," Jamie said, motioning in the direction of the huge fireplace. "She's thrilled to have company."

The older man, a mirror image of his younger brother minus a few gray hairs, spoke in a soft voice. "It's a pleasure, my dear."

As soon as Bernice saw Robert, her heart fluttered, and for a moment, she was sure she was about to suffer another heart attack.

She stood and held a shaky hand out. "Bernice. It's good to have someone in that old place next door." *Damn,* she thought. That wasn't a very smart way to introduce herself. "We're very neighborly and have missed having someone to visit." *There,* she thought. That sounded like something an old Southern lady would say, even though she was just an old broad from New Jersey.

"Please sit down. Jamie made these brownies. She owns a bakery in town. The Sweetest Things, it's called. Downtown

Charleston. If you're in the area, stop in. She makes the best pralines in the South."

The two brothers sat across from Bernice. Jamie brought cups, milk, and sugar to the table, then returned with the pot of coffee. After filling their cups, she served them each a large brownie and wished she had taken the time to ice them, but this would have to do.

"So," Jamie said after she sat down across from the two brothers. "What brings you to Charleston? These old houses are usually passed down from generation to generation, right, Granny? Why, we've had this old place for . . . Heck, I can't remember. It's been in the family since long before I was born."

Bernice gave Jamie the evil eye.

"Atlanta and the traffic. Plus, I lost my wife three years ago. I didn't want to stay there any longer. When Robert told me he was ready for a change, I decided to make it a big one for both of us. I like to tinker around with old houses. When my Realtor found this place, I flew in, checked it out, and as soon as I sold my house, well, here I am."

"You must have been here when Granny was in the hospital, having her bypass surgery."

Bernice kicked Jamie under the table. *The brat.*

Robert's eyes lit up like a candle. "You had bypass surgery, too? I had mine two years ago. Never felt better in my life."

Suddenly, Bernice felt like she'd found a kindred spirit. "Me too. Why don't you tell me all about yours, and I'll tell you all about mine?"

For the next two hours, they all talked about their surgeries and whatever else came to mind. When the phone rang, Jamie was surprised to see how long they'd been sitting at the table. She hurried over to get the phone.

"Toots! Abby's coming home today? Hang on. I'll let you tell her yourself. She's right here."

"Granny, Toots wants to speak to you," she said as she gave Bernice the phone.

Bernice put her hand over the mouthpiece. "Excuse me," she said to her neighbors. "This is my . . . sister. She lives here with me, too."

Chapter 34

Abby refused to wear the clothes she'd worn the night before when the nurse brought them to her, sealed in a plastic bag with her name and room number marked in black letters. She never wanted to see anything that reminded her of Rag ever again. She'd asked for a pair of clean scrubs to wear home. She'd been allowed to take a shower while Chris took care of her discharge paperwork. Wanting to luxuriate under the hot spray to wash away the sweat and grime from hours spent in that closet, she didn't, because she knew she had very little time to accomplish what she wanted to do before Chris returned to the room. She quickly ran the bar of soap over her body. She'd insisted they remove her bandages. Though bruised and tender, she really was no worse for wear. She looked like she'd been the victim of a beating, but her adrenaline was pumping so fast, she barely felt any pain.

Donning the aqua green–colored scrubs the nurse had provided, along with a pair of cotton slippers, Abby raced out of her room before she had any second thoughts about what she was going to do.

At the end of the hall, she spied an information desk. A young girl chewing gum as though her life depended on it was manning the desk.

"Excuse me," Abby said in her best Valley girl–like voice. "My, uh, friend was, like, brought in here, like, uh, last night. And he, like, needed me to bring a few things. His name is Rodwell Godfrey. He, like, uh, forgot to give me his room number. I think he was, like, kinda out of it when he called."

The gum chomper tapped a few keys on the computer, then spoke. "He's on the security floor. Cool," the girl said. "Room two sixty-nine."

"Thanks," Abby said, then hurried away. She didn't have much time. She spotted a bank of elevators and practically ran when she saw the doors swish open. Every second counted.

Having formed something of a half-assed plan, knowing that Rag was being guarded, she crossed her fingers that she wouldn't get caught. The doors opened, and she saw several signs with arrows pointing in all directions. When she saw the sign indicating the room number she was headed for, she walked so fast, she had to force herself to slow down. That was as far as she'd planned. She needed an excuse to go inside the room. Abby saw a waiting room reserved for guests. Inside, there were stacks of magazines and paperback novels. She grabbed several magazines and three books.

Slowly, so as not to draw too much attention to herself, she carried the stack of reading material close against her chest, yet kept her head lowered, just in case someone were to get a good look at her. Her face was a bit swollen, and there were marks that she couldn't hide.

As soon as she saw the guard outside

Rag's room, she knew her task wasn't going to be nearly as tough as she thought. The guard didn't look a day over twenty-one, and Abby knew this couldn't be the former Secret Service agent she'd been told had the unpleasant duty of watching over Rag until the Feds took over. Maybe they were on break, went to the restroom, whatever; it didn't matter. Now was her opportunity, and she'd best take advantage of it.

She saw the guy and figured that since her dumb Valley girl had worked on the gum chomper downstairs, it would probably work on this guy, too. She stood outside the door where he was seated, then cleared her throat. That got his attention. Abby was sure he was playing a game on his cell phone. Some security guard he was. "Hey, howzit goin'?"

"Oh, yes. Fine," the guard said.

"I'm supposed to, like, uh . . . offer the patient some like . . . uh, reading stuff. Do you mind if I step inside the room for a sec?" Abby actually batted her lashes at the kid.

"Uh, sure. Why not?"

"Cool. Thanks, man," Abby said before entering the room.

Inside, Rag was handcuffed to the bed with one hand, and the other had an IV line attached to the inside of his wrist. *Good,* she thought.

He appeared to be unconscious, but she didn't care.

"Hey, you dirtbag." She leaned as close to his ear as possible. She saw his eyeballs move underneath his eyelids. This son of a bitch was no more in a coma now than she was. Just to make sure, she grabbed his earlobe and twisted it as hard as she could.

"Ouch! What the fuck!" Rag said in a voice that spoke volumes. He was not in a coma any longer.

"Hey there. I guess I should ask how you're feeling." She continued to twist his ear. "If you make one little sound, I swear to you, I will cut your balls off. Let me see if I remember this correctly? Hmm, you're going to be on an island somewhere, with millions of dollars, and I was going to be locked in a closet. How's that workin' out for you? Just so you know, that CEO of

LAT Enterprise you spoke with just happens to be my mother, and you, my old friend, fucked with the wrong woman. Just for the record, kidnapping is punishable by death. I'll see you at the trial, but let me give you a word of advice. Save the taxpayers money and plead it out. You might see the light of day before you're a centenarian."

He moaned, and Abby released her grip on his ear. Just for good measure, she doubled her fist and, giving it all she had, punched him squarely in the nose. Blood spurted from his nose. With his one free hand, he reached to stop the flow of blood spewing from his nose.

Abby grabbed his head. "Nope, can't do that. Sorry." Abby spied a roll of gauze on the table beside the bed. She wiped the blood from his face but made sure to use as much pressure as she could. "Don't you dare scream, you pussy. Remember, the balls."

After she'd wiped the blood from his face, she pulled the covers down to the foot of the bed. Knowing the image would haunt her later, but wanting this son of a bitch to experience just a tenth of the humiliation she'd had to endure at his hands, she yanked open the pale blue hospital gown he wore, leaving his genitals exposed for all to see. Wanting to leave a lasting impression, she looked at him, and said, "Remember, the balls, okay?"

Grabbing the stack of magazines and the three books she'd brought inside the room, she left one of the paperbacks, titled *Retribution,* on his tray table.

As she raced out of the room, Abby grinned when she said to the guy, "See ya."

The security here was pathetic. She'd remember this if she was ever hospitalized again. Hurrying to the elevators, she lucked out again when the doors opened the second she reached them. When she reached her floor, she saw Chris walking around in her room.

Shit!

She'd eventually tell him where she'd been, but not just then. Later. For now, she wanted to enjoy the few minutes of fear, pain, and embarrassment she'd caused. Paybacks were a bitch. Account paid in full.

"Hey, I was looking for you," Chris said as he spied her heading to her room.

"I went in search of a Coke machine. Then it dawned on me: I didn't have any money."

Chris looked at her, raised his eyebrows, and shook his head. "Whatever you say, Abby, whatever you say."

With that, a nurse pushing a wheelchair came out of her room. "Miss Simpson, it's hospital policy that all patients leave in a wheelchair."

"Okay, no problem," Abby said. She couldn't help but smile when she thought of the *little* shriveled-up image that would greet the next unlucky soul to enter Rag's room.

Chapter 35

For the hundredth time in a little over twenty-four hours, Toots's eyes filled with tears. Damn, she was becoming a frigging caterwauling old woman. "Phil," she said when they pulled up to the passenger drop-off at LAX, "I can't thank you enough for all the help you've been."

Goebel and Sophie waited in the Escalade while they said their good-byes.

"You'll call me as soon as you're in Charleston? Let me know you landed?" Toots asked.

"I will. And when you return to Charleston,

will you promise me we'll go on that second date?"

"Oh no, I think we're way past that now. After all we've been through, I think we can jump ahead to that third date."

Phil raised his eyebrows up and down Groucho Marx style. "Does that mean what I think it means?"

Toots chuckled. "You'll just have to wait and find out, won't you?" Not only was she turning into a crybaby in her old age, but she could also add prick teaser to the list.

Phil kissed her then, stopping further conversation. Toots's world was spinning. In a good way. "Tell Abby hello, and I can't wait to get to know her better."

"I will. Good-bye, Phil." Before she started bawling again, she jumped into the backseat of the Escalade. "If you say one word, I swear I will slice your tits off with a dull knife," Toots said to Sophie.

Goebel laughed out loud. "Remind me to never get on your bad side," he said as he pulled into the flow of traffic leading out of LAX.

Sophie grinned. "She's all talk."

"Shut up," Toots said, then blew her nose.

"Wait a minute. Aren't you the one that

said 'I'll never get involved with another man,' or something to that effect? Yes, I am sure it was you. And look at you now. You've been on one lousy date with a guy, and now you're acting like a baby because he had to leave just to go cut someone's heart out."

Toots shook her head. "Sophie, you never mince words, do you? The past forty-eight hours have been some of the worst in my life. I would appreciate a little compassion, you old witch."

"Do you two ever say anything nice to each other?" Goebel asked.

Sophie looked at him as though he'd lost his mind. "Damn, I thought this *was* nice, didn't you, Toots?"

Too tired to speak, Toots gave her the single-digit salute. It spoke volumes.

"Fuck you, too," Sophie replied, smiling.

Thirty minutes later, they were pulling into the hospital's patient pickup area. Toots called Chris to tell him their location.

"I can't wait to get Abby home. She is not going back to that house of hers, either. Nor am I allowing her to go to Chris's apartment," Toots stated, sounding like the mother of a runaway sixteen-year-old.

"Like you can stop her. She's thirty, not three," Sophie reminded her, remembering that they had missed celebrating Abby's thirtieth birthday in the immediate aftermath of Bernice's open-heart surgery. "I'm sure the last thing Abby needs is to have you and the rest of us hovering over her like four old mother hens."

"Well, I am her mother. Abby has always listened to me. I am going to insist she stay at the beach house until she recuperates. If Chris wants to stay, too, that's fine with me. I know they're both adults, but sometimes there is nothing like a little bit of pampering. Look," Toots said. "There they are now."

A nurse wheeled Abby outside, where she immediately flew out of the wheelchair as though her ass were on fire. Chris placed his arm across her shoulder and said something to her. Whatever it was made Abby laugh, and that was a good thing. After all her daughter had been through, she still had the ability to laugh, so Toots knew that this, too, would pass.

Toots opened the door, and Sophie jumped out, insisting Abby ride in the front seat.

"I'm fine. I'll just crawl in the backseat with Chris and Mom. God, it's good to be out of that place. I hate hospitals."

Toots hugged her daughter, then said, "Let's get home, Goebel. I know Mavis and Ida can't wait to see their favorite godchild."

"What do you mean, their *favorite*?" Abby asked in mock seriousness. "I thought I was their only godchild."

Sophie, ever the jokester, said, "Listen, kiddo, there are all kinds of things about us you don't know. Give it a few years."

Toots reached over the front seat and yanked Sophie's long hair. "Stop right now! I can't have you ruining my motherly image at this late date!"

"That'll never happen, Mom. I promise. And before I get all teary-eyed, just let me say this. Thanks for being the kind of mom you are, and, Sophie, thank you for being the best, well, one of the best, godmothers a girl could ask for. Again, you have all bailed me out." When Abby was finished, tears were streaming down her face.

"I don't know who's a bigger bawl bag, you or your mother," Sophie said, even though by then her own eyes were filled with unshed tears.

As though on command, Toots, Abby, and Chris all flipped Sophie the bird.

They all laughed, the atmosphere among them relaxed and happy.

"I think you and Chris should stay at the beach house the next few days. That way, I'll be able to watch you and keep you out of trouble," Toots said, realizing her words were just that: words. Abby and Chris could do whatever they desired. Though she hoped they would take her up on her offer. They all needed some family time together, especially now.

"Sure, Mom, if that makes you happy, I'll stay. I just need a few things from the house," Abby said.

"Yeah, I suppose I could hang out with a houseful of women for a day or two. It's not as though I have a long client list just waiting for my advice. Actually, I don't have any clients, at least not in the entertainment area."

Abby appeared stunned. "Really? When did this take place?"

"Since Laura Leighton's last episode. I know you haven't forgotten that little escapade," Chris said. "After that, all the glitz and glamour seemed silly to me. These

Hollywood people are here for two things. Fame and fortune. No one seems to have any morals here, no concern for what's right or wrong. I guess you could say I've had my fill of the place. Maybe I'll go work for a district attorney's office somewhere. Though not in this city. I know most of the people I'd have to prosecute."

"They have a great district attorney's office in Charleston," Toots said, warming up to the idea.

"I don't know what my plans are at this point, but I'll keep that in mind," Chris assured her.

Abby's face brightened. Maybe she should consider this, too? A temporary leave of absence might be just what the doctor ordered. She didn't know how her mother would take this, given all the millions she'd put into *The Informer* to make it the number two tabloid newspaper in the country. But still, it was something to think about.

When they arrived at the beach house, Mavis and Ida, along with Chester, greeted them at the front door.

Abby was barely out of the vehicle when Chester came bounding down the steps.

Standing on his hind legs, he placed both front paws on Abby's shoulders and started licking her as though she were a giant beef stick.

"Hey, boy, I hear you helped save my life," Abby said as she wrapped her arms around the big dog's neck. "It's good to see you, too, my friend." Chester dropped down on all fours, allowing Mavis and Ida a chance to embrace Abby.

"When your mother said you were coming home, I just started making everything I knew was a favorite of yours. I'm afraid there isn't much left in the house right now, but we'll worry about that later," Mavis said, leading Abby to the kitchen, from which all kinds of delectable smells were emanating.

"Smells good in here," Abby said as she walked toward the doors leading out to the deck. Without saying another word to the others, she stepped outside and took a deep breath, grateful that she was able to do so. Thank God they'd found her in time. Drinking in the scene before her—the ocean, the beach, and all the sounds and smells that went along with it—made her realize she'd truly been given a second chance. Did she really want to spend the rest of her life writing articles, if you could even call them articles, about Hollywood's screwed-up starlet of the moment or the latest actor to go into rehab one day and get arrested a week later for possession? Life here could turn on a dime. *One day you're at the top. Then the next, you come crashing down like a falling star.* How important was any of it in the scheme of things? She decided then and there that, if one really understood the meaning of the word, it really wasn't important at all. She supposed you could think of it as a game, but even that glorified it too much. Games had winners, yet all she saw in Hollywood, at least from the perspective of a tabloid, were the losers. She just didn't know if she wanted to be a part of it anymore.

"Hey," Chris called. "Everyone is waiting for you. Come inside, have something to eat, and you'll feel better."

Abby wasn't sure food would cure what ailed her at the moment, but she was hungry. "Of course. I'm ravenous."

Mavis outdid herself. She'd made Abby's favorite: shrimp scampi, a Greek salad, and the garlic rolls she knew Abby would eat one too many of; and then there was dessert. Abby eyed the kitchen table. Plates and cloth napkins. Hmm, this was new. Usually when she came for dinner, they ordered a pizza and used paper plates and napkins. But this was a special occasion, she realized. Her godmothers were just trying to show her how special she really was.

"This all looks scrumptious. I know I'll gain ten pounds at least," she said as Mavis filled her plate.

Chris sat on her left, and her mother to her right. Sophie and Goebel seated themselves directly across from her, and Ida and Mavis sat at either end of the table. For the moment nothing was said. The sounds of silver clicking against china were the only sounds to be heard for the next few minutes, as they all filled themselves with Mavis's goodies.

When they were finished, Toots and Sophie went to the deck for their usual after-dinner smoke. Abby and Chris joined them, though they stayed upwind of the smoke so as not to get a noseful of the nastiness.

"I'm quitting soon, Abby. I promise," Toots said as she puffed on her Marlboro Light.

"Same here," Sophie said. "I'm just not sure when."

Abby just shook her head. "I guess it's just like any other habit. Once you're sick of it, you'll decide it's time to call it quits." Which made Abby think about *The Informer.* Did she really want to call it quits, or was this just a typical survivor-like reaction to all she'd been through?

"True," her mother said. "But I want you to know that I am sincere. I know how much you dislike smoking. Phil said there was a prescription drug on the market that could help me give these up. I might take a look into it when I'm home."

Abby's eyes twinkled, and suddenly she was more grateful to be alive than ever. "Uh, Mom, this Phil. Just how friendly are you two? Should I anticipate a number nine?"

Oh, crud! Toots thought. *Leave it to Abby to call an ace an ace and a spade a spade. No beating around the bush with her.* Of course, she was *her* daughter. She'd expect nothing less. "For your information, young lady, I have had one measly date with Phil. So to answer your question, no, he is not, under any circumstances, being considered as husband number nine. Remember, after Leland died, I swore off marriage?"

"I thought that you swore off men, too. Maybe it was just a misunderstanding on my part," Sophie added, a wicked grin lighting up her dark brown eyes.

"If you two don't stop ganging up on me, I'm going inside," Toots said.

"Hmm, must have hit a nerve," Sophie said as she blew out a giant puff of white smoke. "What do you think, Abby?"

"I don't think I've seen that look in Mom's eyes for a long time, if ever. I know she had it for my father, but I was really too young to understand what all those gaga eyes were about then. Speaking of my dad, this is weird. When I was in that closet, I don't know if I was sleeping or unconscious, but I had a kind of conversation with him, even though I know I couldn't have actually been speaking since Rag had all that duct tape covering my mouth. Still, I would swear we spoke."

Sophie looked at Toots; then Toots looked at Abby.

Hesitantly, Sophie asked, "What exactly did he say?"

"This is the weird part. It was almost like he was trying to apologize for dying when I was so young. He said he was going to make it up to me."

No one uttered a word. The only sounds to be heard were those coming from the beach below. The occasional shout from a parent, a child's cry, and the whooshing sounds as the water sloshed back and forth on the beach.

"Did he say anything else?" Sophie asked, now on the edge of her seat. She lit another cigarette, her hands shaking like a leaf.

"Yes, I believe he did." Abby appeared to be struggling with the memory. "I think he was trying to tell me that he wanted Mother and me to be happy."

"That's it?" Sophie inquired.

"Yes, at least that's all I remember. Sophie, what is it? You look weird."

Sophie shook her head. "There's more to the story than we've told you. When

Rag had you call asking for that ten million bucks, your mom had the money in cash. Dave, who I'm sure you know from his being the head of security at the paper, placed the money in a garbage can in the men's room at the Santa Monica Pier, near the Marine Science Center.

"Everything was coming together according to Goebel and Dave's master plan. The next thing we know, and this is according to the police, two hoods from Venezuela showed up, looking for Rag. I guess he'd ripped off the wife of a wealthy man who has a few unsavory connections. They got to him, not knowing he was in the midst of a kidnapping. Before anyone knew who they were, or what their exact involvement was, Rag was facedown on the pier with a bullet hole in his back. Since he was the only one who knew your location, and he wasn't talking, we . . . we asked your father."

Abby looked as though she'd seen a ghost, which around the beach house was quite normal. "I thought you picked up my hint when I was reading that note, you know, when I mentioned South Central

LA. I guess I just assumed Chester sniffed me out."

Abby plopped down on one of the deck chairs, stunned at the revelation but intrigued since she, too, had had some sort of contact with her father. She'd shrugged it off as nothing more than a dream, or her subconscious desire, as she drifted in and out of consciousness. But now she wasn't so sure.

"Knowing there was no other way to find you, we hurried back here. We decided to try to speak to your father," Toots explained.

Amazed, Abby said, "You did this while Phil was here? The séance stuff, plus Dad?" She shook her head.

"Actually, he was quite open to the idea. He's from Charleston, remember?" Toots informed her daughter.

"Wow! I think I like this guy already," Abby said. "So what did my father say that led you to find me?"

"Just a few words, and they didn't make a lot of sense until Chris's buddies in the LAPD located the pings from Rag's cell phone. Yes, you were in South Central LA.

That much we were pretty sure of, with what you'd said, plus the pings, but your father said, 'Mr. Steve.' We had no clue what that meant until Chris's cop buddy contacted a local police officer whose beat was in South Central. Mr. Steve's is a well-known pawnshop, which just so happens to have a few shitty apartments on the third floor. As soon as we located Mr. Steve's, well, Chester took it from there," Toots said.

"Wow, this is news to me. What I'm not getting . . . Mom, you said you and Phil were in Naples on a date? How did you and my godmothers wind up here?"

"Well, it didn't start out that way. Phil came to the house in Charleston to take me to dinner, and while Bernice was spying on the Patterson place, she heard something that turned out to be Frankie's whimpering. Phil and the rest of us got to the dog. Phil switched into doctor mode right away because he knew that Frankie had a serious spinal injury. He said there was only a short window of time until his injuries became permanent. So it was then he called a friend with access to a Learjet, and we flew Frankie to Naples to see Dr. Michelle Carnes. He had gone to medical school with her father. Knowing it would be a while before Frankie was out of surgery, Phil suggested we spend the night at DiamondHead, his condo on Fort Myers Beach. Then Chris called, and we immediately caught a flight to LA."

"*That* was your first date?" Abby was so stunned, she could hardly get the words out of her mouth. "I would say he's definitely a keeper. Loves dogs, wanted to come and support you, a doctor. Plus, he didn't think Sophie was nuts. This is the kind of stuff fairy tales are made of. Are you sure you all are telling me the whole truth and nothing but?"

"So help me God," Toots and Sophie said at the same time.

For a few minutes, no one spoke. This was turning out to be way more than a simple abduction, if you could even call it that.

Chapter 36

Goebel followed Mavis and Ida out to the deck, carrying a large tray with a pot of coffee and a strawberry cheesecake, one of Abby's favorites. He placed the dessert on the outdoor table, where Mavis proceeded to slice the cake.

"Now, I know this isn't on Goebel's and my diets, but since we're celebrating Abby's safe return, I think it's okay to indulge," Mavis said. "Toots, you want a slice of cake? I know how much you love sweets," Mavis asked her.

Toots didn't answer. Abby's words were still reverberating around in her head, and

Toots wondered if the virtual wall she'd mentally built against another man in her life was on the verge of crumbling.

"Toots!" Sophie yelled. "Mavis is talking to you."

"Sorry. I was woolgathering," Toots said abstractedly. "Sure, I'll take a piece of cake. When have you ever known me to turn down dessert?"

Mavis cut a giant slice and gave it to her, together with a mug of coffee doused with cream and sugar. "If those cigarettes don't kill you, all this sugar is bound to, but we'll discuss it at another time," Mavis said.

Toots wondered if now was the time to speak to Abby, then decided there was no time like the present. "Abby, have you given any thought about taking a leave of absence from the paper and coming back to Charleston?" Toots asked. "After what you have been through, it might be a good time to come home. Josh can run the paper. You said so yourself. You could stay in touch by phone and e-mail. Remember, I was CEO for two years, and not even once did you know this. I'm not asking you to give up your job, Abby. But I think we need to reevaluate our decisions. This paper has been a godsend in one sense, but after what Rag pulled, I'm not sure it's worth all the heartache we've had to deal with the past forty-eight hours. Your safety is more important to me than anything in the world."

"Me too," Chris added.

"And you could come, too, Chris. It would give you a chance to see your father's plantation house. You might even find a position in the district attorney's office." The more Toots talked about the idea, the more excited she became.

"This is a lot to take in right now. I'm not sure of anything yet, but I would like to take some time off. LA is my home now, and I can't just walk away from everything you and I worked so hard to build."

What Abby didn't want to admit to was, she agreed with her mother. This movie-star nonsense was becoming as dull as an old nickel to her now. But could she completely walk away from it? She didn't know. Later, when she was alone, she would truly give it some serious thought. If not forever, then at least until she had some kind of epiphany about some other profession she might want to pursue. Tabloid news was in her blood, and she didn't know if she could give it up completely, but a leave of absence wasn't out of the question at this point.

"You were never a quitter, Abby. I just wanted you to think about this. It's certainly not written in stone," Toots said, though she had to admit she was hoping Abby would be a bit more receptive to the idea. The more she thought about it, the more she wanted to get rid of the paper, perhaps try another media outlet. Maybe Ida's new venture would direct her on another path. And she was half owner of the bakery, though she couldn't bake if her life depended on it. All she could do in that business was act as taste tester.

"It's been a long day. If you all don't mind, I think I'd like to call it a night," Abby said, stifling back a yawn.

"Yes, it has, but, Abby, before you go to bed, would you mind serving as a guinea pig for me?" Ida asked out of the blue. "My new line of cosmetics, Seasons, has healing properties. I would love it if you'd apply a bit to those cuts on your face before you go to sleep."

"Sure, just bring it to my room. I want to

take a quick shower, anyway. I still have hospital grunge that I haven't completely removed." What she didn't tell them was that she had rushed through her shower at the hospital in order to race to Rag's room.

Abby gave her mother and Sophie a good-night hug, thanked Mavis for a meal fit for a queen, and told Goebel good night. As she went upstairs to the guest room where she usually stayed, she called over her shoulder, "Chris, don't forget to come and tell me good night."

"Count on it," he called from the kitchen, where he and Goebel were finishing off the last of the coffee.

Upstairs, she took a shower, only this time she took her time. She'd been more uncomfortable than she'd let on. The hot water felt like heaven as it beat against her sore muscles. Having her hands tied behind her for so long had not only caused the muscles in her upper back to hurt, but had also strained the muscles in her neck. She lathered up three times, then washed her hair twice, wanting to wash away the memories, too, but she knew that was too much to ask for.

She found a pair of her old pajamas in the drawer where she knew she'd find them. She brushed her teeth and combed the tangles from her hair. When there was nothing more to do, she crawled beneath the sheets, loving the soft feel of the high thread count against her skin. Her mom never skimped on anything, and tonight she was exceedingly grateful.

As she was about to doze off, a light knock startled her. She sat up in bed, pulling the covers all the way to her neck. "Come in."

Ida entered the room, carrying several jars of cream. "I just want to rub some of this pumpkin enzyme cream on those cuts. The chemists swear by it, and I do, too. I think I've taken at least five years off my age since I started using my new products." Ida sat down on the bed and opened a jar. "Here, you sit and relax, and I'll be out of here in a minute."

She expertly applied the pumpkin enzyme cream to Abby's face, smoothing an extra layer on the areas where she was swollen and bruised. She also applied a generous amount to her wrists. "I hope you'll see a big change in the morning. Now

I'll go. Good night, dear," Ida said and gave Abby a kiss before turning out the bedside light.

"Night," Abby replied, her eyelids heavy with exhaustion. Her last thought before falling asleep was that Chris had best hurry, or he was not getting a good-night kiss.

Chapter 37

A heavy fog, typical of Malibu, rolled in. In a few short hours, the sun would burn it away, and the Pacific would once again capture the attention of all those who spent their days at the beach, catching a few rays.

As soon as Abby smelled coffee, she perked right up, then winced. She was twice as sore as she'd been yesterday, but the doctor had told her to expect this. In the guest bathroom, she found a bottle of Advil, took three, then brushed her teeth. Splashing cold water on her face, she was totally shocked when she saw her reflection in the mirror.

"Oh my God! Ida is really onto something," she said out loud. Leaning closer to the mirror, she carefully inspected the cuts and bruises that last night had promised to turn all shades of purple, blue, and yellowish green. Then she looked at her wrists. The marks from the plastic ties were almost completely gone. She grabbed a robe from the back of the door, not bothering to stop for a pair of shoes. In just seconds she was downstairs in the kitchen, where she could see that Mavis was busy preparing breakfast.

"Are you the only one who cooks around here?" Abby asked as she helped herself to a cup of coffee.

Mavis jumped.

"Sorry. I didn't mean to startle you. Is everyone still sleeping?" Abby looked at the clock on the stove. It was a little after six. Her mother always got up with the chickens.

"No, your mother and Sophie are on the deck, smoking and having a cup of coffee," Mavis said, her back to Abby as she whipped up something that looked like it might be pancake batter.

"Well, I, for one, can't thank you enough for that dinner last night, and I can't wait to see what you come up with for breakfast." Abby gave Mavis a one-armed hug.

"Thanks, dear." Mavis turned around to give Abby her full attention. When she saw her, she gasped and quickly placed a hand over her mouth. "Oh, Abby! Have you looked in the mirror? Those cuts and bruises, and the swelling, they're practically gone! Quick, show this to your mother and Sophie while I go wake Ida. She'll want to see this right away."

"I know. I couldn't believe it when I saw myself in the mirror. And look at my wrists. They're almost completely healed! I believe Ida is truly onto something."

Abby stepped out on the deck, where Toots and Sophie were smoking up a storm like Puff, the Magic Dragon.

"What do you think?" Abby asked her mother and the second godmother she'd seen that morning.

The two women looked at her, their surprise evident on both their faces.

Sophie was the first to speak. "I'll be damned! Ida was right. That shit is a miracle worker. Come over here and let me have a closer look."

"Not until you both crush out those nasty-ass cigarettes."

Quickly, Toots and Sophie complied.

"Now look at me. Is this a miracle or what? I have never seen anything work like this in my life. Can you imagine all the women who'd give their eyeteeth for something like this!" Abby exclaimed, conveying the excitement Ida must have felt when she came up with the concoction.

Toots examined her daughter's face and wrists. The difference from last night was almost miraculous. "Ida's going to shit herself!" Toots exclaimed excitedly.

"Mother! Do you always have to be so graphic? You're as bad as Sophie. No offense, Soph."

"Oh, none taken, Abby. When you get to be our age, the little things don't matter. Like saying 'shit' if you have a mouthful." Sophie grinned.

"So is this the stuff Ida's going to market on The Home Shopping Club? Because if it is, she'd better have vaults ready, because sales are going to be through the roof. She needs models, to show a before and after," Abby said.

"Oh, that's already taken care of. We're supposed to start this week, but with all the hoopla, Ida made arrangements to stall the network. You know, I used this the other day, and I swear the fine lines around my eyes were less than half, but I was almost afraid to mention anything to Ida for fear she'd accuse me of being as vain as she is. But now, damn, she really is onto something," Toots said to Abby.

Sophie chimed right in. "I tried it once, and I saw a difference, too. As usual, if Ida does anything extraordinary, she wants the world to know about it. This time, though, I think she's really hit pay dirt. Damn her. Why didn't I come up with this?"

The sliding glass door opened. Mavis brought a barely awake Ida out to the deck to see the results of her new product.

"Couldn't this wait? I didn't get to sleep until two in the morning. Those kids on the beach partied all night," Ida complained. "Has anyone bothered to make me a cup of coffee?" she whined.

"You're such an old bitch, Ida. I swear, if

you weren't one of Abby's godmothers, I'd
smack your teeth right down your throat,
and they'd come marching out your ass to
the tune of 'When the Saints Go Marching
In.'"

Coffee spewed from Toots's mouth when
she heard Sophie's latest early morning
greeting. Poor Ida, but she laughed, anyway.

"Mavis, what is it you wanted me to
see?" Ida asked, turning up her nose and
ignoring Sophie's insult. She'd gotten so
used to them by now, they had no effect
on her.

"Look!" Mavis whirled Abby around so
that Ida could see her face and arms.

Ida stared at her goddaughter, her eyes
becoming as round as saucers. She
couldn't believe what she was seeing. The
bruises, the scratches, and the swelling
were all but gone. Had she not seen it with
her own two eyes, she wouldn't have believed it. While she knew the product was
much better than some of the cosmetic
lines currently being touted as the miracle
cure for wrinkles, her line of creams could
truly claim to be the next best thing to a
miracle.

"I knew this was good, but this is even better than I'd expected. I can't believe it. Abby, you cannot tell this to a living soul. We need to . . . I don't know what we need to do, but this is big," Ida babbled, stunned at the results.

"You do have a patent on this stuff?" Abby asked.

"Yes, I do. I was careful during the developmental stages to keep some of the contents a secret. I own full rights to the product. I'm simply amazed at how fast this has worked on you. You're sure you didn't put anything else on your face?" Ida questioned Abby.

"Nope, I didn't even use a cleansing cream when I was in the shower, because I was afraid that it would burn," Abby said.

"When Chris gets up, you might want to talk to him about starting a corporation," Abby said. "Then, if some dumb ass tries to eat the stuff or gets it in an eye that burned or something else goes wrong, the corporation would be liable, and not you personally. Chris would know more about the legal stuff. There is someone threatening to sue the paper on a daily basis. Which reminds me, I need to get Chester home and get to my computer and check on the troops." Abby still wanted a break, but before she took the final steps, she had to make sure Josh could run the show.

Toots rolled her eyes; it had been a little more than two days since Abby was abducted in the basement of *The Informer,* and she was already going back to editor-in-chief mode.

"Toots, your cell phone is ringing. You want me to answer it?" Mavis asked.

"Look at the caller ID and see who it is. I'm not up for any of those automated solicitation calls yet."

Mavis found Toots's cell phone on the kitchen counter. She stepped back through the sliding glass door with the phone and gave it to Toots.

Seeing that it was Bernice, Toots teased, "What do you want, you old hag?" She loved Bernice like a sister and delighted in saying ornery things to her whenever she could. Bernice acted like it pissed her off, but Toots knew better.

"What? A hurricane?" Toots's words caused Abby, Sophie, Mavis, and Ida to stop dead in their tracks. "I haven't paid any attention to the news, Bernice. With

Abby being abducted, watching Jim Cantore on the Weather Channel hasn't been my top priority. Yes, I'll check the news and call you back as soon as I've made a decision." Toots hit the END button on her phone. Another issue that was beyond her control to deal with.

"Bernice says there is a hurricane headed directly toward Charleston," Toots explained. "She thinks I need to get back there ASAP and get the hatches battened down. I wonder why Phil didn't call."

"Shit fire and save the matches! Surely you're not going home when there is a hurricane headed there. That's the last place I want to be," Sophie singsonged.

"I'll go," Mavis offered. "That's your home, and sort of ours, too. You should be ashamed of yourself, Sophie."

"What about the cream? Should I go back to Charleston and do the shooting as we'd planned?" Ida asked.

Toots threw her arms in the air. "I don't know about your makeup right now, but I doubt The Home Shopping Club is going to renege on your contract. Remember, you just postponed it. You didn't cancel it. With a hurricane heading that way, I don't think anyone is going to be worried about their wrinkles. But all bull aside, you are onto something, Ida. You have my full support. Just not now. I need to get back to Charleston. Bernice and Jamie can't handle this by themselves, and Pete is retired now, so he won't be there to help. Looks like it's up to me. I'm going to call my pilot pals and see if they're willing to fly into an approaching hurricane."

"Mom, if you really need me, I can go, but I think I need to take care of a few details at the paper before I take a leave of absence, that is, if I decide to." Abby didn't want to go to Charleston right away but would if her mother needed her. She had come through for her, had actually saved her life. "Just say the word, and I'm there."

"No, I'd rather you stay here. Now that Rag is under lock and key, I think you're safe enough, but I don't want you overdoing it, Abby. That's both your mother and the CEO of LAT Enterprise speaking. Do you hear me?"

"Yes, Mother. Yes, boss."

Always serious in a crisis, Toots picked up her phone and called the pilot she'd used on several occasions. When she explained her situation, he told her he would meet her at LAX in three hours. "Perfect, and thanks."

"We have three hours to get to the airport," Toots said. "Whoever is going back to Charleston best get a move on."

An hour later, they were ready to go. Abby and Chris agreed to stay at the beach house until further notice. The commute to *The Informer* would be a bit of a hassle, but Abby and Chris assured Toots they could handle it.

Chapter 38

Bernice and Jamie spent the next two hours at Publix, purchasing extras. Their list was lengthy. Batteries, candles, and water topped the list. From there, Bernice wiped out the store's entire supply of canned tuna, soup, and Spam. There was no bread at home, but she and Jamie planned to make a quick stop at The Sweetest Things on their way home. They'd take all the goodies, batten down the hatches there as much as they could, then head back to the house, where Wade and Robert had promised to help them unload the car, so

Jamie could return to the airport to pick up Toots and the others.

By the time Toots was due to arrive, the forecasters had predicted that Charleston would begin to feel the effects of the outer bands. They'd been tuned to the Weather Channel. When they saw that Jim Cantore was stationed at Patriots Point in Charleston Harbor, aboard the USS *Yorktown,* they knew they were in trouble. The ship had survived hurricanes in the past, so odds were it would survive this one. Or at least they hoped it would.

Jamie made fast work of grabbing all the baked goods at the bakery, thankful that Lucy, her assistant, had baked a few loaves of bread for her own personal use. Lucy had left some behind, and now Jamie was glad that she had, because the shelves at Publix were wiped out. Too late to board up the front windows, Jamie could only hope that whatever happened, the insurance would take care of their losses. She raced back to the Range Rover, where Bernice waited with the side door opened.

"Dang, Jamie, what all did you bring? That looks like enough baked goods to feed a small country," Bernice said as she helped to arrange the items in the back-seat.

"No point in leaving it behind. Remember, we don't know how long we'll be without access to food. I know that Toots has generators, but we can't eat power," Jamie teased. "But we can eat in the dark if we have to." She made fast work of packing the SUV, then climbed again into the passenger seat. By the time they dropped off all the food, she would have just enough time to get to the airport. Toots had called right before leaving LAX, assuring her it was safe to fly, and since they were on a private aircraft, they wouldn't be going through security, where they could be delayed for who knew how long.

Jamie maneuvered the Range Rover down South Battery, took a left on East Battery, passing the old pastel-colored homes known as Rainbow Row. Most of the homes were over a hundred years old; they'd stood guard over Charleston Harbor since before the Civil War, or the War of Northern Aggression, as the locals liked to call it. Jamie wondered what kind of defense the old homes would put up against hurricane-force winds and the surging water. The area had survived in the past, and she could only hope the old places were still up for the battle.

Thirty minutes later, Wade and Robert helped Bernice put away the groceries.

"I'll be back in no time," Jamie said. "Just stay inside, and if the cell phone rings, make sure to answer it."

Though she knew the three aging adults were quite capable of taking care of themselves, and the house, it felt good to be useful and needed. Since Toots had found her failing bakery and taken her in, her life had been as close to perfect as she'd ever dreamed. She liked the feeling of being part of one big happy family. Being an only child raised by her grandmother, Jamie thanked heaven above every day that there were good people like Toots and the godmothers. They were all her fairy godmothers, and she told them this as often as she could without sounding too mushy.

Jamie arrived at South Aviation Avenue, parking the Range Rover at Landmark Aviation, where Toots's private plane was due to arrive any minute. Inside, it looked like a modern office instead of an airport

terminal. Floor-to-ceiling windows faced
the runway. Television sets were tuned to
the Weather Channel. Several pilots were
seated in the semicircle of plush leather
chairs, glued to the television.

Jamie walked over to the reception desk
and spoke to a young woman dressed in
a navy skirt with a matching jacket. Her
blond hair was pulled up tightly in a bun,
and Jamie thought she looked very pro-
fessional.

"Excuse me. I'm here to pick up Ms.
Loudenberry. Is there somewhere I can
check their arrival time?" Jamie asked. She
had never been to a private airport and
didn't know what the protocol was for in-
coming flights.

The young woman smiled and said,
"Hang on, and I'll check FlightAware. They
track all IFR flights." She ran her fingers
across the keyboard. "It says here they're
less than ten minutes from landing. From
the looks of it, they don't have a lot of time
to spare, as the winds are gusting twenty
to thirty knots already."

"Thanks," Jamie said to the young
woman.

"Have a seat over there. We have complimentary coffee and soda if you'd like. I can get you something while you wait."

No wonder Toots preferred flying privately. The treatment at this aviation center was first class. "No thanks," Jamie said, then walked over to the floor-to-ceiling windows, where she stood next to a handsome pilot, who smiled when he saw her straining to peer at the jet that had just touched down on the runway.

"Are you here to pick up a friend?" he inquired as he scoped her out.

Blushing at his admiring glance, Jamie said, "Yes, I'm here to pick up my business partner and friend. She's been in Los Angeles, and I need to help her prepare for the hurricane. Her house is a historic landmark, so we decided she'd be better off here." She couldn't believe she offered up so much personal information to a complete stranger, but she liked the looks of him as much as he seemed to like hers.

"Would it be too forward of me if I asked for your phone number? I work for Flexjet, and Charleston is my home base. I spend a lot of my time flying millionaires around the world, and I seldom get the chance to talk to a beautiful woman."

Jamie was intrigued, but not enough to give a total stranger her phone number. "I'll tell you what, the next time you're in town, go to The Sweetest Things Bakery, and ask for Jamie. I'm the owner. I'll serve you one of the best pralines in the South, on the house."

He reached inside his jacket pocket and pulled out a business card. "If you change your mind, I'm Mike. I'm here until Saturday. Then it's off to Switzerland."

Jamie took the card, totally blown away. Never in a million years had she thought she'd meet a man, let alone a really good-looking man, when she headed out to the airport. But, you never knew. She smiled at Mike. "I'll keep your card."

He watched the plane taxi up to the window. "Well, Jamie, it appears as though your business partner has arrived. It was nice." With that, he turned and walked down a long hall that led to a pilots' lounge, according to the sign. Jamie was giddy.

Toots, Sophie, Goebel, Mavis, and Ida walked down the small set of stairs that unfolded onto a red carpet that had been placed there by a member of the staff. Again, Jamie was impressed. Toots stopped, spoke a few words to the pilot and copilot, then handed them what appeared to be a wad of cash. Knowing Toots, her tip was more than their weekly pay.

The automatic doors opened. Toots was the first inside. Jamie hurried to greet her.

"I'm glad you're back." She gave her a quick hug. "I have to talk to you about something. It's sort of private."

"Then follow me to the restroom," Toots said.

Jamie handed the keys to Goebel. "I'm parked right in front of the exit. If you want, you can load up while we're in the ladies' room."

Sophie waved to Jamie, then stepped outside to smoke. Ida and Mavis followed Goebel out to the car. They could talk on the ride home. Jamie didn't want to embarrass Toots in front of her friends, just in case the news she was about to tell her ticked her off, or whatever.

In the ladies' room, Toots quickly took care of things, then said to Jamie, "Is Bernice okay?"

"Yes, she's fine. I didn't mean to scare you, but while you were gone, we learned that the Patterson place had been sold. I don't know why the sign was still up before you left. Anyway, the new owners moved in the day after you left."

"Don't tell me this has something to do with Bernice's near-death experience?" Toots said.

"No, not that. But it's a long story. The short version is this. The new owners are two single men, one about Bernice's age, and I'm guessing that the other . . . By the way, did I mention they were brothers? Anyway, the other is about your age. Wade came over the afternoon they arrived, to use the phone. Their power was off. Anyway, Bernice told them she owned the house, and I was her granddaughter, and you were her sister. In case they're still there when we arrive, I just thought I should give you a heads-up."

Toots had expected anything but this, but the idea of Bernice playing lady of the manor presented numerous possibilities, and Toots was going to play it to the max.

"Thanks for telling me. I won't blow her cover, but just between the two of us, I plan to use this against her. In a good way. Now, let's go home, so I can meet my sister Bernice's new neighbors."

Chapter 39

Toots entered her house, with her entourage following closely at her heels. Since they had no luggage to carry in, she went to the kitchen, where she knew most of the action would be taking place. *If* you could call putting groceries away action. As soon as Toots spied Bernice instructing an older man who had to be Robert where to place a bag of canned goods and on which shelf, she went straight for the jugular, letting her know right off there was nothing to worry about.

"Hey, sis, how is it going? I came as quickly as I could, knowing you would need as many hands as possible to prepare *your* house. So, tell me, who is this fine-looking man?" Toots smiled and winked at Bernice.

In a shaky voice, Bernice said, "This is Robert, and his brother, Wade, is . . . somewhere around here. They bought the Patterson house."

"Hello, Robert. I'm Toots, Bernice's younger sister. Did Bernice tell you about her near-death experience? She was allowed to live in order to make sure nothing sinister happens over there. You two aren't serial killers or wanted by the police or anything, are you?" Toots asked as she poured herself a cup of coffee. "Girls," Toots called out as loud as she could, "come in the kitchen. There is someone Bernice wants you to meet." Again, Toots winked at Bernice.

Robert had resumed stacking cans of tuna in the pantry. Wade had yet to make an appearance.

Before anyone else could catch her, Bernice quickly gave Toots the finger. Toots returned fire with both hands.

"How is Abby?" Bernice asked, apparently dying to change the subject.

This changed the tone of their conversation to a much more serious note. "Considering what she went through, she's doing remarkably well. She was going back to the paper today. I think she might take a leave of absence and come to Charleston for a visit. Would you mind if she stayed here for a while? I promise she won't be any trouble." Toots couldn't help herself.

Sophie chose that moment to make her grand entrance. "Did you just ask Bernice if Abby could stay here?" Her tone puzzled, she went on, "Because if you did, then I know Bernice has fallen into an extreme case of dementia since we left two days ago." Sophie saw the older man in the pantry. "Who's that?" Sophie blurted, always a picture of decorum.

Bernice looked like she wanted to strangle Sophie. "This is Robert."

The older man stepped out of the pantry and held his hand out to Sophie. "Pleased to meet you," he said, then went back to stacking his cans.

"WTF is going on here, Toots?"

"Bernice has invited the new neighbors over to help prepare *her* house for the hurricane, and being her little sister, well, I came home as soon as she called," Toots said and winked at Sophie, who caught on immediately.

Toots spoke to Bernice, her tone serious. "Shouldn't we close the shutters now? I hear this hurricane is a monster. I would have thought closing the shutters would be one of the first things you'd want us to do. Goebel is here, so he can check my, I mean *your,* generator in the basement. Unless Robert has done that already."

The words were no sooner out of Toots's mouth when a man came upstairs from the basement. "All seems to be in order," he said as he wiped his hands on a rag. "You must be Bernice's sister. I'm Wade Powell. That old guy in there is my older brother, in case you haven't met."

"We've met, thanks. Bernice didn't tell me you were so handsome, but then again, my big sister always was one for keeping the cute guys for herself."

Toots glanced across the room. Bernice's face was the color of the red cabinets in the kitchen. Mavis appeared out of nowhere, and when she saw Wade, she stood as still as a statue. God, things were happening too fast for Toots, and normally she was one for change.

"Mavis, this is Wade. He and his brother, Robert, who is obsessed with canned goods, bought the house next door."

Wade wiped his hand on his slacks, then held it out to Mavis. "I don't believe I've seen such beauty since . . . ever."

Mavis took his hand in her own, gazing into his eyes like a lovesick teenager.

And the shit just kept right on coming, Toots thought as she observed the two. Odd, though. They all seemed to be pairing off with new men. Maybe this was the reason Bernice had been given a second chance, Toots thought, if you believed in her near-death experience. Maybe it was in the cards that Bernice wasn't going to leave this world without one last roll in the hay, one last chance with a real man. The image brought a huge grin to her face.

Sophie and Bernice watched the couple, too. They didn't say anything for a few more seconds; then Mavis yanked her hand away as though she'd just touched fire.

"It's . . . uh, a pleasure to meet you, Wade. I dress dead people."

"Mavis! Holy shit, you're gonna scare

the guy off before he has a chance to ask you to his place!" Sophie said, giggling.

"Isn't that a coincidence? I owned a chain of funeral parlors before I retired," Wade said, his eyes all aglitter.

"Have you heard of Good Mourning?" Mavis asked, excitement causing her cheeks to color.

"Yes, I have. I think it's a wonderful line of clothing. I always said it was such a waste to buy something to wear that a dead person would never see, anyway. Why not buy something you can wear again and again? Whoever thought of this is a true genius."

Mavis's face was so red, Toots feared she was about to suffer a stroke.

"You've really heard of it?" Mavis asked again, apparently needing confirmation.

"Sure. Why do you ask?"

"Well, I'm the person who came up with that idea. And also, I've—"

"You're the lady who designed those half clothes for dressing the dead, too, aren't you?"

"Yes, yes, that, too," Mavis replied.

"I think I've just died and gone to heaven," Wade Powell said.

Sophie being Sophie offered her two cents' worth, even though it was unasked. "Mr. Powell, you will find we all share many unique talents. Right, Toots?"

Wondering how in the hell she'd get out of this mess of lies, Toots replied, "Yes, and after we know you a little bit better, we'll share those talents with you. Until then, we all need to do what needs to be done before this hurricane hits. Then, when we're finished with our preparations, we're going to have one of the best hurricane parties to ever hit Charleston," Toots announced. She thought about calling Phil but decided to wait.

At least for an hour.

Chapter 40

Thankful her abduction had yet to make the news, Abby returned to *The Informer* early that afternoon, with Chester at her heels. No way would she allow him out of her sight now. He'd saved her life, and she owed the big lug a gigantic steak dinner at least once a week.

Outside the door to her office, Abby was greeted by Dave Thompson and the rest of the security staff.

"It's good to see you, Miss Simpson. I want to apologize for—"

"There's no need. It wasn't your fault. Besides, I'd been in that basement a hundred times, so you're not the only one to mistake the wooden door for a storage closet." Abby watched the other members of the security staff. Unsure if they knew all the details, she decided to assume they did, but she wanted to make it clear that it wasn't to be discussed among them or the newspaper staffers. Before she had a chance to explain her decision, Dave spoke.

"It's being closed up today. Ms. Loudenberry made me promise to do it," Dave said.

"Then let's end this now. Let's get to work. I've got a paper to run," Abby said, suddenly anxious to be anywhere but there.

Dave and the others returned to their duties, while Abby had to force herself to open the door to her office. As she placed her hand on the knob, her hands began to shake. All of a sudden, she felt hot, as though she had a fever. Her throat became so dry, she found it difficult to swallow. Chester pushed on her hand with his muzzle, forcing her to open the door. As she stepped inside, a fear unlike anything she'd ever experienced cloaked her. She took a deep breath. This was worse than when she'd been tied to that chair in the closet.

Sure that she was having a panic attack, Abby sat down in Chester's blue chair. Her heart raced at such a rapid pace, she just knew it was going to pound a hole in her chest. Chester walked over to where she sat, and again, with his muzzle, he nudged her hand. For a second, Abby forgot about herself and realized that Chester was trying to get her attention. Maybe he was trying to distract her?

Abby took a deep breath, then let it out slowly, some of the fear dissipating as she exhaled. Taking another breath, she repeated the process. Her heart rate slowed a bit, and she felt more like herself, though her nerves were taut as a drum, as though something were about to happen, and she should be on high alert. Before she allowed her newfound fear to completely take over her body, she got up, walked across the office, and flipped the light on. *Much better.*

Next, she went to her desk and flipped the single switch that powered all the computers and television sets in her office. At last the room was filled with the hissing and buzzing of the electronics and the low drone of voices coming from the TVs.

She dropped down into her ergonomic

chair, placed her hands on her keyboard, and was preparing to check her e-mail when she froze again. Something was wrong with her. Maybe she was suffering from the aftereffects of her kidnapping or post-traumatic stress. Whatever it was, she did not like it. Shaky, she got to her feet and, without a second thought, ran out of her office, Chester at her side.

Upstairs in the newsroom, all seemed normal, but Abby's vision blurred, making the images appear distorted and blurry. Chester nudged her hand again, and she sat down on one of the chairs reserved for visitors. Before she could stop herself, she took her cell phone from her pocket and hit speed dial.

"Chris, it's me. I don't think I can do this anymore," Abby said, her voice not sounding like her own.

"Where are you?" he asked.

"The paper. I have to leave, *now.*" Abby jammed her phone in her pocket, leaving the newsroom through the employee exit. As soon as she was out of the office and in the parking lot, she took several deep breaths, and the world seemed to right itself a bit. Her cell phone rang.

Chris, she saw on the caller ID and answered.

Concerned, he asked, "Abby, are you all right?"

"Yes, no. I'm not sure," she answered, her voice still shaky.

"Stay put. I'm on my way. I'll be there as fast as I can. Stay on the phone with me, okay?"

Abby nodded, then realized he couldn't see her. "Yes, I'll . . . I'm going to sit in my car." She felt for her car keys and didn't find them. That was when she remembered she'd left her purse in her office. "No, I can't do this!" she said, more to herself than to Chris.

"Abby, you're starting to scare me. Are you in your car?"

"No, I'm in the parking lot. Chester's here with me."

"Get in your car and stay there until I arrive."

Abby raked a nervous hand through her hair. "My keys are in my office, Chris. And I . . . I'm afraid to go in there!"

"Then stay where you're at. Find a spot to sit down."

"Okay," Abby said and scanned the parking lot. Seeing the steps that led upstairs, she sat down on the bottom two, placing her feet on the first step. Chester curled up next to her, protecting her. "I'm on the back steps."

"Okay," Chris said.

What were only minutes seemed like hours as Abby sat cowering on the steps, waiting for Chris to come to her rescue. When she saw his Toyota Camry pull into the parking lot, she'd never been so happy to see him. All the fear she'd just experienced left her body, and she was limp with exhaustion.

Chris barreled out of the car and was at her side. "Abby! You look terrible. What in the hell just happened?" He helped her to her feet and placed his arm around her for support. Chester never left her side.

"I'm sure I've just experienced my first panic attack," she said as she slid into the passenger seat after Chester jumped in and seated himself in the backseat. "I was fine until I went inside my office. The next thing I know, my heart is pounding, my hands started trembling, and I could hardly swallow. Upstairs in the newsroom, everything looked out of shape, sort of surreal."

Chris reached for her hand. "Sounds like a panic attack. I'm not a doctor, but I suspect you're having some kind of delayed reaction to being kidnapped. PTSD, post-traumatic stress disorder. From what little I know, it's not all that uncommon."

Abby appeared to be contemplating his words. "Maybe I should take that leave of absence now, or at least take a few days off. I'm sure I'll be good as new once my body has had a chance to relax for a bit." Abby did not sound the least bit convinced by her own words. "Wait, I need my purse!" Abby said.

Chris hastily parked in a no-parking zone. "You stay here. I'll get your purse."

Minutes later, Chris returned with Abby's purse slung over his arm.

"My purse doesn't go with your outfit," Abby teased, already feeling more like her old self.

Chris knew she was making small talk to ease the moment. He pulled out of the parking lot, onto Santa Monica Boulevard, and into the flow of traffic. Already, it was heavy, but since they were not in a hurry, it didn't really matter.

"You want to stop for lunch?" Chris asked.

"No, Mavis made a big breakfast at the beach house. I'm not hungry yet. I just want to get home. I'll need to check in with Mom to make sure they're okay."

Chris didn't tell Abby that Toots had already called him on her way home from the airport after she arrived in Charleston, but he simply let Abby talk, hoping it would take her mind off the panic she'd just experienced.

Abby looked out the passenger-side window at the landmarks and buildings. They passed by her in a blur. How many times had she driven the same route to work and never noticed that most of the buildings were pastel-colored? Had she been that intent on reporting whatever news Hollywood's current miscreant stars of the month were generating? Again, it all seemed so unimportant to her now. Did she really care if Jennifer Aniston was pregnant or that Lindsay Lohan was headed to jail yet again? Suddenly it all seemed so pointless to her. Who really cared? she thought, but then reminded herself this was all that some people had to look forward to, and maybe it wasn't so silly, after all. But she wasn't convinced that *she* should continue to feed the public their weekly dose of Hollywood gossip. Maybe it was time to reevaluate her career choice. She was, after all, a journalist; she'd worked for the *Los Angeles Times* in the early stages of her writing career. She had left on good terms and knew that if she chose to become a serious journalist again, her old job would be waiting.

"She called me as soon as they arrived. Sorry. I guess I should have said something," Chris told her as he guided the Camry through the streets of Brentwood.

"I figured she was okay. I have the flight thing on my cell phone now, and whenever it pings, if I remember to look, it lets me know that whoever is flying has arrived safely. I've been so screwed up, I didn't even bother to check it," Abby said.

"You look good. I don't know if I mentioned it or not. You were in such a hurry to leave for *The Informer,* I didn't get a chance to tell you," Chris said, nodding at her wrists.

"Can you believe it? Ida is really onto something, big-time. I almost didn't believe my own eyes when I looked in the mirror. Then my wrists"—she held both arms up for his inspection—"are practically healed, too. She's going for the wrinkle factor in her plans to market this, but I'm not so sure she shouldn't aim toward the medical field. I even mentioned that she might want to talk to you about starting her own corporation. You'll probably hear something from her soon enough."

Chris sighed. "I can send her to a buddy of mine who practices corporate law. I don't know that I want to mess with that right now. I've just about given up all my clients after that shit with Laura Leighton. It's almost become meaningless to me, a sort of joke. An entertainment attorney. My dad's probably spinning in his grave. He always wanted me to uphold the law, and look at me now."

Abby was shocked to hear Chris speak that way. Yes, she had known that he'd reduced his list of clients to just a few, but she really hadn't asked him how he truly felt. What amazed her even more was, her thoughts were running along the same line as his. Maybe her mother was right. It might be time for a change. Just what that

change would be, well, she could ask Sophie, but Abby honestly didn't want to know
what the future held in terms of major events
in her life.

Chris pulled into her driveway, and Chester went wild, racing toward the backyard
as soon as Abby let him out of the car.

"Okay, boy, that backyard is all yours,"
Abby said as she took her key ring from
her purse. "Come on in, Chris, and I'll make
a pot of coffee."

"Sounds good. I could use another dose
of the stuff. Since your mom gave me that
Keurig coffeemaker, I need at least five
cups to get me going."

Abby pushed open the door that led
to the kitchen. "Damn, Chris, and here I
thought it was me that kept you charged
up," she teased him, feeling more like herself than she had all day.

Chris pulled her into his arms. "Trust
me, you do."

She leaned her head against his chest,
and Chris knew this woman was his des-
tiny. He planned to tell her this, too. Would
now be the right time, or should he wait,
plan another night out on the town?

"I can't believe it was only three nights

ago that we were at the movie premiere. It seems more like it happened in another lifetime," he said.

Abby poured water into the coffeemaker, then scooped coffee into the filter and clicked the ON button. Within seconds, the scent of aromatic brew filled the kitchen. "I can't believe that low-life piece of garbage would do something so despicable, kidnapping. I always knew he was a scumbag, but I never thought he would stoop that low. I hadn't thought about him in ages. I figured he'd either drunk himself to death or been shot by the husband of whatever wife he had messed with last. The philandering son of a bitch always did have an eye for the married ones. That way, he used to tell me, he managed to remain free of any commitments. Why get involved with someone he would have to provide for when there were all those accommodating fellows marrying women who still preferred to play the field, so to speak? Boy, is he a piece of work."

Chris observed, "What goes around comes around, I guess. The thugs who shot him were sent by the husband of some woman he was screwing in Venezuela. Not sure whether the husband cared about the screwing of his wife or Rag screwing him out of a lot of money. The tragedy, of course, was his thinking he could take you and get away with ten million dollars, and really, he could have succeeded had those two punks not stepped in when they did. Your mom was completely prepared to do whatever he asked to secure your safe return."

"Were you there when he was shot?" Abby asked.

"No. I was at the pier, but Goebel insisted I stay with your mom. We met at Bubba Gump's while Dave, Goebel, and the guys made the drop-off. You know your mother. She would have ripped that son of a bitch to shreds, albeit verbally, had she been there. Truthfully, though, Toots wasn't in very good shape, Abby. I've never seen her like that. I just wished I could have been there to see that bullet knock his ass to the ground."

Suddenly, Abby started laughing. Chris stared at her, thinking she might be hysterical, but then she stopped laughing and just grinned. "If I tell you something, you promise not to turn me in to those cop friends of yours?"

"What did you do, Abby?" Chris asked, a smile as wide as the Pacific on his face.

She poured them each a cup of coffee, then brought the cups to the table. "Remember when you came back to the hospital room, and I told you I had been looking for a Coke machine?"

His eyes twinkled. "I knew it! You were sneaking, weren't you?"

"Let's just say Rag suffered a nosebleed, and his poor little man part, and I do mean little, was exposed for all to see. He made me pee in front of him before locking me in the closet. I just wanted to let him know how it felt to be humiliated that way."

Chris didn't know whether to laugh or be angry. "It's going to be a very long time before he ever takes a piss in private, Abby. I'm sure he'll take whatever plea deal is going to be offered. Life in prison will be much more tolerable for the cowardly bastard than a death sentence."

Abby heard Chester scratching at the French doors in the living room. Apparently, he was too good to use his doggy door today. Getting up to let him in, she pulled the doors aside, and the German shepherd raced through the living room, then hopped up on the sofa. Noticing that Chris's tuxedo jacket was tossed over the back of the sofa, she yanked it up before Chester had the chance to cover it with hair. She took the black jacket and folded it across her arm, and something fell from the inside pocket.

Abby bent down and picked up what looked like a ring box. Shocked, she opened it and saw a diamond ring.

Before she could say anything, Chris asked, "Will you?"

Chapter 41

The shutters were closed; all the lawn fur-
niture and plants were stored in the gar-
dening shed; anything loose was secured.
Toots knew she was as prepared as one
could ever be for a hurricane.

Once Bernice had gotten over getting
caught in her ongoing lie, things progressed
nicely. Their new neighbors were thrilled
at the prospect of a hurricane party, both
claiming they'd never been in an area where
hurricanes were the norm. Toots assured
them that they were safe, or at least as safe
as they could be, and to enjoy the night
ahead.

Wade and Mavis, along with Coco, whom they had discovered hiding in the basement after Mavis realized the little pooch hadn't been there to greet her, hadn't taken their eyes off one another. Apparently, talking about dead people excited them both, and for once, Coco was on her best behavior.

Bernice and Jamie had made enough food and desserts for a small army. Pralines from the bakery, in every flavor, muffins, and cupcakes. Sandwiches with chips and pickles, olives, and peppers were just a few of the items they were going to have at their hurricane party. When Toots saw that their party preparations were ready, she found some booze that had belonged to that cheap ass Leland. She took the rocks glasses from the hutch in the dining room and made a minibar on the kitchen counter. There was beer and wine, but Toots knew she and the girls would hit the hard stuff tonight. With Abby safe at home and Rag headed for a very long term in prison, it was definitely time to celebrate. There was just one thing left to do.

Call Phil.

"Hey, it's me," Toots said into the phone. "How'd the emergency go?"

"Looks like they're gonna live a few more years, so I guess that's a good thing. What are you up to? How is Abby?" Phil asked.

Toots could hear the concern in his voice and more than appreciated it. He was truly a good guy. "The last I heard, Abby was fine. I was called away on an emergency myself this morning. Seems there's a hurricane headed toward Charleston, and someone had to batten down the hatches." Toots let her words hang, hoping he'd catch on.

"You're in Charleston?" Phil asked.

"Yes, I am. And the reason I'm calling, we're having a hurricane party. I thought you might want to join us. We've got new neighbors here who just happen to be without electricity, so they've joined us. I thought maybe you could come over before the storm hits."

Phil laughed. "I guess in all your preparations, you haven't seen the latest report. It seems this hurricane has made a turn and is now headed directly for New York City. I guess the 'cone of uncertainty' strikes again. We should only get a bit of tropical storm–force winds and some heavy rain.

If the party still stands, I can be there in half an hour. By the way, Dr. Carnes called. Frankie is doing fantastic. I'll tell you about him as soon as I see you."

"Sounds like a plan to me," Toots said, grinning. "I'll be waiting." She clicked off, then went to the kitchen, where everyone was gathered around the table, filling paper plates with food that Phil was sure to disapprove of. Nothing heart-healthy in sight. They spent the next half hour stuffing themselves with the finest pralines in the South and the best country-ham sandwiches money could buy.

Toots clapped her hands to get everyone's attention. "Listen up. It seems that in all of our merrymaking, we have neglected to listen to Jim Cantore from the Weather Channel. I just spoke with Phil, who informed me this hurricane has taken a turn and is currently expected to make landfall in New York City! So, we're no longer having an official hurricane party, but we're going to celebrate the little storm we're about to get. We sure as hell could use the rain."

Everyone started talking at once. Then

Sophie banged her spoon against a glass. "This calls for a toast, wouldn't you all agree?"

They all agreed, and Sophie took the bottle of hundred-year-old scotch and poured a liberal amount into ten rocks glasses that Toots had lined up along the counter like shot glasses. When she finished, she and Sophie passed out the glasses.

"Now, Sophie, what is it we're toasting?" Toots asked, not caring one way or another. They were having a good time, and now more than ever, she truly appreciated the loved ones in her life. Tears filled her eyes as she thought about just how blessed she'd been. Yes, there had been a few rough spots along the way, but she wouldn't change a thing. Life was good.

Just as Sophie was about to speak, the doorbell rang, and Toots had the sudden thought that it was about to get better. "Wait! Hold the toast!" She placed her glass on the counter and practically raced to get the front door.

She pulled the heavy oak door aside, and standing there like a drenched puppy was her new man, or whatever they called them nowadays. In her day, they called them boyfriends. "You're just in time to join us. We were about to make a toast," Toots said, guiding Phil to the kitchen.

"To what, might I ask?" he said.

"I haven't a clue," Toots said when she entered her kitchen, a room she truly loved, the room that like no other said "home." She clapped her hands together a second time. "Everyone, this is Phil, Dr. Phil Becker, the famed cardiologist, and if it weren't for him, my dear older sister, Bernice, wouldn't be here today. I say we toast him!"

Glasses were raised, and introductions made. The rest of the evening was spent telling old stories, learning new ones, and making new memories with the new men in their lives.

Toots realized she'd had a little too much to drink, and seeing that the rain was nothing more than a light drizzle, she stepped outside to smoke. Sophie spied her across the room, where she gave Goebel a healthy kiss, then joined Toots on the wet steps, where they both plopped down, their rear ends soaking up the moisture.

"You know what, Toots?" Sophie asked, then took a drag from her cigarette.

"What's that, Sophie?"

"Life doesn't get any better than this," she said.

Toots nodded in agreement. Then, as they stood to go back inside, her cell phone vibrated in her pocket. Who would be calling her at this hour?

Looking at the face of her phone, she saw it was Abby. Her heart raced for a moment. The last time she'd received a late-night call, it had been Chris, telling her Abby had been abducted.

"Hello?" she said, instantly sober. "Abby! Are you all right?"

"Mom, are you sitting down?" Abby asked.

"No, but something tells me I should be." Toots sat back down on the wet porch steps, with Sophie plopping back down beside her.

"Oh, Mom! This is the best news! Chris has asked me to marry him, and I said yes!"

Momentarily stunned, Toots was at a loss for words.

"Mom, are you there?" Abby asked.

"Yes, yes, I'm here. Abby, I don't know

what to say except this is the best news I've had in forever! God has answered my prayers. I have always hoped this day would come. You have made me the happiest mom in the world!" Toots exclaimed.

Sophie pinched her. "What is it?"

Toots placed her hand over the phone. "Shut up, Sophie. Chris asked Abby to marry him, and she said yes. We've got a wedding to plan."

"Abby, I just told Sophie. I think she's dumbfounded." Toots laughed, her world so perfect at that exact moment, she was afraid to do or say anything else, fearing it would break the spell.

"Mom, Chris wants to speak to you."

"Hey, old girl, I hope I have your blessing. I know if Dad were alive, he'd be thrilled. I was going to ask Abby to marry me the night of the premiere, but, well, you know what happened. I just wanted to tell you how much I love your daughter, and I will devote my life to making her happy."

"Well, Chris, all I can say is, this news has made me the happiest woman alive. You both have my blessing. I love you, you know that, right?"

"Oh shit, Toots, don't go getting all mushy on me." Chris laughed. "Here's Abby."

"Mom, I just wanted to share my fantastic news!"

"Wait, wait! Have you set a date?" Toots asked excitedly.

"No, but you'll be the second to know when we do. Gotta go, Mom. Tell the other godmothers for me, okay?"

"Sure," Toots said. "Love you, Abby."

"One more thing, not to put a damper on my news, but we just learned an hour ago that Rag accepted a plea. He won't see the light of day ever again. And I love you, too, Mom," Abby said before clicking off.

Toots and Sophie raced inside the house, not caring that their tushes were soaking wet. For the third time that night, Toots clapped her hands to get everyone's attention. "I just received a phone call from Abby, my daughter, for those of you who have never met her. Apparently, she's just accepted a marriage proposal from Chris, my stepson, and no, don't ask, but it's a good thing!"

Mavis and Ida gushed like two old hens. Sophie poured them all another glass of scotch, and they toasted Abby and Chris's engagement numerous times throughout what was left of the evening.

Everyone huddled in groups of two: Sophie and Goebel, Bernice and Robert, Mavis and Wade, Toots and Phil, leaving Ida attached to her cell phone. From this modern-day messenger pigeon they all learned that Dave Thompson was coming to Charleston in three days. It seemed that all the members of AARP at the party were about to fall head over heels in love.

Once again.

Chapter 42

Six weeks later . . .

Ida paraded around The Home Shopping Club studio as though she were royalty. And in a sense, she was. For the previous four weeks, Ida, Toots, Sophie, and Mavis had arrived at the studios in Wilmington, North Carolina, at 6:00 AM each Saturday to tape the progress of Ida's new line of skin care and makeup, which she'd aptly named Seasons, as it was being marketed to women who were a bit, well, *seasoned.* That day, for the first time, they were going to go on the air live. This would be Ida's national debut, and Toots, Mavis, and

Sophie would reveal their amazing progress over the past six weeks. The Home Shopping Club would play each taped session, showing the amazing results of Ida's skin-care products. If they were as successful as expected, then she would follow with her line of makeup, which had the same ingredients as those in the skin-care line.

They had arrived at the studios in Wilmington, North Carolina, at 3:00 AM for the team of experts Ida had hired to do their hair and makeup. Each one would be representing a different product in the line.

Sophie had used the face cream, and her results had exceeded the expectations of the chemists involved, and the marketing firm Ida had hired was begging for free samples.

Mavis, with her sensitive skin, who was more prone to wrinkling beneath her eyes, had used the specially prepared eye cream. Her results had exceeded all expectations as well.

Toots, who had the best skin, was starting to show signs of aging in her décolletage area. A gentler version for this tender area had proved once again that Ida was a true genius in her designated area of entrepreneurial expertise.

"Beauty at Any Age" was the motto touting the line.

All were seated in tall chairs, facing the cameras and surrounded by the bright lights in the studio.

"What if people don't like this stuff?" Sophie asked as her makeup artist applied a touch of gloss to her lips. Their faces would be free of cosmetics in order to show the viewing audience just how remarkable the changes were.

Before Toots could answer, one of the hairstylists spoke. "Are you kidding? We see thousands of products come and go, and none of us have ever seen something that works as fast and as amazingly as Seasons. I don't care what their age. If women don't jump on this stuff, they're out of their minds. I think the entire staff has already set aside several bottles of this cream. Frankly, we have never seen anything like it. I think the only thing you will need to worry about is how fast you can produce the stuff."

Ida listened as the hairstylist practically salivated when she spoke of the line.

"How many units do you have ready?" Toots asked while yet another stylist twisted her auburn hair into an updo.

"We have two hundred thousand units ready for shipping. Depending on today's sales, we're prepared to produce the product on an as-needed basis. I'm hoping to keep the production lines running twenty-four/seven," Ida said. "I'll break even at one hundred thousand units. Anything beyond that is pure profit. Too bad I can't market this with Drop-Dead Gorgeous."

"Ida, that's terrible!" Mavis said, though she was smiling. "I've learned a thing or two since I started Good Mourning, and one of them is that you can never say never. Who would have thought when we were sewing those clothes by hand that a year later, I'd have two warehouses doing nothing but sewing? I have to say I never expected to become a wealthy woman. You remember when Herbert came through and said he was proud of me? That's given me more motivation to try other things."

Mavis paused as her stylist sprayed her hair. "Wade is going to come out of retirement, at least for a while. Since Ida's so busy with her live customers, he's quite good at making the poor souls look almost as nice as Ida can, so he's going to assist me the next time I'm called to do a dressing out."

"Ugh," Sophie said. "That's just disgusting. I don't see how either one of you can spend your working hours with dead bodies. Though I do recall that one time when I had to give you two a hand."

Mavis and Ida both gave Sophie looks that should have killed or, at the very least, kept her quiet, but Sophie, loving to joke, continued with her explanation. "No one even knew I assisted you two, either. I never said a word."

"Then why are you saying it now, when we're about to appear on national television?" Ida asked. "I think it's rude, and beyond mean. This is supposed to be . . . my day! Why you would want to ruin it is beyond me!" Ida shouted. When she realized some of the camera people were staring at her, she lowered her voice. "If you tell, Sophia Manchester, I promise I will tell Goebel that you . . . you were a lesbian in high school!"

Toots's eyes widened, Mavis's mouth

formed a perfect O, and Sophie roared with laughter.

"Oh, shit, Ida, I'm just fucking around. Oops, I mean screwing around. I promised you and Mavis I would never tell, and I won't. If you want to tell Toots, then that's up to you. I was simply remembering that time I assisted you two," Sophie said.

Toots, more curious than ever, said, "I'm sure eventually one of you will blab. I'm a patient woman, remember?"

The director began to shout to the crew, and an assistant carrying a clipboard, with a headset on, announced, "Okay, ladies, we're about to go live in two minutes. All you have to do is sit there, smile, and look pretty. Our announcer will do most of the talking. Then Ida will tell the audience about each different product as the camera focuses on you. Now, no cussing, okay?" she said with a big grin.

Toots, Sophie, and Mavis nodded, all knowing this really was Ida's moment to shine. And theirs, too, in a sense. They wouldn't do anything to mess this up. Though Sophie and Toots delighted in pulling Ida's chain, they loved her as much as they loved one another. Mavis, sweet

Mavis, could always be counted on, no matter what.

"Okay, everyone into position," the director called. "We're live in ten, nine, eight, seven, six . . ."

The female host of the Saturday morning segment said, "Welcome to The Home Shopping Club. Ladies, you will want to get to the phone when you see what we're about to offer. A new line of skin-care products, Seasons, will revolutionize skin care as we all know it. We only have two hundred thousand units available today, so without further delay, I'm proud to introduce Ida McGullicutty, Seasons founder and the creator of this amazing product."

"Thank you, Carol. I'm so excited to be here," Ida said as she'd previously been instructed during rehearsal.

"Each of our models today has used a specific product designated for a particular area. For the past four weeks, these women have allowed us to show them without any makeup, without any touch-ups, as you will see. Let's watch their transformation."

The television monitors showed Sophie, Toots, and Mavis, starting at week one and ending with live shots of them in the studio. While the camera highlighted each woman's area of application, Ida narrated exactly what product they'd used and how to use it to achieve maximum results.

"Lines are opening, ladies and gentlemen. Each product you've seen comes in a set of three. This product is not offered in stores. The original retail price is two hundred fifty-nine dollars, but today, on The Home Shopping Club, we're practically giving the product away for fifty-nine dollars and ninety-five cents plus shipping and handling. The first hundred callers will receive free shipping. Okay, ladies, time starts now."

The clock at the bottom of the screen showed thirty minutes. The number of sales was registered on the left side of the screen.

While the viewers saw the amazing progress once again, Carol spoke to Ida live as sales skyrocketed. "Ida, tell us your story. How did you develop Seasons?"

Ida went through her rehearsed lines, telling the viewers how she'd always had an interest in cosmetics. That it was through her natural curiosity and science that she and her team were able to develop these products and that pumpkin enzymes played a big role in the products' success.

"Ida, excuse me. I'm being told that the phone lines in our call center are jammed. We only have twenty more minutes left for this item. If you can't get through, keep trying, as you will not want to miss out on this introductory price."

Ida looked at the girls, mouthing, "Can you believe this?"

They all smiled when the camera panned back to Carol. Sophie gave Ida a thumbs-up sign, and Toots and Mavis just grinned.

Once again, Ida was instructed to continue talking about the product. "The enzymes in the pumpkin have soothing properties as well. They're good for scars, scrapes, and skin rashes, too."

Before Ida could continue to promote the many healing properties of her products, Carol broke in. "Ida, I'm sorry to have to interrupt you, but I have just been informed that we have sold out! For those viewers unable to get through due to the overwhelming demand, I've just been told by the producers, we're going to try to feature Seasons again in the near future. Please stay tuned. Up next . . ." Carol announced the host for the next segment and quickly helped Ida and the girls make their way off the set.

Epilogue

April, the next year . . .
Charleston, South Carolina

Giant oak trees dripping with Spanish moss canopied the short path leading to the plush garden where Abby's wedding was scheduled to take place. The gardens were flush with spring's blooms. The azaleas were every hue of pink under the mid-morning sun; the camellias, red, white, and orange, exploded from verdant stems like wild arms reaching out from the earth. The scent of night-blooming jasmine still clung in the morning air.

Toots wanted one last moment alone in the garden to ensure that everything was as close to perfect as possible for her daughter's wedding day. Toots drew in a deep breath, taking in the fresh air, the chirping birds, and the sounds of crickets rubbing their legs together. And every once in a while she could hear the croak of a frog. Had she asked Mother Nature to create an absolutely perfect venue, this is what she would have wanted.

Abby and Chris wanted a simple wedding, with only those they were very close to attending. Toots had been completely shocked when Abby took an indefinite leave of absence from *The Informer,* leaving it in Josh's capable hands. Chris had decided that it was time to return to his father's estate, which had been in his family for over two hundred years. He was temporarily, at least, abandoning his legal career. When they told Toots that they would be returning to Charleston to live, she and the godmothers could barely contain their excitement. And with the wedding gift Toots had given them a few weeks ago, they were considering the possibility of setting up a foundation for the care of abandoned animals whose medical needs went beyond the ability of existing shelters to handle. With the help of Dr. Becker, who kept insisting they call him Phil, they had contacted specialists on the East Coast to explore the possibilities.

And now, at last, the day had arrived. It was time to go inside and dress for the wedding. Tapping on Abby's door, the bedroom she'd had as a child, Toots felt the tears coming again but blotted them with a tissue as she'd already had her makeup expertly applied. Ida's miracle creams had truly taken years off her appearance. She tapped lightly on the door, and Abby called, "Come in."

Sophie, Mavis, and Ida were helping their goddaughter into her wedding gown, which was a simple cream-colored sheath with a scooped neckline. Her blond hair was piled artistically on top of her head, with loose tendrils around her face. She wore her mother's diamond earrings and a simple gold diamond necklace given to her by her godmothers. On her wrist she wore a single gold bangle given to her by Chris. On the inside, he had had their wedding date inscribed in a simple script. She wore a cream-colored veil that reached the top of her shoulders. Abby was a simple woman, not one for frivolous accessories.

Toots had been honored when Abby asked her to serve as her matron of honor. Yes, they all knew it was unusual, but they didn't care. Sophie, Mavis, and Ida would act as her bridesmaids. Each wore an elegantly cut tea-length dress in a pastel green.

Abby's bouquet was a single white rose with baby's breath and a sprig of greenery from their night-blooming jasmine.

"You look like an angel," Toots said to her daughter. "I wish your father were here to see you, but something tells me he's watching over you, and he approves."

"It's time, Mom," Abby said. "Sophie, tell Goebel I'm ready for him to escort me down the aisle, or the garden path."

They all laughed, each a little bit nervous.

The five women carefully helped Abby down the stairs to the garden, where it had been prearranged that Goebel would wait with her out of sight.

Lucy, Jamie's assistant, had offered to provide the music. Abby heard the soft, melodic sound of the young woman as she sang her and Chris's favorite song. As soon as she finished their song, she began to play the traditional wedding march.

Toots, knowing this was her signal, walked slowly down the garden path leading to the priest who had christened Abby. He'd flown in from New Jersey just to perform the ceremony. Toots couldn't have been more pleased.

She walked down the path, all eyes focused on her. When she reached the altar they'd had specially constructed, she felt her eyes tear up when she saw Chris and Phil waiting. Chris was her stepson, and he was about to become her son-in-law as well, and she, his mother-in-law as well as his stepmother. Yes, this was not the norm, but there was not one thing that was normal about this loving group of women who'd shared the raising of Abby.

Sophie, followed by Mavis and Ida, walked down the path to the altar. Jamie, who had remained behind, stepped onto the path, leading Chester, who wore a matching tuxedo collar, followed by Coco, wearing a diamond-studded collar with a pale green, silky half dress. Then there was Frankie, dressed in a matching collar, with a mini white top hat secured on his small head. Mike, Jamie's date, laughed as he saw her walk the animals down the aisle.

Neither Abby nor Chris had known that the animals were sharing their special day, and both laughed when they saw the trio of canines as Jamie escorted them to the altar.

Wade and Robert were seated in the chairs placed on either side of the pathway, along with several of Chris's and Abby's friends from high school and college.

Father Cauble proceeded to read a verse by Kahlil Gibran that Chris and Abby had chosen.

"May your marriage bring you all the exquisite excitements a marriage should bring, and may life grant you also patience, tolerance, and understanding. May you always need one another—not so much to fill your emptiness as to help you to know your fullness. A mountain needs a valley to be complete. The valley does not make the mountain less, but more. And the valley is more a valley because it has a mountain towering over it. So let it be with you and you. May you need one another, but not out of weakness. May you want one

another, but not out of lack. May you en-
tice one another, but not compel one another. May you embrace one another, but
not encircle one another.

"May you succeed in all-important ways
with one another, and not fail in the little
graces. May you look for things to praise,
often say, "I love you!" and take no notice
of small faults. If you have quarrels that
push you apart, may both of you hope to
have good sense enough to take the first
step back. May you enter into the mystery
that is the awareness of one another's
presence—no more physical than spiri-
tual, warm and near when you are side by
side, and warm and near when you are in
separate rooms or even distant cities. May
you have happiness, and may you find it
making one another happy. May you have
love, and may you find it loving one another."

After Father Cauble recited their chosen
poem, he proceeded with the traditional
wedding vows.

"Christopher Clay, do you take Abby
Simpson to be your wedded wife to live together in marriage? Do you promise to love,
comfort, honor, and keep her for better or

worse, for richer or poorer, in sickness and in health, and forsaking all others, be faithful only to her so long as you both shall live?"

Chris spoke with confidence. "Yes, I do."

"Abby Simpson, do you take Christopher Clay to be your wedded husband to live together in marriage? Do you promise to love, comfort, honor, and keep him for better or worse, for richer or poorer, in sickness and in health, and forsaking all others, be faithful only to him so long as you both shall live?"

Abby said, "I do."

"Does the couple wish to exchange rings?"

Each placed a simple gold band on the other's finger.

"By the powers vested in me by the State of South Carolina, I now pronounce you husband and wife. You may kiss the bride."

Chris took Abby in his arms and kissed her passionately.

"I now introduce Mr. and Mrs. Clay."

Lucy played the wedding march exit, while Chris and Abby raced down the path, followed by Chester, Coco, and Frankie.

It was official. Abby's dream had finally

come true. Inside the house, her mother had spared no expense for her small reception. What made it even better was that Toots and Phil were madly in love, Goebel and Sophie were engaged to be married. Wade and Mavis were contemplating moving in together, and good old Bernice and Robert were inseparable.

As Toots, Sophie, Mavis, and Ida had done since they met over fifty years ago—only this time Abby was included—they placed their hands on top of one another's, lifted them to the sky, and said, "When you're good, you're good!"

JAMIE'S HEALTHY BROWNIES

baking spray
¼ cup organic salted butter
¼ cup unsweetened cocoa powder
¼ cup unsweetened applesauce
2 large eggs
1¼ cup Splenda
1 cup all-purpose flour
¼ tsp baking powder
½ cup unsweetened chocolate baking bits
¼ cup fat-free milk
½ tsp vanilla extract

Preheat oven to 350°F and spray an 8"×8" baking pan with baking spray.

Melt butter in a small saucepan over low heat and mix in unsweetened cocoa powder. Add applesauce. Mix together until smooth, and then remove from heat and let cool.

Beat eggs in a large bowl and mix in the Splenda, flour, and baking powder. Add the chocolate mixture and stir thoroughly.

Fold in the unsweetened chocolate

baking bits, milk, and vanilla extract, and then pour the batter into the pan.

Bake for 30 minutes, or until slightly undercooked. Brownies will set as they cool.